PERFECT

BOBBY

THANK YOU

Thank you for reading PERFECT STORM 1, the first installment in the Perfect Storm survival thriller series by Author Bobby Akart. Join Bobby Akart's mailing list to learn about upcoming releases, deals, contests, and appearances. Follow this link to: BobbyAkart.com

PRAISE FOR BOBBY AKART AND PERFECT STORM

"An international bestseller from an author who's as current as tomorrow's headlines!"
"Bobby Akart is a genius at creating disaster scenarios."

"Mark Twain once wrote, *there is something fascinating about science*. Mr. Akart gets it!"

"As with any of the best novels, this book really captures your attention and makes it hard to put down at the end of the day."

"Bobby Akart continues to deliver the top thrillers of the year. Year after year after year!"

"The way this author brings every character to life is a gifted Masterpiece."

"I am speechless. By far the most edge of your seat, acrylic-nail-biting book ever. E V E R.
The characters suck you in on a roller coaster ride of emotions."

"Bobby Akart continues to give his readers spell-binding scenarios that are so close to real life, it's scary as all get out."

"An incredibly well written story by this gifted writer who can weave a story like no other."

PERFECT STORM 1

by
Bobby Akart

OTHER WORKS BY AMAZON CHARTS TOP 25 AUTHOR BOBBY AKART

The Perfect Storm Series

Perfect Storm 1

Perfect Storm 2

Perfect Storm 3

Perfect Storm 4

Perfect Storm 5

Black Gold (a standalone terrorism thriller)

Nuclear Winter

First Strike

Armageddon

Whiteout

Devil Storm

Desolation

New Madrid (a standalone, disaster thriller)

Odessa (a Gunner Fox trilogy)

Odessa Reborn

Odessa Rising

Odessa Strikes

The Virus Hunters

Virus Hunters I

Virus Hunters II

Virus Hunters III

The Geostorm Series

The Shift

The Pulse

The Collapse

The Flood

The Tempest

The Pioneers

The Asteroid Series (A Gunner Fox trilogy)

Discovery

Diversion

Destruction

The Doomsday Series

Apocalypse

Haven

Anarchy

Minutemen

Civil War

The Yellowstone Series

Hellfire

Inferno

Fallout
Survival

The Lone Star Series

Axis of Evil
Beyond Borders
Lines in the Sand
Texas Strong
Fifth Column
Suicide Six

The Pandemic Series

Beginnings
The Innocents
Level 6
Quietus

The Blackout Series

36 Hours
Zero Hour
Turning Point
Shiloh Ranch
Hornet's Nest
Devil's Homecoming

The Boston Brahmin Series

The Loyal Nine
Cyber Attack
Martial Law
False Flag
The Mechanics
Choose Freedom
Patriot's Farewell (standalone novel)

Black Friday (standalone novel)
Seeds of Liberty (Companion Guide)

The Prepping for Tomorrow Series
Cyber Warfare
EMP: Electromagnetic Pulse
Economic Collapse

Copyright Information

ACKNOWLEDGMENTS

Creating a novel that is both informative and entertaining requires a tremendous team effort. Writing is the easy part.

For their efforts in making the Perfect Storm series a reality, I would like to thank Hristo Argirov Kovatliev for his incredible artistic talents in creating my cover art. He and Dani collaborate (and conspire) to create the most incredible cover art in the publishing business. A huge hug of appreciation goes out to Pauline Nolet, the *Professor*, for her editorial prowess and patience in correcting this writer's brain farts that happen more frequently with age. Thank you, Drew Avera, a United States Navy veteran, who has brought his talented formatting skills from a writer's perspective to create multiple formats for reading my novels. A round of applause for Kevin Pierce, the beloved voice of the apocalypse, who brought my words to life in audio format.

Now, for the serious stuff. While the Perfect Storm series is based on scientifically plausible events, certain parts of the story have been fictionalized for dramatic purposes and they're not intended to reflect on any actual person or entity.

Accurately portraying the aftermath of a devastating perfect solar storm required countless hours of never-ending research and interviews of some of the brightest minds in the world of planetary science.

Once again, as I immersed myself in the science and history, source material and research flooded my inbox from around the globe. Without the assistance of many individuals and organizations, this story could not be told. Please allow me a moment to acknowledge a few of those institutions that without their tireless efforts and patience, the Perfect Storm series could not have been written.

Many thanks to the preeminent researchers and engineers who provided me assistance, tutelage, and scientific background at the following:

The Space Weather Prediction Center in Boulder, Colorado

The Aerospace Corporation in El Segundo, California

The Haleakala Observatory, home to the Daniel K. Inouye Solar Telescope, in Maui

NASA's Jet Propulsion Laboratory in Pasadena, California

The Geophysical Institute at the University of Alaska, Fairbanks

A tidbit of note. Longtime reader and friend, Neal Burgoyne, was gracious enough to allow me to use his real name as a fictional character in the Perfect Storm series. This is a fictional depiction of a good friend. His cat, Yang, is also very real although I hope his demeanor isn't as I portrayed.

At our home, we fly three historic flags across the columns across the front. One is the Benington Flag commemorating an important battle during the Revolutionary War that took place in upstate New York near its namesake, Bennington, Vermont. The British forces were led by General John Burgoyne who'd dealt the colonists several defeats including at Fort Ticonderoga. His success ran out at the Battle of Bennington where the American forces stood fast and repelled the British.

I know the real Neal Burgoyne well enough to assure you, he's no Torie but rather, a red-blooded American Patriot.

Finally, as always, a special thank you to The Team, my loyal friends who've always supported my work and provided me valuable insight from a reader's perspective—Denise Keef, Joe Carey, Shirley Nicholson, Bennita Barnett, and Colt Payne.

Thanks, y'all, and Choose Freedom!

ABOUT THE AUTHOR, BOBBY AKART

Author Bobby Akart delivers up-all-night thrillers to readers in 245 countries and territories worldwide. He has been ranked by Amazon as #25 on the Amazon Charts list of most popular, bestselling authors. He has achieved recognition as the #1 bestselling Horror Author, #1 bestselling Science Fiction Author, #5 bestselling Action & Adventure Author, #7 bestselling Historical Fiction Author and #10 on Amazon's bestselling Thriller Author list.

His novel *Yellowstone: Hellfire* reached the Top 25 on the Amazon bestsellers list and earned him multiple Kindle All-Star awards for most pages read in a month and most pages read as an author. The Yellowstone series vaulted him to the #25 bestselling author on Amazon Charts, and the #1 bestselling science fiction author.

Since its release in November 2020, his standalone novel *New Madrid Earthquake* has been ranked #1 on Amazon Charts in multiple countries as a natural disaster thriller.

Mr. Akart is a graduate of the University of Tennessee after pursuing a dual major in economics and political science. He went on to obtain his master's degree in business administration and his doctorate degree in law at Tennessee.

With over a million copies of his novels in print, Bobby Akart has provided his readers a diverse range of topics that are both informative and entertaining. His attention to detail and impeccable research has allowed him to capture the imagination of his readers through his fictional works and bring them valuable knowledge through his nonfiction books.

SIGN UP for Bobby Akart's mailing list to learn of special offers, view bonus content, and be the first to receive news about new releases.

Visit www.BobbyAkart.com for details.

DEDICATIONS

With the love and support of my wife, Dani, together with the unconditional love of Bullie and Boom, the princesses of the palace, I'm able to tell you these stories. It would be impossible for me to write without them in my heart.

This story was written during a difficult time in our lives. For my long-time readers, you know that our English Bulldogs, Bullie and Boom, affectionately known in my stories as the princesses of the palace, are the center of our universe. At Christmas in 2021, Boom Chukka suffered a significant tear in her gastrointestinal tract caused by chewing a pressed rawhide bone.

Because of Dani's watchful eye, she noticed Boom-Boom's gums turn more and more pale. I also noticed that her poop became black and tarry. Both of these were symptoms of internal bleeding. I relay this to you because, one day, you might experience this with your beloved pups.

Internal bleeding is nothing to be trifled with. Without urgent care, your fur babies can die within days, if not sooner.

We rushed Boom Chukka to our vets in Georgia. The entire team, led by Drs. Rambo and McNair, came to her rescue. By the early evening of New Year's Eve, her packed cell volume (PCV) and hematocrit (HCT) fell below twenty percent where thirty-five percent is normal. Thanks to a dog-to-dog blood transfusion from Dr. McNair's dog, Liza, Boom-Boom was able to survive long enough to transport her to the University of Georgia Veterinary Hospital in Athens.

With the help of God watching over our entire family during this difficult time, Boom Chukka fought to live another day. As of this writing, Bullie and Boom are the ripe age of twelve years, and eight months. However, they firmly believe they're one-year-old pups.

I urge you to love those who are closest to you, including your four-legged, bestest pals.

AUTHOR'S NOTE

March, 2022

For years, I've tackled the disaster thriller genre. As an author, the hardest part might be choosing how to destroy the Earth, therefore imperiling all of mankind. Look at all the options I've written about: asteroids, nuclear electromagnetic pulse attacks, pandemics, earthquakes, volcanoes, bioterrorism, cyber warfare, pole shifts, etc.

However, in a class by itself, is severe space weather. If its ominous name didn't clue you in, severe space weather can cause some serious complications to life on our planet. Much like earth-based weather, it's uncontrollable. It also has the potential for massive destruction and disruption of modern technology. Imagine the collapse of power grids; radio blackouts; satellite interference or even destruction; and airline operations ceasing, all in less than a minute. Without electricity, how would you communicate with your family, call 9-1-1, get clean water or keep food from spoiling? With a radio blackout, how would airplanes land safely? Massive solar flares have the potential to change life as we know it.

Now, if I haven't gotten your attention, let's take a look at the science and a little history, shall we?

Severe space weather is the result of large-scale eruptions of plasma and magnetic fields from the Sun's corona. Known as coronal mass ejections (CMEs), these eruptions can create magnetic storms in the magnetosphere and Earth's upper atmosphere, which can damage power lines, cause blackouts, and even dislocate Earth's radiation belts, damaging satellites.

Thankfully, such magnetic storms are classified as low frequency, but high impact. To be an impactful magnetic storm, CMEs from the solar disk must be fast and massive, launched from near the center of the Sun and directed toward Earth's magnetic field. CMEs also need to have a strong magnetic field with the opposite orientation of Earth's own magnetic field. Although classified as low frequency, when these conditions are met, CMEs are high-consequence occurrences. Here are some examples.

In recent history, the collapse of the Hydro-Quebec grid occurred in March 1989 leaving the province of Quebec without electricity for 9 hours. The outage closed schools, businesses, public transportation and grounded flights at Dorval Airport. Citizens found themselves stuck in traffic on darkened roads without street signals and many workers were stranded in office buildings, elevators and stairwells. The storm was felt in other parts of North America as well, with approximately two-hundred solar storm-related events reported including the failure of a transformer at a New Jersey nuclear power plant.

Amazingly, the 1989 magnetic storm that struck Quebec pales in comparison to other magnetic storms in our history.

The strongest storm in recorded history to directly impact our planet came in September of 1859. The CME behind the Carrington Event, as it became known, was first seen by Richard Carrington, a British amateur astronomer. Nearly eighteen hours after it was observed, the powerful CME impacted the Earth's magnetosphere, triggering a severe geomagnetic storm that disrupted telegraph networks around the world. The rare, fast-moving (CMEs normally impact Earth around 36 hours after being observed) CME hit the planet with highly charged particles enveloped the Northern Hemisphere. Telegraph operators were electrocuted, and fires were ignited as flames traveled along the telegraph lines.

The 1921 Geomagnetic Storm, also known as the New York Railway Storm, included geomagnetically induced currents that would have been 10 times more intense than those responsible for the 1989 Quebec solar storm. Taking place over several days in May 1921, the New York Railway Storm is widely considered the largest recorded in the twentieth century. It is this perfect solar storm event that forms the scientific basis for my book series.

SUNSPOT CREDITED WITH RAIL TIE-UP

New York Central Signal System Put Out of Service by Play of Northern Lights.

The sunspot which caused the brilliant aurora borealis on Saturday night and the worst electrical disturbance in memory on the telegraph systems was credited with an unprecedented thing at 7:04 o'clock yesterday morning, when the entire signal and switching system of the New York Central Railroad below 125th Street was put out of operation, followed by a fire in the control tower at Fifty-seventh Street and Park Avenue.

This is the first time that a sunspot has been blamed for such a piece of mischief. From other accounts it appeared

The New York Times
Published: May 16, 1921

later events showed ... the American
represent the will of the American
people," Signor Orlando declared.

SUNSPOT AURORA PARALYZES WIRES

Unprecedented Disturbance Is Attributed to Solar Manifestations.

BROADWAY LIGHTS DIMMED

Theatre Crowds Returning Home Amazed at the Brilliancy of the Skies.

WASHINGTON, May 14.—The unusually severe aurora borealis of ... an immense sun

ELECTRIC DISTURBANCES AFFECT FRENCH WIRES

Aurora Not Visible, Its Absence Being Attributed to Atmospheric Conditions.

Copyright, 19?' by The New York Times Company

By Wireless to THE NEW YORK TIMES.

PARIS, May 17.—The disturbance which interrupted telegraphic transmission in the United States last week has been making itself felt also in

WHAT IF FICTION BECOMES REALITY?

A word of caution when thinking about history and the timeline of events. It's easy to dismiss any discussion of past catastrophes when one considers events like super volcano eruptions taking place every seven-hundred-thousand-years as in the case of Yellowstone. Massive solar storms occur far more frequently. Let's look at a recent event from just ten years ago.

On July 23, 2012, two CMEs erupted from an active patch of sunspots on the far side of the sun which is monitored by the Parker Solar Probe that circles the sun ahead of Earth in the same orbit. Emerging about fifteen minutes apart, the CMEs quickly merged into one massive shock wave of charged particles that washed over the probe's sensors.

Behind the shock wave, this energy raced along at about 2250 kilometers per second—five times their normal speed at Earth's distance from the sun—and the magnetic field strength there was more than ten times that normally seen at Earth's orbit.

If pointed in our direction, such a combination would have produced the strongest geomagnetic storm to have struck Earth in history. It could have knocked out satellites and earthbound power grids, researchers say. Fortunately, the event, a prime example of a *Perfect Storm*, was directed into a region of space where the solar wind and the magnetic field had been weakened by a solar flare 4 days earlier.

While the flare occurred in Earth's orbital plane, the solar matter missed us by the equivalent of nine days. Similar to the Carrington event, the particles traveled from the sun to the Earth in just seventeen hours. Had Earth been in the way at the time, the global damage toll would have crested the $10 trillion mark: the first fourteen-figure natural disaster in history. It was only luck that caused this perfect storm to miss us.

I add this example as a word of caution to us all. These severe solar storms happen with regular frequency. We dodged a powerful catastrophic solar flare in 2012. Next time, we might not be so lucky.

REAL-WORLD NEWS EXCERPTS

NEW STUDIES WARN OF CATACLYSMIC SOLAR SUPERSTORMS

~ *Scientific American, September 24, 2019*

New data suggest the New York Railroad Storm could have surpassed the intensity of the famous Carrington Event of 1859.

A powerful disaster-inducing geomagnetic storm is an inevitability in the near future, likely causing blackouts, satellite failures, and more. Unlike other threats to our planet, such as supervolcanoes or asteroids, the time frame for a cataclysmic geomagnetic storm—caused by eruptions from our sun playing havoc with Earth's magnetic field—is comparatively short.

It could happen in the next decade, or in the next century, or tomorrow. All we know is, based on previous events, our planet will almost definitely be hit relatively soon, probably within 100 years.

Jeffrey Love of the U.S. Geological Survey and his colleagues reexamined the intensity of the 1921 event, known as the New York Railroad Storm, in greater detail than ever before.

The Carrington Event is particularly famous for its effects on Earth, sending geomagnetically induced currents coursing through the planet's nascent electric grid and starting fires worldwide. A new analysis published in Space Weather a month before Love's paper, however, shows the effects of the 1921 New York Railroad Storm were just as severe, if not more so.

The 1921 event unfolded in two phases, unleashing an opening burst of disruption before intensifying into a full-fledged superstorm.

Although the Carrington Event has long been the canonical storm for forecasting what might one day come our way, maybe now the New York Railroad Storm and its impacts should be equally revered. "I think the 1921 storm is maybe worthy of just as much discussion," Love says. "Looking at these two storms, they are, far and away, the biggest ever recorded."

RESEARCHERS INVESTIGATE WHAT HAPPENS IF PERFECT SOLAR STORM HITS EARTH

~ *The Space Weather Journal, January 2021*

For years, scientists have been wondering what's the worst the Sun could do.

A study by the NASA Jet Propulsion Laboratory and the Indian Institute of Geomagnetism introduced the concept of a perfect interplanetary coronal mass ejection, stating that it could generate a magnetic storm with intensity greater than the Carrington storm.

The Carrington Event was the largest geomagnetic storm on record, which produced auroral displays as far south as the tropics. The study found that a repeat interplanetary shock of a perfect storm scenario would arrive at Earth within 12 hours and would eventually hit the magnetosphere at 45 times the speed of sound. In response to the shock, a geomagnetic storm around twice as powerful as the 1859 Carrington storm would happen.

"None of this if fantasy," Dr. Tony Phillips of SpaceWeather.com notes. "The Solar and Heliospheric Observatory (SOHO) has observed CMEs leaving the sun at speeds up to 3,000 km/s. And there are many documented cases of one CME clearing the way for another."

A GIANT SOLAR FLARE IS INEVITABLE AND HUMANITY IS COMLETELY UNPREPARED

~ *Big Think, October 19, 2021*

For the past 150+ years, the big ones have all missed us. But at some point, our good luck will run out.

In 1859, when solar astronomer Richard Carrington was tracking a particularly large, irregular sunspot. All of a sudden, a "white light flare" was observed, with unprecedented brightness and lasting about five minutes. Approximately 18 hours later, the largest geomagnetic storm in recorded history occurred on Earth. Aurorae were visible worldwide, including at the equator. Miners awoke in the middle of the night, thinking it was dawn. Newspapers could be read by the light of the aurora. And troublingly, telegraph systems began sparking and igniting fires, even though they were disconnected entirely.

This turned out to be the first-ever observation of what we now know as a solar flare: an example of space weather. If an event similar to 1859's Carrington event occurred here on Earth today, it would result in a multitrillion dollar disaster.

Most of the space weather events that have occurred throughout history would have posed no danger to humans on our planet, as the only discernable effects they would have would be to cause a spectacular auroral display. But today, with the massive amounts of electricity-based infrastructure that now covers our planet, the danger is very, very real.

The major issue is with the infrastructure set up for large-scale production and transmission of power; there will be uncontrollable surges that will knock out power stations and substations and pump far too much current into cities and buildings. Not only would a big one — comparable to 1859's Carrington event — be a multitrillion-dollar disaster, but it could also potentially kill thousands or even millions of people, depending on how long it took to restore heat and water to those most direly affected.

EPIGRAPH

Within any important issue, there are always aspects no one wishes to discuss.
~ George Orwell, Author

Here comes the sun. Here comes the sun, and I say, it's all right.
~ the quiet Beatle, George Harrison

Tyranny and anarchy are never far apart.
~ Jeremy Bentham, English philosopher

Civilization is hideously fragile.
There's not much between us & the horrors underneath, just about a coat of varnish.

~ CP Snow, English physical chemist

We all live in a state of mind that it won't happen to me.
Until it does.
Because you never know when the day before is the day before.
Prepare for tomorrow.

~ Author Bobby Akart

PART 1

Wednesday
And so it begins ...

CHAPTER ONE

Wednesday
Central Park
New York City, New York, USA

The sun threatened to boil the planet, or at least it felt that way. Temperatures in New York City had set record after record. It was the talk of the town, but, as they say, the show must go on. Not surprisingly for the uniformed NYPD officer leaning against the fender of the patrol car, his hefty frame poured buckets of sweat across his blue shirt. His partner impatiently waited in line at a hot dog cart near the entrance to Central Park.

The two were 10-63, temporarily out of service, while they ate a quick lunch. They'd spent the morning responding to domestic disputes between hotheads or chasing off mischievous kids who opened up fire hydrants, allowing thousands of gallons of water to pour onto the street. The cool water provided some respite from the overbearing heat, but it also threatened to run the city's already-depleted water supply dangerously low.

The officer took his attention away from his smart phone to look at the sky. The forecast for the rest of the week was the same as the first of the week. Hazy, smog-filled skies producing ozone warnings. Obnoxiously blinding sunshine promising heatstrokes to the unsuspecting. Cops on edge as tempers flared while the heat index soared.

His partner returned with their hot dogs. "I don't wanna eat here," she said, rolling her eyes as she surveyed her surroundings. "I mean, look at these people. They abandoned the overpasses and moved into the park. The mayor wants them removed, but nobody's got time for rousting the homeless."

Her partner surveyed the ragged tarps and lean-to shelters made of cardboard. He imagined a scene straight out of *The Wizard of Oz* in which a sudden wind and thunderstorm washed over Central Park. Bye-bye, Toto. See ya in Kansas.

"No such luck," he mumbled to himself, barely loud enough for his partner to hear him.

She wasn't done complaining, munching her hot dog as she spoke. "The hoity-toity of the Upper East Side aren't used to homeless roaming their streets. The nineteenth is constantly responding to calls about people peeing on their planters and crapping in their shrubs."

With a mouthful of his lunch, her partner was quick to point out, "It's not like they have a choice. Do you think anyone's gonna invite them inside?"

"No, but where did they crap when they lived under the overpasses?"

"The city came through with the porta-potties. You know. A real humanitarian effort." He sighed. "Anyway, we're staying here. The CO said no excessive driving, remember?"

His partner rolled her eyes again, her signature look of disapproval, and took another large bite of her hot dog. She chewed as quickly as possible in order to offer her two cents' worth, when their day suddenly exploded with activity.

It was like a bag of popcorn starting to cook in a microwave. First, a few faint pops could be heard. Then the popping sounds turned to the unmistakable reports of gunfire. A barrage was let loose, impossible to separate the individual rounds being fired much less discern the number of shooters.

A cacophony of shots rang out, confusing the patrol officers as they ducked for cover. Pedestrians screamed. The homeless scattered. The windows of their patrol car exploded into thousands of bits of glass.

Palms sweaty, the male officer fumbled to key his mic. "Shots fired! 10-13!"

"I'm hit!" his partner shouted from the other side of the patrol car.

He scrambled on all fours to reach her. As he clawed his way towards his partner, a bullet tore through his calf muscle. The burning sensation was immediate as the searing pain of his leg being torn apart reached his brain. His face contortions revealed the agony he was experiencing.

Together, the two officers leaned against the side of the patrol car and pushed the intense pain out of their minds. They readied their sidearms, their eyes darting back and forth in preparation for an attack that would never come.

A man's voice bellowed through a megaphone, blasting the words that could be heard through the trees of Central Park.

"Cut! Print that! Moving on!"

CHAPTER TWO

Wednesday
Central Park
New York City

Asher Doyle smiled, not because the scene was a success but because he was tired of working with these two actors. To be sure, the casting director had done one helluva job choosing a heavyset, sweat-prone male to be coupled with a complaining, judgmental female partner. Their true personalities fit their roles to a T.

"Doyle!" the director barked. "Front and center!"

Asher grabbed his script book and rushed to the gathering of production team members near the director's air-conditioned trailer. The heat-weary group sucked on bottled water as the director addressed the production team of *Blue Bloods.* The hit CBS drama had been one of the highest-rated television programs for years. Asher, a screenwriter, had been fortunate to land a job with the police procedural drama.

Blue Bloods was unique in that it focused equally on the personal conflicts of the characters and the drama associated with fighting crime in the city that never sleeps. Asher's father, a former NYPD detective who later became deputy commissioner of Public Information, had been a hero to him in many ways.

Asher's dream was to become a police officer, but his parents, envisioning a life fraught with danger for their son, had steered him toward a degree in journalism at New York University. After college, his dad had arranged an internship with the screenwriting team, and Asher caught the bug. Between the excitement of being associated with a talented slate of actors, including Tom Selleck, and the realism of shooting a scene for the program, Asher found a career that called upon all of his life experiences.

"You've got my notes for next week's Sunday dinner scenes, right?" his director asked without looking up from a clipboard full of forms thrust at him by a production assistant. He scratched his name without reading them.

"I do," replied Asher. He reached into his messenger bag and retrieved three bound copies of the script. "I wrote Sami into the scenes as you asked."

Asher was referring to Sami Gayle, who played the role of Nicky Reagan, daughter of Erin Reagan. She had a reoccurring role on the program during the beloved Sunday dinner scenes when the family gathered at Frank Reagan's home. Gayle had quit the show years ago to pursue other endeavors in San Francisco; however, her character was being revived, albeit for only a short time. She would be killed in the fifth episode of the season during a smash-and-grab robbery in SoHo.

The director took the revised script. "Go ahead and send it to everyone via email. We're going to shoot the scenes next week and then wrap until after Labor Day. I, for one, have had enough of this damned heat."

Several members of the team voiced their agreement. The director's assistant stepped forward to provide everyone a reminder of the upcoming schedule. "We shoot the chase scenes tomorrow in Central Park. Call time is high noon, people."

"Of course it is," complained one of the crew.

"What about Friday?" asked another.

"Same. Noon both days. We'll wind up by seven tomorrow and six on Friday. The city's already bitchin' about us filming on Friday afternoon. There's some kind of event at the Central Park Zoo, and they want the East Seventy-Second Street entrance cleared no later than seven."

"Yeah, sure," moaned one of the set designers.

The new head of cinematography shook his head. "Do they have any idea what it takes to break down these multi-cam setups?"

The director ignored the complaints. Asher managed a slight grin. For years, *Blue Bloods* had dealt with the city's demands. The twenty-million-per-season tax break received from the state and the inconveniences of filming were easily offset by the revenues generated by filming the program's twenty-two episodes throughout the city.

Asher, who by nature was workmanlike when on the set, didn't engage the other members of the production team as they complained. He, for one, was glad to be there. He consistently maintained a professional decorum while working with the production team and actors. Despite his quiet nature when working with a group of Type A personalities, he was a valued member of the team for many reasons. In addition to his talent as a screenwriter, he was born into a Catholic family. *Blue Bloods* was one of the few programs that routinely included religious tenets through the Reagan family, whose characters were Catholics.

Asher was also the team's liaison with the brass at One Police Plaza. As the son of a decorated detective, he was provided more deference when it came to street closures than a production company imported from Hollywood.

The meeting broke up. Asher removed his Ray-Ban sunglasses

and wiped the sweat from his face. The inside of his NYPD cap was soaked in sweat. He'd lived in New York his entire life and had experienced all the Big Apple had to offer. However, he couldn't recall a time when it was this hot for so many days in a row.

Something had to give.

CHAPTER THREE

Wednesday
Haleakala Observatory
Island of Maui, Hawaii

"Come on, Yang! Don't be a pouty puss. I'm only gonna be gone for a few days."

Professor Neal Burgoyne continued stuffing clothes in his duffel bag while he kept an eye on the Weather Channel. A record heat wave had swept over the Continental U.S. Naturally, New York was the center of attention, as was often the case when unusual weather affected the most densely populated city in America.

Burgoyne kicked a pile of pillows out of his way and knelt in front of a dresser to peek underneath. He prepared himself for Yang, the usually feisty cat, to spring out from under the piece of furniture. The adopted feral cat was astute enough to know when Burgoyne was leaving for a trip. He rarely pulled the duffel off the top shelf of his closet. It meant Yang would be left alone in the professor's apartment with only Animal Planet playing on the television to keep him company.

"Jeez," muttered Burgoyne. "Where the hell are you?"

For the seventh time, he counted three fingers on his hand and then yanked on his thumb. He needed three days of travel clothing and one *Sunday best*, as he called it, for his presentation at the symposium he'd been invited to.

If it were up to him, he would've appeared by videoconferencing. However, he was the guest of honor thanks to his work at the Daniel K. Inouye Solar Telescope at the Haleakala Observatory. Known as DKIST, most of the facility was used for the study of the Sun. DKIST boasted the world's largest solar telescope with a four-meter aperture that allowed sunlight to pass in for analysis. Named for the longtime senator from Hawaii, DKIST was also a teaching facility. Burgoyne's curricula had been critically acclaimed by others in his field. Well, most of them, anyway. Over the years, he'd managed to attract his fair share of detractors.

Burgoyne rarely adorned his salt-and-pepper head with a hat. However, the heat wave enveloping New York prompted him to adopt headgear with a wide brim. The well-worn, wide-brimmed fedora gathered dust on the shelf next to his equally rarely used duffel bag.

He made his way across the modest apartment. He glanced behind the sofa and side chairs in search of his best friend, silently cursing Yang's elusiveness.

Burgoyne reached into the dark closet for his hat and was greeted with a hiss. His arm recoiled, and the expletives began to fly.

"Dammit, Yang! What the hell's that all about?"

Yang leapt off the shelf and landed on all fours six feet below. He took off in a rush, bounding across the rug until he slid under the bed like a baserunner stealing second.

Burgoyne exhaled as he retrieved the hat. "That was pretty rude, buddy. Keep it up and I'll stay a week. You know, maybe see a show or eat at some fancy restaurants."

Burgoyne was lying, and Yang most likely knew it. Both of them suffered from separation anxiety when the professor's duties took him away. Yang was his constant companion whether in the classroom or within the observatory.

He was about to kneel at the foot of the bed to engage his ornery cat when his cell phone rang. The distinctive ringtone, pulled straight from the *Twilight Zone* television show, indicated his research assistant and fellow transplant from upstate New York, Kelly Baxter, was calling.

"Hey, Kelly," Burgoyne answered immediately.

"Professor, I think you need to stop by here before you catch your flight."

Burgoyne frowned. He and his assistant were on a first-name basis. "What's with the formality?"

"Um, sir. There is someone here from KITV. She's a producer or something like that."

Burgoyne tucked his phone between his cheek and shoulder. He hated the concept of hands-free speakers.

"Okay, that's exciting. Tell them to go away."

He zipped up his duffel and set up Yang's electronic feeder. On the few occasions that he traveled, he wondered why he bothered with the feeder. The petulant cat would go on a hunger strike anyway in order to guilt his human companion into staying home the next go-around.

"Well, they want to ask you to appear on *Good Morning America* this Friday."

Burgoyne let out a hearty laugh before he responded in a series of simple, two-word sentences. "Bull shit. Been there. Done that. Forget it."

He'd appeared on the ABC program years ago and had been broadsided by a simultaneous guest appearance by Bill StickANeedleInMyEye, as Burgoyne called him, the Science Guy. The know-it-all mechanical engineer had somehow convinced American journalists he was an expert in anything related to science. Like that Tyson fella, the astrophysicist, the science guy had the gift of gab and a schtick that made him ideal for television.

Burgoyne had butted heads with the science guy during that last interview and practically stormed off the set at the end of their segment. He left the studios without saying goodbye and hightailed it back to his comfort zone in Maui on the first available flight.

"Okay, I'll tell her."

"Wait. Kelly?" he asked. "What do they want to talk about?"

Burgoyne listened as Baxter engaged the producer. After a moment, she came back to the phone.

"The Perfect Storm. Same topic as your presentation."

Burgoyne thought for a moment. Not that he relished the opportunity to appear on national television, he was always raising private funds for DKIST. This topic, although controversial, would give him exposure to money outside the scientific community.

Baxter took advantage of his pause and added, "She promised it would be just you. Nobody else."

Burgoyne nodded and smiled. They remembered his reaction to the last blindside. "Fine, tell them I'll do it. After they're gone, let me know. I wanna stop by and have you keep an eye on something I was studying last night."

"Yes, Professor. Aloha."

Burgoyne laughed and whispered to himself, "Whatever." After giving Yang one last chance to exchange goodbyes, to no avail, the lanky professor adjusted his ponytail, donned his fedora, and marched out the door toward the observatory.

CHAPTER FOUR

Wednesday
Haleakala Observatory
Maui, Hawaii

It was an impressive scientific achievement. The most powerful solar telescope in the world, located at DKIST, gathered images from the Sun's surface and lower atmosphere multiple times per second. Not only did it generate spectacular imagery of the Sun, it also provided unparalleled predictive capabilities of the intense activity on the solar disk.

Burgoyne had been part of the team at DKIST since the state-of-the-art telescope had opened its eyes for the first time in December 2019. The first data points generated were beyond the expectations of the scientific community. The buzz surrounding the beautiful images and videos caused Burgoyne to swell with pride. He readily accepted the accolades thrown in his direction. However, he immediately realized the telescope could serve a more important purpose—protecting the planet from a disaster that was most assuredly coming. Back-to-back catastrophic solar flares.

A key goal of solar astronomy was to study the correlation between the Sun's activity and the space weather that causes solar storms. Then, based upon the timing and intensity of solar matter hurled from the Sun, scientists around the globe would determine whether the conditions existed on Earth for significant damage to occur.

At DKIST, Burgoyne's team focused on measuring the magnetic field of the Sun at its photosphere, chromosphere, and across the solar corona, which was usually hidden by the bright light of the Sun's surface. The data received by these measurements could help predict solar flares and coronal mass ejections that could devastate electronics on Earth.

Burgoyne became known for his analysis of the magnetic field of the Sun and its alignment in relationship to the Earth. He hypothesized that advance prediction of a coronal mass ejection, or CME, would enable mitigation protocols to be initiated, designed to protect the world's power grids.

Burgoyne waited behind a large growth of hibiscus plants until he saw the television producer pull away from the observatory's entrance. He didn't want to get involved in an unnecessary conversation because he needed the time to speak with Baxter and the other scientists manning the telescope.

He walked briskly down the hill, watching his footing on the rocky surface mostly devoid of vegetation. His mind wandered to his trip, lamenting the fact he'd be smelling vehicle exhaust and the sweaty bodies that would undoubtedly fill the streets of Manhattan.

The professor was met inside the lobby of DKIST by Baxter and two recently graduated scientists. "Good morning, Neal. I'm sorry about the sudden phone call."

Burgoyne smiled. "That's fine. I changed my mind after thinking about our funding drive. We need to introduce new entities to the important work we do here. The usual nonprofit donors are stretched pretty thin. We need corporate America to step up to the plate. The

GMA appearance will give me an opportunity to speak to more than just the usual brainiacs."

The students chuckled at the odd use of the term. Either of them could have responded with *pot, meet kettle*. However, they wisely held their tongues. For all of Burgoyne's eccentricities, he was a brilliant scientist. He was constantly absorbing knowledge from any available resource. His somewhat reclusive lifestyle allowed him to study the Sun while reviewing the work of his peers without cluttering his brain.

"You wanted us to keep an eye on something?" said Baxter inquisitively, reminding the professor of their phone call.

Burgoyne nodded and pointed toward the hallway leading to his office. "Come with me. We have two active regions developing that require additional monitoring."

Baxter hustled to keep up with Burgoyne. "Have they been given designations by the SWPC?" The Space Weather Prediction Center in Boulder, Colorado, was responsible for assigning four-digit region numbers when solar watchers identified a strong and active magnetic field. These active regions were often associated with sunspots, the source of the violent flares and CMEs emanating from the solar disk.

"Not yet," replied Burgoyne. "I expect they will once the two regions rotate back into view."

"Professor, did you notice them during the last time they were in view four weeks ago?" asked one of the students. Unlike Earth, which rotates on its axis every twenty-four hours, the Sun rotates on average every twenty-seven days.

They entered his office. Burgoyne took a deep breath before tossing his duffel bag onto a chair. His mind searched the memory banks as he contemplated ways to cancel the trip. He'd much rather be sitting in the observatory's control room, studying images and data while sipping Kona Coffee.

"No. This is based on information from the Parker space probe. It was buzzing around the disk at its usual three hundred thirty miles per hour. As the probe slingshotted itself closer to the surface last night, it revealed the two developing active regions."

"What about size?" asked Baxter.

"I expect them to be immense. Both of them. And ..." He paused as he considered the possibilities. "They're located in perfect alignment along the Sun's equator."

Baxter studied her mentor and nodded slowly. She was not a skeptic. The professor's hypothesis regarding the potential of a Perfect Storm were deemed to have astronomical odds. Yet, as she had pointed out numerous times to the others at DKIST, it had happened before. Therefore, it could happen again.

"Sunshine!" said Burgoyne loudly, startling Baxter. His computer immediately left sleep mode, and four monitors, stacked two over two, sprang to life. "Let's see what we have."

For a moment, he studied data from the SWPC as well as from the National Center for Atmospheric Research, or NCAR. Both organizations gathered information from scientists around the world and acted like a clearinghouse for solar data. They were able to disregard anomalies while acting as a final arbiter when issuing geomagnetic storm warnings. A single source to disseminate credible information back to facilities like DKIST.

"Well, just as I suspected," he mumbled. Burgoyne pointed toward a monitor that displayed a time-lapse graphic titled *sunspot number and latitude in degrees*. The graphic created waves of both blue and red across the screen. He pointed at the monitor. "Parker has provided an analysis of the bands of magnetism drifting across the surface. Red and blue indicate oppositely charged magnetic bands. Do you see how they march across the equatorial region of the solar disk?"

Baxter responded. The new additions to the team knew when it was time to be quiet. "The number of black spots is incredible. They're annihilating each other."

"That's right. These oppositely charged bands are powerful, smashing together and kickstarting the development of the active regions. The fact they are rolling across the equator is troubling. It's the hottest part of the solar disk, and solar flares emanating from the central latitude lines of the Sun are the most powerful."

One of the students took a chance to engage her professor. "They appear close together. Could they merge into one?"

Burgoyne furrowed his brow. "Possibly. This is why I need you three to be on this twenty-four seven. This could either develop into a massive coronal hole that will spew devilish winds, or it could generate back-to-back CMEs."

Baxter stood upright, eyeing the graduate students. They nodded in response to her making eye contact. "We'll keep an eye on the Sun's rotation compared to Earth's rotational position. Continuously."

Burgoyne sighed. "Good. When dealing with the Sun's inner dynamo and its eruptions, timing is everything, as we all know."

CHAPTER FIVE

Wednesday
4th Floor, Random House Tower
1745 Broadway
New York City

Lauren Doyle picked through her turkey cobb salad, pushing the red onions out of the way. When the editorial assistants took everyone's lunch order, she'd made a point to have the deli eighty-six the red onions, restaurant parlance for removing an ingredient from the customary recipe. She worked in an up-close-and-personal environment and didn't need to repel her authors with dragon breath. Today, they forgot.

Her mind wandered as the author droned on about his accomplishments as a writer in an attempt to impress Penguin's executive managing editor, or to be braggadocio. To be sure, the man had been successful as an independent author. So much so that the Big 5 publishing house with offices worldwide had spared no expense to fly him up for the meeting and stick him in a swanky hotel.

Lauren would be one of five editors assigned to the author. She'd started with Penguin as a mechanical editor, or copy editor, whose job it was to review a manuscript's punctuation, capitalization, and other style rules.

Over time, her role at Penguin became more focused. Soon, she was only assigned authors in the thriller and science fiction genres. Then, with the success of apocalyptic movies, she worked exclusively as a developmental editor for authors writing disaster fiction.

Her job was to think big picture. Every aspect of the story, from character development to subplots, was scrutinized by her. Her authors either loved her or they hated her. Not all of them were open to suggestion. Most had big egos due to their success; otherwise, they wouldn't be sitting in the posh conference room next to Meredith Cross, the publisher's executive editor.

"Here's the thing." The author was summarizing his position. "There's no doubt in my mind that this impressive editorial team will make me a better writer. I've enjoyed talking with Lauren this morning as she educated me on the benefits of working with a publishing house."

"Then you understand why your career is ready for this next step," interjected Cross. Lauren's boss was putting a hard sell on the author, a somewhat unusual tactic for her. Ordinarily, she allowed others to go through the interview process.

"My decision to move forward will be purely financial," the author continued. "First, you've indicated that an agent would be in my best interest. I get that. They know their way around here and have the legal team to assist with contracts. However, the agent will get ten percent of my royalties."

Lauren nodded internally. It was possible he didn't need an agent. Especially since he'd managed to gain entrance to the fourth floor without one.

"Plus, you will get half the remaining ninety percent. The math is simple. I'd be taking a heckuva pay cut."

"Movies or streaming is a possibility with us," countered Cross. "The exposure you'll get for your work through us is incalculable."

Lauren admired the author's self-assurance. Her mind wandered again as he provided the editorial team a dozen reasons why it would not make economic sense for him to sign on. Most authors would be profusely thanking Cross and looking for the contracts to execute. Not this guy.

Many of the questions from the Random House team turned to their curiosity of the subject matter of his novels. *What kinds of threats do we face? Which one concerns you the most? What is the likelihood of that happening? Don't you think people would pull together to help one another?*

He calmly answered the questions. The sincerity and belief in his convictions were obvious. All of the potential scenarios were either based on plausible science or historical fact. Certainly, he explained, there were probabilities to consider, but as he put it, being ready for a catastrophic event was like purchasing insurance against something like Superstorm Sandy. Hopefully, you'll never face a catastrophe, but if you do, you'll have a better chance at survival than most.

As he spoke, Lauren thought about her own refrigerator and pantry. They were, quite simply, empty. Except for pita chips and hummus or other snacks, they were a typical double-income, no-kids family in New York. Their sustenance came from takeout.

What shocked her the most was his belief that society would collapse in a matter of hours rather than days as most asserted. Lauren and Asher had often spoken about how stressed Americans had become. Whether because of the recent economic downturn or the rabid, partisan political environment, it seemed the country had been divided into tribes. Left versus right. People of color versus whites. Haves versus have-nots.

Weren't we all the same when it came time for a crisis? Maybe, she thought to herself, once upon a time. She was only a kid when 9/11 devastated New York City. Asher had lost family members in the aftermath. She'd lost an uncle. The pain the city had endured was indescribable.

Yet, around the country, Americans rallied together. Everyone hung a flag on the front of their homes. Some clipped them to their car windows. Lapel pins of Old Glory could be seen throughout her building. However, with the passage of time, the showing of patriotism faded away until fifteen years later, a prominent player in the National Football League knelt during the national anthem as a form of protest. His actions generated a media and political firestorm that raged on for a decade.

Lauren visibly shook her upper body as if a chill had run down her spine. She wanted to forget about how dangerous New York City had become since then.

As the conversation continued, her thoughts turned to Asher and their upcoming tenth anniversary celebration. He'd texted her earlier to let her know he could be freed up by six on Friday evening. She knew he was filming near Central Park, so she began to look at dinner possibilities around there. She didn't want to appear rude or draw the ire of her boss by searching for options on her iPhone. This meeting would be over soon enough.

"Why don't you speak with your wife and let us know," said Cross unemotionally as she stood, signaling an end to the interview. Lauren sensed her boss was annoyed with the way the interview had gone. She was not used to rejection. Rejecting authors and their manuscripts was the publisher's prerogative.

After a few disingenuous pleasantries were exchanged, the room emptied. Lauren remained to finish her salad, when a special news alert appeared on her phone. She studied it and then looked at the door. Perhaps they should throw more money at this guy.

CHAPTER SIX

Wednesday
NY1 Studios
Chelsea Market Building
New York

Howie Gordon waited patiently while a production assistant adjusted his tie and a member of the makeup team patted his forehead dry. At the top of the hour, he'd teased the weather forecast from outside the NY1 studios in the heart of Manhattan's Meatpacking District. The story of the day continued to be the excessive heat that had beset the five boroughs, and the entire Northeast, for that matter.

He inwardly grumbled when he was asked to do the live lead-in from the busy sidewalk. *What is the point?* he wondered to himself. *Everybody knows it's freakin' hot. Hot enough to boil Hell's teakettle, for Pete's sake.*

However, today he had a new spin on the heat wave. He was going out there, as they say. His dramatic drop-off after he'd teased the segment sounded ominous even to him.

Does this heat wave portend something far more catastrophic?

Ooh. Ah.

Hurricane Howie, a moniker bestowed upon him years ago when he participated on a reality television show, could imagine everyone scooting up on the edge of their seats at home. Eagerly awaiting the answer to his foreboding query.

He returned inside to prepare for his segment. The cool air did little to prevent the perspiration beading up beneath his full head of hair. The aging process had been kind to Howie, as he had avoided male-pattern baldness while acquiring a silver-fox tone of gray. His good looks and Midwestern smile made him a favorite in the New York media market.

Despite the air conditioning, it was still necessary for him to press his earpiece in a little tighter, as sweat had moistened the rubber tip. He always relied upon the countdown given to him by the producer. However, the cue from the talking heads generally elicited a comment or answer to a question, so he needed to pay attention to their banter.

The female anchor wrapped up the news segment and turned her attention to Howie. "New York was all a-sizzle yesterday as it reached a record when temps hit an agonizing one hundred six degrees, tying a record set on July 9, 1936. Well, we all know man-made climate change is a major contributing factor to this record heat, but our chief meteorologist, Howie Gordon, seems to have an additional theory. Howie?"

"That's right, Annika. But first, let me say if our fellow New Yorkers ran out of polite words to describe how hot it got Tuesday, they're gonna be speechless over the next several days."

Howie leaned into the camera as he added, "And New Yorkers will need to get creative to beat the potentially one-hundred-ten-degree temperatures in store for today through the weekend."

With the green screen as his backdrop, Howie went through his normal weather forecast. He smoothly switched between computer-generated graphics and images with the subtle press of the clicker in his left hand. After he wrapped up the forecast with the warning to the viewing audience that there was no end in sight to the record heat and drought conditions, he pushed the clicker into his pocket and clasped his hands in front of him.

"Now, a common question I get from our viewers is whether solar flares like those creating the beautiful auroras in our northern latitudes have an effect on our temperatures." He paused to gather his thoughts, his mood becoming pensive.

"Along the way to this phenomenal gig on *The Morning Show*, I was the chief meteorologist in Anchorage, Alaska, where space weather was discussed about as often as the Earth's weather. Most people don't think about what's happening around our solar system as weather, but it is.

"In Anchorage, I got to know the scientists at the Geophysical Institute at the University of Alaska. The institute was one of hundreds of organizations that worked closely with the Space Weather Prediction Center located in Boulder, Colorado, to create forecast models for the intensity and location of auroras. They also taught me a thing or two about the relationship between solar activity and our planet's temperatures.

"These solar flares and coronal mass ejections, as they are called, bombard Earth's outermost atmosphere with tremendous amounts of energy. Now, most of that energy is reflected back into space by the planet's magnetic field. For that reason, they told me, the energy does not reach our planet's surface and usually has no measurable influence on surface temperatures. You see, the energy released by these solar storms is different from the visible and ultraviolet light that penetrate Earth's atmosphere. Instead, the storms hurl bursts of powerful, electrically charged particles through space. They stream through the Earth's upper atmosphere but don't cause heat waves."

Howie took a deep breath because he expected the executive producer was scratching his head at the point of his whole dissertation. Howie felt the people of New York had to know what might come their way.

"In the next few days, it's possible these solar storms could grow in magnitude, releasing enough energy to spread highly charged particles to the lower latitudes. In fact, here in New York, we might experience the beautiful auroras I was accustomed to seeing in Alaska. But with the beautiful night skies, another hazardous situation may impact all of us.

"The charged particles can rain a substantial amount of radiation on satellites, and the increased electromagnetic activity can also disrupt power grids and radio communications. In other words, power outages and blackouts are possible due to these solar storms. Under the current heat conditions, that can be devastating to many New Yorkers."

Howie had said enough. Apparently, those in the control room agreed, as they quickly cut off his mic and turned the cameras onto the shocked duo squirming nervously in their chairs. He was certain an ass-chewin' awaited him when he left the weather desk. However, he didn't care. Over the years, Howie's gut had served him well, and there was something about solar cycle 25 that raised alarms inside him. People needed to be prepared.

CHAPTER SEVEN

Wednesday
Cubbison's Farm
Harford, Pennsylvania

"Luke! Pull!" shouted John Cubbison from his perch atop the track hoe. The massive excavator rumbled underneath him as he barked his orders. "This is the last one!"

His nineteen-year-old son shifted the levers of the family's bulldozer. His twin brother, Matthew, provided a thumbs-up, indicating the heavy-duty chain had been secured around the massive tree stump.

The Cubbison men, including John's father, Grandpa Sam, as everyone called him, had excavated a new pond on their property along the creek bed that bordered the northernmost part of the farm. They were adding more cattle and needed additional pasture together with a water source.

The dozer lurched forward, and the stump fought to hold on to the earth in a perfect example of the *irresistible force paradox*. The deep rooting system of the mighty oak tree might have been only four feet deep, but it spread laterally for dozens of feet. The oak had survived storms and high winds for years. It was once an immovable object. Until, that is, the twenty-thousand-pound Cat D3 bulldozer began its work. The unstoppable force groaned as the tug-of-war commenced. The dozer's tracks fought for a grip on the newly uncovered moist soil of the pond's banks.

The stump began to give way. Under the ground, the roots of the red oak cracked and lost their grip on the earth. Luke utilized all the horsepower the D3 had to offer, urging it forward with his John Deere cap as if he we were persuading a horse to gallop across the prairie.

"Stand clear, Matthew!" admonished Grandpa Sam, who'd worked Cubbison's Farm since he was waist-high to his daddy. Matthew scrambled up the bank just as the tap root broke free, sending rich, fertile soil and stones into the air.

"Hell yeah!" Luke shouted as the D3 won the battle and slowly chugged up the slope toward higher ground. He replaced his cap in order to shield his face from the bright, blistering sun.

His father wasted no time in moving the excavator forward to pull dirt into the hole left by the stump. Twenty minutes later, their pond was formed and ready for the creek to be diverted to fill the shallow three-acre dent in the earth.

With the heavy equipment shut off, their respective engines crackling from the heat generated during the final excavation effort, Grandpa Sam summoned everyone under the widespread canopy of an American beech tree. As the guys gathered together, he tossed them bottles of water from a cooler and began to lay out the sandwich fixin's.

The Cubbison family, in addition to owning a variety of livestock, also operated a farm-to-table market along the highway bordering their property in Susquehanna County located in Northeastern Pennsylvania. What was once a farmer's vegetable stand decades ago had become a regionally known market and restaurant. John's wife, Emma, had taken on the task of running the market when Sam's wife had passed away. The business had thrived under her watchful eye, drawing visitors from throughout the Northeast.

The guys eagerly sliced the fresh loaf of bread baked for the occasion. Their hearty appetites urged their hands into action, spreading the homemade pimento cheese across the slices until each took a man-sized mouthful. Only Grandpa Sam had the ability to speak as the younger generations chowed down.

"We're almost done," he began as he wandered away from the three Kawasaki Mule side-by-sides. He pointed to the two saplings with fluorescent orange strips tied to them. "The terrain between the flags is perfect to divert the creek. With the overflow we created on the other side of the pond, heavy rains will allow the water to continue flowing toward the State Game Lands."

The Pennsylvania State Game Commission owned and managed nearly two million acres of property used for hunting, trapping, and fishing. The Cubbisons had obtained a permit to divert the creek with the proviso that the water overflow picked up on the other side.

"Whadya think, Grandpa? A couple of hours?" asked Luke.

It was unfair to call Luke the favored son of the twin boys. He was clean-cut. Polite. An A student in high school. The obvious heir apparent to the running of the Cubbison farming operation when his time came. His brother, Matthew, on the other hand, was the polar opposite.

Luke loved farming, and his persona reflected it. Matthew, who'd grown rebellious as he got older, worked the farm because it was his best option at the moment. Luke was a great student, but Matthew barely graduated. Luke loved the outdoors. Matthew preferred playing video games. Luke was an ardent country music fan. Matthew like heavy metal. The two were fraternal twins rather than identical twins. Luke had been born just minutes before Matthew, a fact that Matthew seemed to resent. They each had their own unique personalities despite living under the same roof their entire lives. That said, they were loved equally by their family.

Sam shrugged as he returned to his tailgate lunch. "I suspect so.

Besides, your mother looked me in the eye when we left the house this morning and told me to have everyone back by three for shaves and showers."

"I'm not shavin'," grumbled Matthew, who sported a full beard and mustache.

"Except you, of course," said his grandfather.

"So the plan is to head up to Binghamton?" asked John. Binghamton, New York, was the closest large city to the Cubbisons' farm. Interstate 81, which ran just east of Harford, could get them there in less than an hour.

"That's right, son," replied Sam. "My granddaughter seems to think the overalls aren't good enough for New York City folks."

Luke laughed. "Are you gonna have to wear a suit? And hard-soled shoes?"

Matthew chimed in, "Where the heck you goin'? The opera?"

Their dad stepped in to protect Sam from the onslaught of teasing the boys seemed to be ready to administer. John was supposed to be the one escorting his daughter, Catherine, to New York. The pond dig had taken longer than expected, and there was a large party to be catered at Cubbison's that required his help. Sam was more than willing to take Cat to New York. However, he didn't think a new wardrobe was necessary.

"Boys, lay off your grandpa. Mom and Cat will get him outfitted in something appropriate. They're gonna be doin' a lot of walking and, I think, going to visit at least four museums. Right, Dad?"

"Cat has an itinerary lined out that would put one of those tour guide operations to shame. That young lady intends to see it all while we're there."

"I would've taken her," said Matthew with a somewhat sour tone. He had ulterior motives, of course, that both of his parents had fleshed out in short order. Matthew wanted to take a taste of the nightlife the Big Apple had to offer since it had recently lowered its legal drinking age to eighteen.

"Grandpa Sam has always wanted to travel into the city," said John.

The sixty-seven-year-old shrugged. Not really, but his love for his granddaughter forced him to overcome his reservations. New York City, the once vibrant city known for its exclusive retail stores, flashy Broadway shows, and its high-flying financial district, had fallen on difficult times in the past decade. Crime had risen exponentially as the NYPD had been neutered and prosecutions had waned. Some foreign state departments had issued warnings for their citizens contemplating travel to New York to take extraordinary personal safety measures upon arrival.

Grandpa Sam had quipped there was nothing that he and his concealed handgun couldn't handle until John had reminded him that guns were banned in the city to keep everyone safe. Although the two men shared a laugh, they realized the irony wasn't very funny.

"Well, you all know how much I enjoy studying history. Cat has promised lots of it in the museums we'll be touring. With the itinerary she's made up, Sunday will be here before we know it."

John stood and wiped his mouth with the sleeve of his shirt. Despite the heat, he always wore a long-sleeve chambray shirt in the summer to protect his skin from the sun. Over the years, the dermatologist had removed several noncancerous moles from his chest and arms.

"Let's knock out this last part so we can get back to the house. We don't want your mom swinging her rolling pin at us, do we?"

CHAPTER EIGHT

Wednesday
Cubbison's Farm
Harford, Pennsylvania

Emma Cubbison always considered herself as cool as a cucumber. Calm. Composed. In control. The idiom was based on the belief that in hot weather, the inside of a cucumber remained cooler than the outside air surrounding it. Emma was uncharacteristically perspiring profusely as she began to set up the tables for Friday night's Founder's Day soiree hosted by Cubbison's Farm-to-Table. It would be the largest gathering of the year in Susquehanna County and attended by all the local self-important muckety-mucks.

"Cat!" she hollered at her thirteen-year-old daughter across the lawn. "Go ahead and start bringing the glass vases."

Catherine, called Cat since she was a baby scampering around the Cubbisons' farmhouse, was on her summer break from middle school. She grudgingly obliged her mother's request. "Mom, you do remember it's only Wednesday, right?"

Emma was nervous about hosting the annual dinner. In the past, the dinner had been held at one of the eateries in the county seat of Montrose located half an hour from Scranton. The newly installed president of the Chamber of Commerce, a California native, had taken to Emma upon her arrival in the small community. Emma's farm-to-table operation at Cubbison's Market had intrigued her. She surprised everyone when she chose it for the location of this year's Founder's Day dinner.

Farm-to-table dining was a California dining concept meant to promote the produce and livestock of local farms. In theory, most produce loses its nutrients within twenty-four hours of harvesting. Small, local restaurants began to tout the locally grown food as an alternative to that shipped all across the country by jobbers like Sysco and Kraft.

Emma had started the operation as a subsidiary of the Cubbisons' highly successful farmer's market located on the country road fronting their land. Just two miles from Interstate 81, Emma served meals on Friday and Saturday nights to a packed house, figuratively speaking, as the dining was strictly outdoors, pending favorable weather. A billboard on the heavily traveled interstate drew travelers to their market, resulting in multiple expansions over her twenty-six-year marriage to John.

Emma addressed her daughter as she arrived with the first case of vases. "Honey, I know it's Wednesday. Tonight, we have to go to the mall and have a send-off dinner at Applebee's. Tomorrow morning, I gotta get you and Grandpa Sam ready for the trip. I'll have my hands full preparing the food while keeping your dad focused on watchin' over the market while I do so."

Cat studied her mom. She was her mother's *mini-me*. Both were thin with flowing blonde hair. Despite Emma's very active days, she refused to cut it short as so many women do. To be sure, there came a point in life when fussin' over hair day in and day out seemed superfluous. Following her college days in California, Emma had adopted a beachy waves hairstyle. It was what had attracted John to her when they first met. She vowed to always provide him a vision of her younger, less wrinkled self.

"Mom, I'm already packed. I mean, pretty much."

"Your grandpa hasn't started because we have to get him some proper clothes. Plus, your father wants to have a discussion with both of you before you leave."

"Discussion?" asked Cat.

"Honey, just humor him, please. He's worried about the two of you in the big city. Especially New York."

"We'll be fine. We don't have anything planned for nighttime."

Emma smiled and patted her daughter on the head like a child although she was blossoming into a beautiful young woman. "We know that. He just wants to make sure there are no oopsies."

"Oopsy?"

"Yeah, you know. Lapses in judgment that might get you two into a pickle. Sadly, you can't count on anyone coming to help if you get, um, well ..." Emma's voice trailed off. She didn't want to break her daughter's spirit.

She'd been so proud of Cat when she'd become the youngest girl in Harford Fair history to win the Queen Contest. Her three-hundred-word essay on the topic What My Fair Means to My Community had been praised by the judges. Also, Cat's dynamic, mature responses during the personal interviews had impressed everyone.

In addition to receiving the customary award certificate and ribbon for being chosen as the Fair Queen, Emma had earned an all-expenses paid-trip for two to New York City to visit its renowned museums. Naturally, her dad had been planning to escort her until Emma had begun to feel overwhelmed about the prospect of hosting nearly a hundred local politicians, business owners, and professionals for the Founder's Day dinner. She wanted John's help, and Grandpa Sam was ready to fill in as Cat's chaperone.

"Mom? Do you want me to get the rest of the vases? What about flowers? They won't last in this heat."

Emma snapped out of her sudden contemplation of her young daughter's trip to the city. It would be difficult to focus on the dinner while she worried about Cat's safety. She'd have to keep up a façade for the sake of her family and the guests.

"You're right, honey. Vases only. I'll cut some stem flowers from the garden at the last minute."

Cat smiled and nodded. She jogged back toward the she-shed, as John called it, to retrieve the rest of the vases. Her blonde hair was pulled back in a ponytail and swished back and forth like the tail of a palomino pony playing in the field.

"I really don't want you to grow up," she mumbled to herself as her eyes followed her daughter into the small Dutch barn painted red. "My mom didn't shelter me, so I'm not gonna shelter you."

Then Emma looked toward the sky and the blazing midday sun. "God, I'm counting on you to keep her safe. Do you promise?" She waited for a response but didn't get one.

CHAPTER NINE

Wednesday
Applebee's Grill + Bar
Binghamton, New York

"Sam Cubbison, you are a royal pain in the ass to shop for," said Emma playfully as the family exited their Chevy Suburban SUV at Applebee's. She and Grandpa Sam had that kind of relationship. In many respects, Emma reminded him of his dearly departed wife's feistiness. He enjoyed the fun-loving ribbing between them.

"I don't think so," Sam countered. "I just have certain standards to uphold, including in my professional attire."

As the group of six milled around outside the Applebee's entrance, waiting to be called by the hostess, the two-hour-long shopping excursion was the topic of conversation.

"Dad, there is more to clothing than Carhartt and Wranglers."

"Not really," Sam said, shaking his head. He'd walked in and promptly walked out of stores like American Eagle and Hollister. He'd given Eddie Bauer slightly more time before declaring the Oakdale Mall to be a bust.

He'd never let on that he'd already made the decision to shop elsewhere as they approached the mall. Gearcor, a retailer known for work clothing, had an outlet down the street. He'd purchased clothing and shoes there in the past. They carried his favorite brands, including Carhartt, Wolverine, Timberland, and Danner. Once inside the store, he became far more cooperative, actually enjoying how Emma and Cat doted over their choices for him.

"Hey, sis, wanna do a TikTok in front of the entrance?" asked Luke. TikTok was a video-sharing app popular with young people.

"Really?" replied Cat, somewhat surprised her older brother would be willing to put himself out there in front of prospective cute girls inside the restaurant.

Luke and Cat had always been close ever since she'd fallen off a horse while on his watch. When they were riding through some trails in a woodsy area of the farm, her horse had been startled by a rattlesnake, causing her to be thrown off her saddle. While she lay on the ground, stunned from the impact of the fall, the rattler slowly approached her. Luke sprang into action, pulled his Mora knife, and rammed it through the body of the snake. Although the snake was still alive, the knife had impaled it, preventing it from advancing on the frightened Cat. The incident had created a tight bond between the two.

Luke was genuinely enthusiastic. "Yeah, come on. We've practiced 'Fancy Like' at home. Let's do it here."

Country artist Walker Hayes's first hit was a song titled "Fancy Like" that quickly became known as the Applebee's song because aspects of the restaurant were included in the lyrics. The Hayes family, including the artist's teenage daughter, had created a country line dance to the lyrics that took the world by storm. The videos of the family dancing to "Fancy Like" went viral, and soon everyone was creating home videos to upload to social media.

Cat looked to her other brother. "Matthew, will you play it on your phone so we can stay choreographed?"

Matthew smirked and shook his head. "Sorry, not on my playlists. Like, never."

His father scowled at his son's dour attitude and offered to cue it up for the kids. "Cat, if it's on your phone, I'll—"

Cat shook her head. "No, Daddy. I need you to run the video. Mom?"

"I'm on it," she replied as she scrolled through her iTunes downloads. Seconds later, the two were dancing in perfect coordination, laughing, and smiling at the camera. Several of the restaurant guests sitting in booths near the window began to film the family as Luke and Cat performed on the sidewalk outside the entrance.

When it was over, everyone exchanged high fives. Even Matthew. And, needless to say, there were several orders placed for the Bourbon Street Steak with an Oreo shake. It was a family outing that would be remembered, and longed for, as the difficult years ahead passed them by.

CHAPTER TEN

Wednesday
Undisclosed Location
New York City

Dirk Kantor stared down at the stack of Benjamins on the dark mahogany table. Well, to call it a stack was an understatement. It was more like a pile of money. He'd counted it in front of his employer, continuing his practice of trusting no one. Next to the proposed payment was an envelope full of dossiers on several unknown mercenaries who'd accompany him on the job.

Kantor was an expert thief. A burglar extraordinaire. Known worldwide for his ability to enter the most secure of facilities, expertly penetrating their defenses in order to kidnap a target or, in this case, simply gather information.

However, the client was certainly out of the ordinary. In fact, the client's business immediately made him suspect. In all his years of using his skills to steal from others, he'd never been hired by a law firm before.

After some basic research, he'd learned this was no ordinary law firm. His employer represented some of the most well-known politicians in America. They were adept at managing political campaigns as well as destroying the hopes and dreams of their opposition. Oppo research, as it was known in the political biz, had become just as essential as touting the accomplishments of their politician clients.

Known as the politics of personal destruction, it had existed for ages in America but reached new levels with the advent of the internet and cell phone cameras. The firm was able to reach back decades, in some cases to high school, in search of a tweet on Twitter or a Facebook post that might be construed as homophobic, xenophobic, racist, misogynist, sexist, or some other form of -ist word. Oftentimes, this background research could tank a nomination or destroy a political career.

Kantor knew the game. He'd been tasked with breaking into politicians' homes to insert hidden cameras and microphones in the past. But this was the first time he'd been asked to break into the accounting firm of a sitting president.

When he was first approached by the law firm, he got up and walked out of the K Street restaurant in Washington, DC. He responded to their offer with three words that instructed his suitor to perform a sexual act upon himself that was physically impossible to do.

Yet they persisted in their entreaties. Kantor was their man. He would have a team to protect him during the task. All they wanted were the contents of the target's tax filings. The president had refused to present them to Congress, and the head of the select committee investigating his financial dealings was certain there was wrongdoing being hidden from public scrutiny.

When the firm's attempts to secure the records through more common nefarious means, like bribing an IRS worker or an employee of the accounting firm, failed, the call was placed to Kantor.

"Name your price," they'd said. So he did. It was an outrageous sum of money. Far more than what was warranted since it was doubtful he would have to risk his life. When they readily accepted his demand, he silently cursed himself for not asking for more. Nonetheless, he was on board, and half of his payment sat on the table next to him.

He'd been careful, researching the firm and their connections. Still, he preferred to play it alone. It was safer that way. If something went awry, which was bound to happen, Kantor had his cabin in the woods of West Virginia. He had an ample stash of money, weapons, food, and precious metals to ride out the storm of a botched heist.

In his line of work, Kantor recognized there were multiple ways the shit could hit the proverbial fan. The fan wasn't turned on yet, but it was certainly about to be plugged in, with a fresh pile of human excrement sitting in a pile nearby.

"I don't need these guys," he mumbled to his liaison at the law firm. He closed the file folder and pushed it past the money toward the man. "I work better alone."

"You'll need personnel to watch your back while you accomplish the task."

"These guys are trained killers. Regardless of the nature of the information sought, it's still a straight-up burglary. I don't need a bunch of gunslingers. I mean, did you notice that most of them received dishonorable discharges from the military?"

Kantor knew the type. He was former Delta Force stationed in Afghanistan long after the U.S. military forces had supposedly pulled out. He'd made a series of career-ending mistakes that could have court-martialed him at best, imprisoned him at worst. Instead, he was given the opportunity to join a counterintelligence squad made up of misfits like himself. They were always into self-dealing and self-preservation. Whoever the guys were in the folder, he couldn't trust any of them. He knew the type.

The liaison ignored his question. "It's a condition of employment. A job that, as you say, is a straight-up burglary that you are being paid an inordinate sum to perform."

Kantor leaned back in his chair, attempting to strike a defiant pose. There was only one way to be safe, and that was to go it alone.

"Too many people might draw attention. Look at their pictures. Their mugs have operator written all over them."

"We'll provide the cover and disguise," the man countered.

"What? Are you gonna put them in blue coveralls and have them push around a maintenance cart? The security team at 30 Rock ain't stupid, friend."

His interviewer remained firm. "We cannot budge on this. You do your job, and we'll do ours. That said, my employer expected some pushback from you on this issue." He slowly reached into his coat pocket, causing Kantor's body to tense. He eased his hand toward the concealed weapon under his untucked shirt. The liaison assuaged his fears as his eyes darted from Kantor's face to his right hand. "There will be no need for that."

He carefully set five bitcoins on the table next to the stack of cash. The physical form of the most widely traded cryptocurrency had a value of seventy-nine-thousand dollars each.

"What am I supposed to do with those?" asked Kantor.

"Another four-hundred-k to sweeten the pot," the man replied. He stared down at the golden coins before continuing, "Each of the bitcoins has a private key on the back to store your personal wallet address. Or you can establish multiple accounts. Mr. Kantor, this negotiation is over. Will you perform the task?"

Kantor allowed a slight smile. He wasn't happy with the addition of the thugs, and he expected they might have orders to kill him once the tax records were secured. He'd try to make allowances for all of those contingencies. The money was phenomenal, making the job a risk worth taking.

"I'm in. We'll be a go for this Friday night." He scooped up the cash and the bitcoins. It was time to prepare.

PART 2

Thursday

CHAPTER ELEVEN

Thursday
Marriott Marquis Hotel
Broadway
New York City

The heart of the city. The soul of the Big Apple. The center of the universe as far as New Yorkers were concerned. For decades, iconic Times Square, the liveliest part of Manhattan with its huge, illuminated advertising video screens and nonstop New Year's Eve party feel, had been the star of many a movie and novel.

Cat's prize package included a three-night stay at the Marriott Marquis in Midtown Manhattan overlooking the intersection of Seventh Avenue, Forty-Second Street, and Broadway. It was centrally located to all the points of interest on Cat's itinerary, allowing the two of them to walk to their destinations in order to avoid the city traffic or the infamous subway.

The heat index was not a deterrent to Sam and Cat's plans to tour the city on foot. They were used to working outside and were both in good physical condition. Although Sam was in his late sixties, years of working the farm and walking the fields provided him the stamina to trek the city sidewalks of New York.

"Can you believe how much the parking costs around here?" asked Sam as he stared out across the cityscape from their forty-seventh-floor window. "Forty-eight dollars! Just to park for a day. That's insane."

Cat emerged from the bathroom of the two-room suite wearing khaki shorts, a white Gap tee shirt, and Converse sneakers. She was dressed for an all-day outing with her backpack slung over her shoulder, filled with travel brochures she'd received by mail. The internet gave her the ability to lay out her course. However, she liked the touch and feel of the old-school trifold informational pamphlets.

"Wait 'til we buy our first hot dog from one of the street vendors," she said teasingly. "I went on one of those travel websites to get prices for stuff like that. That's why I've been saving my money. You know, to help out with expenses."

Sam immediately felt remorseful for complaining about the cost of parking. This was a once-in-a-lifetime opportunity for his granddaughter. He didn't want to spoil it with needless negativity. He walked over to her and studied her from head to toe.

"You have really grown up, missy. We're all very proud of you."

Cat hugged her grandfather. After he had turned over the operations of the farm to John and Emma, he had more time to spend with his grandkids. Truth be told, Cat was his favorite; however, he tried not to let it show.

"Thanks, Grandpa Sam. Are you ready?"

"You betcha. How do I look in my khakis and collared shirt? Right out of a Macy's catalog, don't you think?"

Cat stifled a laugh. "For sure. Say, should we grab a couple of waters out of the fridge?" The hotel offered a stocked refrigerator. Items taken were added to the guest's bill.

Sam thought for a moment as he calculated the value of the seven-dollar bottles of water bearing the hotel's logo. He inwardly smacked himself on the side of the head to put the thought out of his mind.

"I'll get 'em. It's hot as blazes outside, and isn't our first stop the furthest from the hotel?"

"That's right. It's a couple of miles through Central Park to The Met. I thought we'd see the best one first."

With water in hand, Grandpa Sam urged her to lead the way.

They soon learned that a brisk two-mile walk in rural Northern Pennsylvania might be accomplished in forty minutes, give or take. In the city, stoplights, pedestrian traffic, and panhandlers served to provide many obstacles. It took almost an hour and a half to make the trek up Seventh Avenue into Central Park. Along the way, they took photos of famous landmarks like Carnegie Hall and the Central Park Carousel, an amusement ride that featured fifty hand-carved horses. Naturally, Cat had to take a turn while Sam filmed her. Along the way, they talked about what they observed.

"I can't believe all the homeless people," Cat began as she clutched her backpack strap a little tighter. "But then you'll see limousines or expensive-looking cars drive right past them. On one corner is a man with alligator shoes, and on the other is a woman with only socks on. And they were torn."

As if on cue to accentuate her point, two women walking through the park for exercise brushed past them as they continued to the Metropolitan Museum of Art.

Sam had noticed the same. "They're all in a hurry, it seems. I don't wanna say they're rude, but folks don't make eye contact. It's almost like they don't want to waste time smiling."

Cat looked around Central Park. The heat of the day seemed to keep people inside, so she imagined it was less crowded than normal. "I like Central Park. If I had to live here, I'd want a house looking at the park."

Grandpa Sam laughed and pulled Cat close for a hug. He could only imagine what that would cost. Thus far, he had been pleasantly surprised with their first day in New York. It wasn't the cesspool his son claimed it was. Sure, it was crowded, and life here moved at warp speed compared to Harford, PA. At the end of the day, they were all people, just like him. Only there were about nine million of them.

His musings were interrupted as Cat suddenly stopped.

"Wow!" she exclaimed.

CHAPTER TWELVE

Thursday
The Metropolitan Museum of Art
New York

Those who say *everything is bigger in Texas* have never visited the Metropolitan Museum of Art. In a cultural sense, The Met was kind of a big deal. Not only was the museum complex itself impossibly large, it had one of the most well-curated collections of art and artifacts in the world, which spanned over five thousand years of history.

Cat was awestruck at the sight of the entrance. The granite façade towered over Fifth Avenue. Dozens of steps led upward to the massive entry doors flanked by columns and red banners bearing the gold logo of The Met.

For a moment, she stood there. Looking upward. Admiring the architecture and the magnificence of it all. Her mind raged with inner conflict. Part of her wanted to race up the steps and start the tour immediately. The other part of her wanted to explore every detail of the grand entrance, trying to picture its construction and the craftsmen who built it.

Sam seemed to read her mind. "Cat, why don't we take several pictures and a video. Then we can check out the rest." He paused and surveyed the structure. He shook his head in disbelief at the enormity of the museum. It might take a week or so, but they'd get through it all.

Once inside, Cat relaxed and began to take in the magnificence of it all. She methodically moved from room to room, vignette to vignette. Nothing was uninteresting to her young, curious mind. Even Sam was impressed by the collections, especially the antiquities. He was in awe of how well preserved the Iranian storage jar from 3700 BC was. Or the oldest piano in existence, dating back to the early eighteenth century.

Cat loved the paintings. Rembrandt. Monet. Van Gogh. All of the great Masters of Art were represented. They came across one exhibition that seemed to attract the curiosity of other visitors. One of the museum's curators was giving a brief presentation of five paintings.

"Let's go in here," whispered Cat to her grandfather. She took his calloused, time-worn hand in hers and gently tugged him into the vignette. The curator was beginning the presentation.

"In the art world," she began, "the European masters are the best known. However, America has produced its share of renowned artists as well. Names like Norman Rockwell, Jackson Pollock, and Samuel Morse, to name a few. This month, we are honored to present the works of Thomas Cole, one of America's preeminent landscape painters.

"As a child, Cole immigrated to the U.S. from England in the early eighteen hundreds. He developed a worldview that depicted the growth and fall of an imaginary city. Perhaps a great empire's capital.

"Each painting reveals a different stage in the empire's growth. At first, *The Savage State* was the land in its most raw form. The scene reveals nature at its finest. Pristine. Unaffected by man."

"Then, as the hunter-gatherers of ancient days grew in numbers, they progressed spiritually and culturally, banding together to form small communities. This is reflected in his work *The Pastoral State*."

"As time passes, man reaches the peak of civilization. Known as the *Consummation of Empire,* this painting depicts the city in all of its glory. Exquisite marble structures surround the water. Magnificent ships bring in goods from afar. A joyous crowd celebrates their scarlet-robed king and victorious generals. However, the opulence portends doom for the empire's future."

"In Cole's fourth painting, *Destruction*, man battles man for control of the city. Perhaps it was a conquering army or simply the collapse of society that brings destruction. Regardless, the once proud empire devolved into debauchery, jealousy, and hedonism, resulting in its downfall."

"And, lastly, to drive home the point of where Cole believed man was headed, the final painting shows the results of man's destruction. Desolation reveals the once proud empire was reduced to rubble. As daylight fades away, all that remained were ruins of the once vibrant empire."

The curator paused to allow the museum visitors to reflect on the five paintings affixed to the wall behind her. "One might say that Cole was overly pessimistic about the enduring qualities of man and the ability of nation-states to rise above the destruction of one another, or themselves. However, as a historian, I can leave you with this thought.

"In the history of mankind, all of the great empires have eventually collapsed. Whether it was the great Roman Empire or the Ming Dynasty or the reign of Napoleon in France. There has never been an empire that has avoided this fate. Which leads me to posit this question.

"Do you think America will collapse someday? Will our nation be the lone exception to this timeless trend of rise and fall? I suppose time will tell, but I will say many a theorist believes, despite our great advances in information and technology, we are in a state of decline at present."

She clasped her hands together and managed a smile. After thanking her guests for listening to her presentation, she slowly walked away, leaving the visitors dumbfounded, mouths agape, and one elderly man wearing a U.S. Navy Veteran cap wiping away tears.

Sam led Cat back into the large hallway leading deeper into The Met. Neither said a word for several minutes as they moseyed along, mindlessly taking in the exhibits. The presentation of Cole's *Course of Empire* had a profound effect on them both. Sam had seen the decline as well. His life spanned decades, some of the most culturally tumultuous in America's history. As for Cat, she was too young to make that assessment although she had learned one thing from her science and history studies in school.

If it had happened before, it could happen again.

CHAPTER THIRTEEN

Thursday
International Symposium on Astronomy, Space Science and Astrophysics
Jacob Javits Center
New York

Professor Neal Burgoyne was actually enjoying himself. He had the opportunity to reunite with former colleagues and even accepted praise from one who had publicly ridiculed him for his theories on solar activity. Upon further research, the scientist from NASA's Jet Propulsion Laboratory had confirmed Professor Burgoyne's hypotheses.

The conference was one of three being held in the sprawling Javits Center that week. The gynecologists were gathering in one wing of the center while the travel agents were holding their annual show in the other. It was an odd combination of attendees who roamed the halls of the Javits Center on that Thursday. Professor Burgoyne was enjoying himself as he took part in his second-favorite pastime besides studying the celestial heavens—people watching.

He was to deliver the opening-day keynote address that afternoon. Naturally, the organizers expected him to stay through Saturday for the duration of the conference. He was booked into his hotel until then, but inwardly he would seize any excuse to return to his beloved Maui.

To their credit, the conference had successfully gathered the leading academic scientists, researchers, and astrophysicists from around the world to attend. He was going to grab their attention early, and then he was going to make his case.

The eccentric professor and astrophysicist waited offstage as another presenter talked about the need for additional funding to explore the Martian surface. A noble cause, to be sure. However, Burgoyne thought, how about funding a project to counteract a threat that could change life as we know it? Maybe, just maybe, the right person would hear his plea.

Burgoyne took the podium and offered some initial background comments on his career and his present work. He sang the praises of DKIST and revealed some of the new innovations his team had incorporated into the study of the Sun. Then he paused, surveyed the audience, and made eye contact with his nemesis who'd once besmirched his theories. Undeterred, he began with a controversial topic.

"As scientists, it is not that difficult for us to denounce the existence of God and the teachings revealed in the Bible. However, over time, scientists from around the globe have found tangible evidence of many passages. To be sure, some of the prophecies may seem scientifically implausible, or even impossible. However, I would like to direct your attention to one of the Old Testament's most famous prophets—Moses."

Burgoyne lifted the wireless microphone from the podium and began to casually walk the stage. He wanted the audience of scientists to relax as he relayed his theories as if he were telling a story.

"I've often found it interesting that the story of Noah is found in Genesis, the most basic explanation of the earliest days of man's existence. The Bible no sooner laid the foundation of man's journey than, through Noah, it described our potential annihilation. It certainly reminds us all that things don't last, and at any given time, catastrophe may strike.

"God warned Noah of a great flood that would consume the Earth. He was tasked, in just seven days, to prepare for this catastrophic event by gathering two of every living creature. Of course, we can all find holes in the story if we choose. It's always easy to attack a written work by picking at it like vultures.

"However, I offer the story of Noah to remind you that for eons, mankind has been struggling with the concept of impending doom, an apocalyptic event, if you will, that can bring their lives as they know it to an end.

"So how does this relate to what we do as astrophysicists? Are we supposed to become doomsayers, prophesizing the end of all mankind? I don't think so. However, I do believe we owe a duty to our fellow man to prepare for those catastrophic events, albeit somewhat unlikely, that can place our lives in peril, cause destruction, or even death."

He glanced at Dr. StickANeedleInMyEye, who smirked. Burgoyne ignored his irritatingly smug look.

He continued, "We are all familiar with the extraordinary weather event brought to the world's attention in the movie *The Perfect Storm*. In the meteorological sense, the perfect storm moniker was created in 1991 when a highly unusual weather anomaly resulted in a nor'easter converging with a hurricane moving up the east coast from subtropical waters.

"The storm event took many lives and caused millions of dollars in damages. Weather forecasters believed it to be a one-of-a-kind storm event, but later studies showed that a similar convergence had taken place multiple times around the world at different times in history.

"This leads me to a discussion that is more relatable to everyone in this room. There exists in space weather the potential for a perfect storm of another ilk. One caused by the celestial body that gives us life but which is certainly capable of taking it away. I am talking about a perfect solar storm. A worst-case coronal mass ejection that provides our planet a direct hit.

"All of us who've studied the Sun have queried, *what's the worst the Sun could do?* I have an answer for you. Imagine how quickly this could occur. A CME explodes from the solar disk at three thousand kilometers per second, aimed directly at Earth. Directly behind it, another CME of equal magnitude and speed follows. One clears the path for the other.

"Our colleagues at SOHO have recorded similar events to what I describe on numerous occasions. Make no mistake, the perfect storm is real. In recorded history, it has been observed, but Earth was not directly in its path." Burgoyne paused to return to the podium before continuing.

"We're all familiar with the Carrington Event of 1859. The perfect storm scenario I am referring to would be twice as strong. The technological advances of our modern world, if left unprotected, would not be able to withstand the onslaught of energy thrust upon our planet's atmosphere.

"Our models at DKIST found that a massive geomagnetic disturbance associated with a perfect storm would exceed values observed during recent extreme events such as Carrington and the Quebec power grid collapse in '89. However, there is another example that is not as well-known but significant, nonetheless.

"It was May 1921, and the Sun was becoming more active as the solar cycle ramped up. It began with a calm, relatively benign solar flare. One that might generate a warning today of potential communications disruptions or GPS inaccuracies. Then the whole world exploded with colorful auroras caused by a co-rotating active region. The two ARs were in almost precise alignment near the Sun's equatorial region.

"The Sun's multiple outbursts went cannibal as the second, faster

CME overtook the slower one. It created the first documented perfect storm although it wasn't called that at the time.

"The space weather event was known as the Great Storm of May 1921 or, locally, as the New York Railroad Storm. For days, the highly charged particles descended close to the planet surface. The entire signal and switching system of the New York Central Railroad was fried. Fires spread throughout the communications system, just as they had during the Carrington Event.

"However, the impact of this perfect storm event was not limited to the Northeastern United States. Across Europe, telephone, telegraph, and cable traffic were put out of commission. In Pasadena, California, where the aurora reached its zenith, most anything electronic, albeit limited at the time, was rendered inoperable.

"I give you these examples for a reason. Noah was warned of the great flood and given seven days to build his ark. When the perfect solar storm strikes Earth, and it will someday, we will have barely thirty-six hours to allow our emergency managers to prepare, if not less.

"And the catastrophic effect would not be limited to terrestrial targets. A CME strike of this size would push the planet's magnetopause downward until it was only two Earth radii above the surface. The net effect is satellites in low-Earth orbit would find themselves exposed to a hail of energetic, highly charged particles in the form of what I call a *super fountain* of oxygen ions.

"Imagine dropping a massive boulder into a calm sea. The displacement of water would plunge upward. The perfect storm scenario will do the same to the oxygen ions, potentially, and quite literally, resulting in the satellites being sucked down to the planet surface."

Okay, Professor Burgoyne thought to himself. *Catch a breath. Either they believe you or they don't. The naysayers have never seen the research. Those who understand the scientific theory behind the perfect solar storm are like the Vegas gambler who prefers to play the odds.*

For them, the good news is that the perfect CME storm is rare. One perfect CME has to follow another, and both have to be Earth-directed. It is the very definition of a HILP—a high-impact, low-probability catastrophic event.

It all added up to something that doesn't happen with regularity. However, it had before, and it will again. The question was when.

CHAPTER FOURTEEN

Thursday
Cubbison's Market
Harford, Pennsylvania

"Have you heard from our travelers today?" asked John the moment his wife had provided her customers their receipt. It had been a busy sales day for a Thursday. Not that Emma wanted to turn away business; she really could use the time to prepare for the Founder's Day dinner. John eased behind the cash wrap and gave his wife a bear hug from behind. He kissed her on the neck, and she reacted as she always had, even after twenty-six years of marriage. She shuddered in delight.

"Your rudely independent daughter has only texted me a few times," replied Emma as she playfully wiggled out of his grasp. She grabbed the phone and presented to John as if to say, "*See, here's the proof.*" Instead, John shrugged.

"That's more than I get from her. At least Dad touched base by phone. He was exhausted, as Cat seems intent on runnin' him ragged. That said, honestly, I think he's having the time of his life. He admitted the whole Big Apple thing was a little overwhelming. However, he said he was up to the challenge."

Emma furrowed her brow and wiped the sweat off with her forearm. She'd been working inside the market, where a cooling fan was positioned near the cash wrap. Still, it was hot. "That's good to hear. Cat did promise me a phone call tonight after their day was done. They were gonna hit another museum, then go into Macy's. She wanted to see what all the hype was about. Seriously, those were her words."

John laughed. "You wanna know how many times I've prayed that our daughter doesn't grow up. I wanted to keep her under thirteen. You know what I mean?"

"Too late for that milestone. What's the next goal? Sixteen. Before she can drive?"

"Honey, she can already drive the farm trucks through the pasture. She's helped during feeding time in the past."

"You let her drive?" Emma placed her hands on her hips and stuck her chin up. "When was this?"

"It's your fault."

"How do you figure?"

"Well, she's got your height in her genes, so it's no problem for her to see over the dash. And, like her mother, she won't take no for an answer."

Emma moved toward John with her fists balled up. He quickly retreated around the counter and then grinned when two women entered the market. He politely greeted them before winking at his wife.

In response, she mouthed the word *later*. She clearly wanted to know about her child's driving exploits. She turned her attention to her customers.

"Welcome, ladies. Where are you folks from?"

"Hi. We live in Scranton. We've just attended a wedding in Ithaca, you know, New York. We thought it might be a pleasant drive to return through the country. We'd heard about your place and thought we'd come in."

"Well, fantastic. We love our little neck of the woods. The rolling fields, barns and silos are a fixture of Northern Pennsylvania. Here at Cubbison's, we grow everything fresh and only sell to customers like you. Well, of course, we serve dinner outside on Friday and Saturdays when weather permits."

One of the ladies reached into her handbag and retrieved a cell phone. "It's all so colorful. Um, may we take some photos?"

"Absolutely!" replied Emma cheerily. "Let me give you my card that has all of our social media addresses. Feel free to tag us, and I'll share your post with others."

The woman smiled and nodded and began taking pictures. John wandered back to the cash wrap, presuming he'd avoided his wife's wrath, for now. The woman's companion approached the couple and spoke in a hushed tone of voice.

"May I ask a question?"

"Sure," replied Emma.

"About twenty miles back, we drove past a small community that truly struck us as odd."

John was intrigued. "How so?"

"Well, please don't think bad of me. But, um, well, the people who lived there didn't look like you folks. I mean, I've lived in Scranton all my life, and it isn't exactly Philadelphia, but it's not rural like Harford. You know?"

John and Emma nodded, unsure as to how they should respond.

The woman continued. "Anyway, the town was full of Middle Easterners. You know, people dressed in those burka things. The men wore odd clothing. It was so out of place that it kinda concerned us."

John was aware of what the woman was talking about but had no interest in getting into a discussion with her. Years ago, after the U.S. had pulled its military forces out of Afghanistan, a void was left, resulting in the government's immediate collapse and takeover by the Taliban. Tens of thousands of refugees fled the Taliban rule and were airlifted to the United States. They were settled around the country, including in Northeastern Pennsylvania.

Many of the locals were oblivious to the federal government's actions. When the state's congressional representatives became aware, several complained that the refugees had not been vetted by the State Department. Some of the refugees, it was feared, might have been Taliban who'd infiltrated the transplants.

It had been several years since the resettlement had taken place, and other than a couple of cases alleging child molestation, the refugees had stuck to themselves. John quickly responded in a way that would signal Emma to avoid the conversation.

"I'm not familiar with that. I'll ask around, and I appreciate you for bringing it to our attention."

The woman shrugged. "I just thought it was odd, you know. It's not that I object or anything like that."

"Of course not," said Emma in a sarcastic tone that only John could detect. He tried to tap her right leg with his foot, but she quickly lifted her heel to avoid the contact. She had no intention of taking it further.

A few minutes later, the two ladies departed but were replaced by a carload from the Susquehanna Valley Chamber of Commerce. They wanted to discuss the final arrangements for the Founder's Day dinner. John quickly excused himself and slipped out the back door in search of his sons. They had some sprucing up to do.

"Okay, guys. Let's get the entrance and parking area in shape. Your mom will close up after these people leave, and then I want you to take a tractor with the rock rake attachment. Luke, make sure you fill in any potholes and keep it as even as possible. Matthew, take one of the farm trucks to the hay barn and bring a dozen rectangular bales to the front parking area. We'll stack them and add some potted flowers that your mom set aside."

"Are you gonna be up here, too?" asked Luke.

"I'm gonna wash Old Jimmy."

"It needs it," said Matthew. "It's covered in an inch of dust."

John sighed and nodded. He retrieved the end of the hose from the farm hydrant and turned on the water. He was spraying the family's pride and joy before he was close enough to make a difference.

A few years after Emma took over the market, she announced to the family at dinner that the growing business needed a mascot. Sam chuckled and suggested a goat. Emma hurled a dinner roll in his direction, which simply opened up the floor for more suggestions. The kids, much younger at the time, began suggesting every farm animal they could think of. Cat, a toddler at the time, suggested Minnie Mouse, to which her dad pointed out that Minnie already had a job.

Emma then explained she was considering something besides a living, breathing creature. Some farm-to-table businesses had a windmill or a babbling brook or even snowcapped mountaintops in their marketing materials. She wanted something that represented both their restaurant operation and the old-school farmer's market they operated. It was Sam who came up with the suggestion.

"I sure wish I had that old '57 pickup. It would've been perfect."

"I remember that truck. I learned to drive in it when I was a kid. Three on the tree, baby. Right, Dad?"

"Three on the tree?" asked Emma.

"Yeah. The truck had a manual transmission. Rather than having a floor shifter, the gearshift lever was mounted to the steering column."

"That's it!" Emma exclaimed. "Find me a pickup like that."

John and Sam exchanged looks and then burst out laughing. Sam stifled his laugh to respond. "Miss Emma," he began, "I'm afraid they're all dead."

"Huh? The trucks are dead."

John explained, "Honey, it would be near impossible to find one running that doesn't cost a fortune. There might be a rusted-out body somewhere or another."

"For our anniversary?" she'd asked with a sweet smile that was irresistible to her husband. He couldn't refuse her.

It became a family project they'd never forget. The rebuild project took nearly a year. The rolling stock of pig iron and sheet metal came from all over the country, typically delivered in fifty-five-gallon drums or on open pallets. As was often the case during a restoration of a vintage vehicle, parts were a challenge.

Sam had a sufficient recollection of his first 1957 GMC truck that he knew which other brands were interchangeable with the original. For example, despite Emma claiming to be satisfied with just a body, the guys undertook to install an engine and transmission. They located a '58 Pontiac 336 engine and a rebuilt Carter carburetor. The transmission came from a Chevy, and the seats were out of a '55 model GMC truck.

To top off the vintage look, vertical side bracing was inserted into the truck bed's stake pockets and provided a varnished finish so they would shine. Finally, a barn-red paint job completed the look so it would match the buildings at Cubbison's Farm.

Sam and John kept the truck running, frequently changing out the expansion freeze plugs to protect the engine from the sometimes harsh Pennsylvania winters. The freeze plugs prevented the coolant inside the engine from freezing resulting in a cracked engine block. It had been a labor of love and a frequent participant in the Founder's Day parade in Montrose and at the county fair.

Just as John completed washing Old Jimmy, the contingent from the Chamber of Commerce left. Emma closed the door and followed them into the parking lot. She waved goodbye and approached John with a scowl on her face.

"What's wrong?" he immediately asked.

"They wanna add two more tables of six."

"Can we handle the extra guests?"

"Yeah, I guess. I charged 'em extra."

John smiled and pointed toward the truck. "Wanna take a spin?"

"No, thanks. There's more."

"Oh?"

"They agreed to allow Saint Joe Winery to provide several cases of Ruby Red and Saint Joe White to be served with dinner."

"Alcohol? They'll all get drunk, and we'll never get them to leave."

Emma sighed. "Yep. That's about the way I saw it, too."

CHAPTER FIFTEEN

Thursday
Haleakala Observatory
Maui, Hawaii

Kelly Baxter rubbed her eyes until the sockets were sore. She was exhausted as she dutifully studied the series of computer monitors affixed to the half wall in the center of the Haleakala Observatory. She'd performed countless calculations and models to determine the precise time when the active regions she'd been instructed to monitor by Professor Burgoyne would reveal themselves. She was beginning to doubt herself and, to an extent, her boss.

It was an odd moment during the relationship of the Sun and the Earth. The Sun's magnetic field goes through a period of time, approximately eleven years in length, in which its stormy behavior rises to a maximum, causing its magnetic field to reverse. Once the solar cycle, as the eleven-year period is called, reaches its peak, the Sun settles back down to a minimal amount of activity before another cycle begins.

Professor Burgoyne had developed a theory that the solar cycles could overlap one another. As one cycle begins to wane, another overlaps it. The last solar cycle can stubbornly hold on, producing occasional sunspots and clogging up the Sun's upper layers with the remnants of its decaying magnetic field.

The present cycle would start ramping up, struggling to break free of the last cycle's refusal to end. It was accepted science that the solar cycles tend to overlap slightly. There was no precise stop and start.

However, Professor Burgoyne's hypothesis was that not only can the solar cycles overlap, they can interact as well.

Under his theory, there was the potential for an intense Termination Event, as he deemed it, when the new cycle breaks free of the old. During this brief interaction, the solar activity would be well above average intensity. In fact, according to his analysis, both the Carrington Event in 1859 and the New York Railway Storm of 1921 took place during transitions from one solar cycle to another.

Before he left, he instructed Baxter to study the solar disk carefully. The conditions were ripe for a Termination Event. Now, after near continuous monitoring of the data, Baxter wasn't sure. And then everything changed.

She was about to turn over the monitoring to a graduate student when a dark space appeared precisely at the equatorial region of the Sun. It was as if something had taken an eraser and removed the blinding reddish-orange appearance of the Sun and replaced it with a void.

This void was known as a coronal hole, a region of the Sun's upper atmosphere that was cooler and far denser than the rest. Despite its cool nature, superheated hot gases were emitted through the coronal hole. Through the dark void, solar winds burst out of the Sun and into space.

Baxter turned her attention to her notes. Her eyes darted between the legal pad and the monitors. She frantically switched to space weather monitors from NOAA, NASA, and Stanford. They all reflected the same activity.

The two active regions she was instructed to monitor were coming into view. And it was massive because the two had consumed one another to create a behemoth of a portal to release the Sun's wrath.

CHAPTER SIXTEEN

Thursday
NY1 Studios
New York

Howie Gordon was feeling the energy in the NY1 studios that evening. Every news reporter got hyped up as any significant news story was breaking, even if it related to the weather. Like the rush of adrenaline law enforcement officers feel when they approach a crime scene, journalists feel a similar excitement when they bring breaking news to the public.

Since his arrival in New York, there had not been a weather story worthy of the lead at six in the evening. This would mark his first appearance at the evening hour. After spending a considerable amount of time on the phone with his friends at the Geophysical Institute in Fairbanks, Alaska, as well as a contact he maintained at the SWPC located in Boulder, Colorado, Howie had no trouble abandoning his usual playful Midwestern nature. This was serious business although the executive producer was downplaying the event.

After a brief opening segment by the evening news anchors, they turned their attention to Howie. "Well, sir, the irony of this weather event is not lost on us. I was watching your segment yesterday morning when you discussed this very possibility. Now, it appears you are something of a modern-day Nostradamus."

Howie managed a smile and a chuckle. "I don't know if I'd go that far. As I said, these things have happened before, and the science hasn't changed. They can happen again." Howie turned his attention from the news desk to the dedicated camera that remained focused on him.

"This solar event is truly breaking news, as the Space Weather Prediction Center has announced the appearance of a massive opening in the Sun's atmosphere. Predictions are uniform across all of the space-monitoring resources I have available to me. We will be experiencing two or three nights of spectacular auroras.

"For those who live in our northernmost latitudes, like I did while I worked in Alaska, we called the auroras the northern lights because, typically, the auroras are confined to the polar region. Well, we're in for a phenomenal light show of our own. I'd call it the Night of the Northern Lights right here in New York and possibly as far south as the Sunbelt States.

"However, for New Yorkers, rest assured it will be a spectacle like no other. I've personally enjoyed the northern lights throughout my career by traveling to parts of Canada and Alaska not frequented by most people. It's awe-inspiring and, frankly, very spiritual."

One of the news anchors interrupted him. "Howie, it appears we are in for quite a treat tonight and tomorrow. Are you able to give us an idea of when this aurora will peak?"

Howie nodded his head and returned his attention to his camera. "Late this evening, we will see the first sign of the beautiful hues of green, blue, purple, and possibly red. Naturally, those in the northern part of the state near the Canadian border will be treated to the aurora sooner. Tomorrow night, however, the power of the sun will be on full display. I'm told the solar winds will engulf the Earth just after sunset, around eight o'clock."

The news anchors continued to interact with Howie. "What is the best way for our viewers to take in this spectacular event?"

"Well, we live in a city of steel and stone mountains. Those on the sidewalks might be able to see the sky although the lights emitted by the city that never sleeps can hamper that effort. My suggestion is to gather on the rooftop of your building. I've already seen social media posts of parties being arranged. A buddy of mine who owns a bodega near my flat in Brooklyn said he's been receiving special orders of Sol Beer, a Mexican brew with a picture of the sun as its logo."

The news anchors laughed and looked at one another. "I'm glad our viewers are getting in a festive spirit for this celestial event. Howie, because this is such a strong storm, is there anything we should be worried about? I mean, for example, should we wear special glasses like during an eclipse?"

Howie desperately wanted to roll his eyes but restrained himself. He was glad for the question, however. Yes, he'd been read the riot act the day before after he'd discussed the potential catastrophe brought by powerful solar storms. He had not intended to go there tonight although it was warranted. Yet, thanks to a stupid question, the opportunity presented itself.

"That is a good question, but the answer is no. The aurora and the solar flares that cause them are not harmful to your retina. However, as I brought up yesterday, these powerful storms have the potential to disrupt communications, global positioning satellites, and, in some cases, our electrical power grids."

"If that happens, what should we do until Con Edison fixes things?"

Howie shouted back in his mind, *Nothing, you dope! We'll be screwed!*

"FEMA suggests keeping at least three days of food, water and medications on hand to prepare for a catastrophic event. I'd suggest to our viewers they do more than that."

"A week? Or more?" asked the anchor.

"More. Maybe months," Howie replied unemotionally.

The news anchors had run out of follow-up questions.

CHAPTER SEVENTEEN

Thursday
Marriot Marquis Broadway
New York

Sam and Cat were exhausted from their day of sightseeing. All the boxes on Cat's checklist for the day's itinerary had been checked right down to hitting the famous food carts for hot dogs and pretzels. They had both flopped on the hotel suite's sofa, watching Howie Gordon's reporting on the upcoming solar event.

"Whadya think, Grandpa Sam? Can we check it out, too?"

"You know, let's look at the hotel's information book to see what's on the roof." He studied the three-ring binder he found in the nightstand next to the bed. He found the restaurant list, which included The View, a revolving restaurant and lounge on the top of the building.

"They do have a restaurant up there, but there doesn't appear to be any kind of observation deck. Lots of windows, though."

"Maybe we can eat there?" Cat asked innocently.

Sam perused the menu and imagined placing an order. An appetizer of charred Mediterranean octopus. Dinner could be herb crusted venison loin topped with braised red cabbage and a side of roasted pumpkin with sage.

No, thanks.

"Let me call the concierge and ask for some other options. I'm not sure we can meet The View's dress code."

Sam placed the call downstairs and found the concierge to be very pleasant and helpful. She'd recently transferred to this hotel from Atlanta. She clearly enjoyed her job, as she must've spent a considerable amount of time studying things to do in Manhattan.

"May I suggest the rooftop observation deck at 30 Rockefeller Center? You might recognize 30 Rock as the home to NBC."

"Yes. Is that close by?" asked Sam.

"Yes, sir. It's within walking distance, about halfway between here and Central Park."

Sam cupped his hand over the phone. He whispered to Cat, "Don't we have a museum near Central Park on tomorrow's list?"

"First thing," she whispered back.

"Can we move it to the end?"

Cat's face contorted as the adorable young girl performed her mental calculations. She simply provided Sam a thumbs-up. Before he could return to the call, the concierge spoke to him.

"Sir, if this is of interest to you, might I assist you in purchasing tickets? The Top of the Rock is frequently sold out and might already be in light of the news."

"Yes, please do. Do you need my credit card?"

"No, sir. With your permission, I'll bill it to your room and print the tickets here at my desk. You can stop by at your convenience to pick them up."

Sam thanked her and disconnected the call. Despite their exhaustion, both of them jumped off the couch and exchanged high fives. Then they checked their watches before pulling two dining chairs to the window of their room. The weatherman said the aurora would peak tomorrow night. However, they planned on catching their first glimpse of the northern lights tonight. Grandpa Sam even sprang for two bags of Boomchickapop from the hotel's guest cupboard, disregarding the twelve-dollar price tag per bag.

PART 3

Friday

A spectacle like no other.

CHAPTER EIGHTEEN

Friday
Times Square Studios
Good Morning America
New York

Professor Burgoyne was not camera shy. In fact, he possessed every bit of the gift of gab as those who were frequent contributors to ABC's *Good Morning America* regarding topics of scientific interest. The difference was that some of his theories regarding the heavens were, as they say, *out there*. Pardon the pun.

On this particular occasion, he was anxious for his segment to get started. Not because of nervousness. But, rather, because he wanted it over with so he could hustle to LaGuardia and get on the ten a.m. United flight. He'd have a brief layover in Denver before traveling nonstop to Maui.

As the Thursday events at the Javits Center were winding up, he'd begun to receive urgent text messages from the observatory. Baxter had gathered all hands on deck to monitor the data from the Sun while keeping Burgoyne abreast of the information.

He'd considered bolting up from his seat on the symposium's stage to catch a red-eye back to Hawaii. Then he remembered the potential exposure he'd get from his *GMA* interview. By prior agreement, he was assured by the producers he would not share the interview stage with anyone else. It was the first segment to be aired following the seven a.m. opening news of the day and the presentation of the nation's weather.

Although he'd decided to remain in New York, he had his assistants at DKIST rearrange his flight to depart a day and a half early. Burgoyne knew the havoc a solar storm of this magnitude was capable of wreaking. This was not the place to be if the worst-case scenario took place.

GMA anchor Robin Roberts interacted with her co-host, Michael Strahan.

"Michael, you've seen New York City all abuzz in the past."

"I have," said the NFL Hall of Famer. "When the Giants won Super Bowl 42 in '08, the energy in the city was incredible. We were still recovering from the attacks of 9/11, and the victory over the heavily favored Patriots came as a momentous win. Not only for our team but for all New Yorkers."

"This is a different kind of buzz, isn't it?"

"It sure is. I mean, the celebrations and ticker-tape parade following our victory was incredible. You could feel the love, you know? What's coming tonight is being deemed a once-in-a-lifetime event. I've not experienced this kind of excitement and anticipation since I moved here in '93."

Roberts nodded in agreement. She turned her attention to their guest. "As it so happens, we have with us Dr. Neil Burgoyne, who is the head of the Daniel Inouye Solar Telescope and Observatory in Hawaii. Good morning, Professor. You're a long way from home."

"I sure am, but I appreciate the opportunity to join you this morning," Burgoyne responded, quickly disregarding any nervous jitters.

Roberts provided Burgoyne an open-ended question, which

allowed him to ramble. "Professor, when we booked you for this segment, this spectacular event wasn't on anyone's radar. Well, I suppose it was on yours. Am I right?"

"Studying the Sun is what we do at DKIST, Robin. That's an acronym for our facility. Our goal is to do more than contribute to the vast resources relied upon by NASA and the Space Weather Prediction Center. We also undertake modeling of potentially catastrophic solar storms."

"Catastrophic is an ominous adjective, Professor," interrupted Roberts. "What does catastrophic look like?"

"Yeah," began Strahan, who tried to make light of the subject. "Could it get any hotter than it already is in New York City?"

Professor Burgoyne was lightly annoyed but kept his composure. "No, Michael. What we are talking about is energy rather than the Sun's harmful ultraviolet rays. The enormous amount of energy associated with back-to-back ejections of plasma from the Sun could have a devastating impact on our intricate electronics.

"Think of the powerful blast from lightning strikes. In a fraction of a second, a large bolt of lightning produces about ten to the ninth power joules of energy. A large solar flare consists of multiple discharges of electromagnetic radiation and can be four times the power of a direct hit by lightning. In addition, the solar winds engulfing the Earth can last for many days."

"So what's happening right now, Professor?" asked Roberts.

"Quite frankly, Robin, it's a perfect storm scenario. The end of the Sun's solar cycle number twenty-four is meeting an abrupt end just as the new cycle, number twenty-five, is beginning. The massive upheaval on the solar disk yesterday resulted in a Termination Event. In astrophysics parlance, that is a term associated with this sudden switch from one cycle to another."

"What does this perfect storm scenario portend for us?" asked Roberts.

"Yesterday, a massive cloud of solar matter erupted from the Sun's equatorial region, zooming into space, where it passed one of

NASA's two Solar Terrestrial Observatories, commonly referred to as STEREO.

"Our team in Hawaii recorded this coronal mass ejection as traveling over three thousand kilometers per second. It was the fastest speed ever recorded since STEREO was launched in '06. But the Sun wasn't done yet. Minutes later, along the same active region on the solar disk, a second blast was detected.

"The Sun delivered a one-two punch so powerful it surpassed the near-miss event that occurred in July 2012."

"Near miss?" asked Strahan.

"That's correct," replied Burgoyne. "A perfect solar storm occurred on July 23 of that summer. It missed Earth by a margin of nine days. The strength of that storm was comparable to the so-called Carrington Event of 1859, which is widely known to be the strongest to hit the planet directly in modern times.

"What we have today is not that dissimilar from the July 2012 perfect storm event. The two separate, back-to-back ejections reached an exceptionally high strength as the first ejection cleared the interplanetary medium around the Sun to make way for the full power of the second ejection."

"Hey, this is above this old football player's head," interjected Strahan with a toothy grin. He became more serious. "Everyone is clearly excited about the aurora display tonight. On this program several years ago, you talked about a storm that hit New York back in 1921."

Burgoyne explained, "Well, as of this moment, we don't have sufficient data on the power of this perfect storm, although our modelling at DKIST suggests there is sufficient energy associated with the dual CMEs to encircle the Earth five times. If that comes to pass, the New York Railway Solar Storm of 1921 will pale in comparison. Today's solar storm will rival the effects of the Carrington Event."

"Lights out?" asked Strahan.

Burgoyne avoided appearing alarmist for fear of being marginalized by viewers. "Potentially, yes. The EMP Commission, um ..." His voice trailed off as he responded. "EMP stands for electromagnetic pulse, the highly charged energy that strikes the planet during a solar storm.

"In 2001, largely in response to the major blackout in the Northeast following a solar storm that struck Quebec in the spring of 1989, Congress set up a commission to study the impact on America in the event of a much stronger solar storm. The '89 outage only lasted nine hours, but it could've been much worse. Well, um, especially under the present conditions."

"How strong was the Quebec storm?" asked Roberts.

"The first solar flare was an X4.5, while the second one was a weaker M7.3," replied Burgoyne. He continued his response by putting the Quebec event into context. "The Carrington Event in the mid-eighteen hundreds was likely off the charts. Today's sensors are only able to calculate up to X28 before cutting out. Many scientists believe the Carrington Event was in the neighborhood of an X45. It followed a weaker solar flare, in that instance."

"And this one?" asked Roberts.

"The first solar eruption was an X18. The second was so powerful it overloaded the sensors, leaving us without a precise measurement. By extrapolation, one can assume it was X30 or greater." Burgoyne paused before adding, "A similar scenario to the Carrington Event."

The set became quiet for a few moments. Roberts grew pensive as she studied her notes and glanced at the clock identifying a countdown to their local news break. "Professor, if this perfect storm, as you call it, materializes with the potential intensity you've described, what will you do?"

Burgoyne furrowed his brow, pausing before he responded. He diverted his eyes away from Roberts and looked directly into the camera.

"Get as far away from here as possible."

CHAPTER NINETEEN

Friday
American Museum of Natural History
Central Park
New York

"This has certainly been a popular exhibit today," greeted the art curator for the American Museum of Natural History. A gathering of visitors, including Sam and Cat, had stopped to study a series of lithographs displayed on easels in a semicircle. "Most of our visitors flock to see the life-size T-Rex or *Mammuthus*—the mammoth skeleton found in Indiana."

"I wasn't familiar with the work of Rockwell Kent," offered one patron as he surveyed the lithographs. "Naturally this series titled the *End of the World* caught my eye as I walked by."

"And this lithograph in particular," said another visitor, pointing to one of the sketches. "*Solar Flare-up*. Apropos, considering today's exciting news. Don't you think?"

The amiable curator smiled and stepped next to the sketch the woman referred to. He provided some background to the burgeoning crowd.

"Kent was commissioned by *Life* magazine in 1937 to produce a series of lithographs to accompany an article in an upcoming issue about the Hayden Planetarium. The planetarium once stood behind this museum. It officially closed in 1997 and was demolished to make way for the Rose Center for Earth and Space." He paused to strike a pose in front of the artwork, clasping his hands in front of him as he spoke.

"The November '37 issue of *Life* featured an article titled the 'Four Ways in Which the World May End.' Kent perceived the world was threatened by a variety of means and drew upon his worldview when he created these sketches. We're honored to have the original lithographs for this exhibit."

"Are these based upon the Bible?" asked Cat.

"No, not necessarily," replied the curator. "Mostly, Kent believed catastrophic events related to other celestial bodies in the form of a cosmic cataclysm that could destroy life on Earth. For example, this one, called *Lunar Disintegration*, imagines the Earth and Moon colliding. Next, *Solar Fade-out* envisions that eventual day when our sun burns out, ballooning into a red giant before consuming Mercury and Venus. Soon thereafter, Earth will become a scorched, lifeless rock, stripped of its atmosphere before the oceans are boiled off."

Sam lowered his brow and provided the curator a death stare. He wasn't interested in frightening the bejesus out of young Cat. To her credit, she appeared unaffected by the graphic description and asked about the fourth lithograph.

"What about this one?"

"That's *Degravitation*," replied the curator, who broke eye contact with Sam. "That envisions the Earth losing its gravitational pull. With no gravitational pull, the atmosphere would dissipate into space, the Earth would stop rotating, and we would all feel weightless. Eventually, the strong gravitational pull of the Sun would suck us—"

Sam interrupted him. "Well, thank you, sir, for the explanation. Cat, let's go find the dinosaurs." He firmly placed his arm around Cat's shoulder and pulled her away from the *doom and gloom* exhibit, as he thought of it.

"Grandpa Sam, I had another question," Cat protested. "We're going to have a solar flare, the weatherman said. The drawing showed people dying and the plants all dead."

Sam gathered his thoughts and took a deep breath. "The artist was just exaggerating, Cat. You know, to make the *Life* magazine people happy. We get solar flares all the time, and nothing comes of it. Well, except tonight, of course, when we get to experience the beauty of our world."

Cat grimaced before reluctantly shaking her head. When she got home, she planned on learning more about these solar flares.

They toured the remainder of the museum, hitting all the high points before exiting back into Central Park. They decided to make a loop around the Jackie Kennedy Onassis Reservoir, the largest body of water on the island of Manhattan, before moseying back toward the hotel to freshen up. After they walked past the Central Park Zoo, they emerged near Fifth Avenue. Something caught Sam's eye, causing him to grab Cat's hand and pull her along down the sidewalk.

"Hey! Check this out!"

Sam had caught a glimpse of a placard taped to a street sign. At the top was the logo of the *Blue Bloods* television program. He and Cat eagerly read the notice.

"Wow! They are actually filming today." Sam was beside himself.

"Right now, I think," added Cat.

She opened up the Google Maps application on her phone and typed in the address. She chose directions as if they were walking. The small blue dots appeared on her phone's screen, leading them several hundred feet ahead toward Fifth Avenue.

"It's close?" asked Sam.

Cat, expert trip planner and tour guide extraordinaire, looked at her watch. There was time to go see.

"Close enough," she replied. This time, she had a firm grip on her grandfather's hand as she gave him a tug in the direction of the television production.

Minutes later, they came upon a small crowd of onlookers hoping to catch a glimpse of Tom Selleck or Donnie Wahlberg. While those two famous actors were nowhere to be found, filming was taking place, which excited them both.

They walked through the trees in search of a knoll that might overlook the cordoned-off, temporary film studio. It appeared they were setting up for a shoot-out between the NYPD and a carload of bad guys.

While starstruck Sam watched the activity with wide eyes, Cat filmed from afar, pleased to add this to her personal video blog of the trip. This, the thirteen-year-old decided, was truly a trip of a lifetime.

CHAPTER TWENTY

Friday
Central Park
New York

Asher Doyle was melting. He could swear that was the case. He recalled some athletes could lose six or seven pounds during the course of an outdoor sporting event. He wasn't playing softball on one of the twenty-six fields found throughout Central Park. However, he was dressed, in character, as a member of the NYPD Emergency Service Unit who perform rescue, SWAT and other high risk tactical operations. The tactical gear complete with body armor weighed a ton, it seemed. He vowed to keep off the pounds he was in the process of losing due to the profuse sweating his body endured.

This afternoon marked the end of filming an action scene that began with an armed robbery, followed by the getaway vehicle occupants firing on police officers during their lunch break, and culminating with a chase scene through Central Park to this point where the NYPD had the bad guys pinned down behind two wrecked vehicles.

Because of the delays and the excessive heat, the American Federation of Television and Radio Artists union, AFTRA, had stepped in to limit the amount of time their actors were allowed to film. Production had to continue, so the director began to enlist members of the production team to play extras without speaking parts.

Asher, because of his NYPD lineage, was always a logical choice for these types of roles although he knew very little of what a beat cop went through. Because of his father's career, his knowledge related to what the commissioner dealt with at 1 Police Plaza. Still, he had the clean-cut look and certainly knew how to carry himself to lend authenticity to the scene.

His part of filming wrapped as the production team prepared for the final shoot-out. Asher hurried toward the temporary tent housing wardrobe, where he stripped out of the NYPD gear. He glanced past the caution tape and caught a glimpse of an older man accompanied by a teenage girl moving closer to the filming. The young girl was filming the activity, something that was discouraged by CBS security. Seconds later, a plain-clothed, off-duty officer hired by the production team approached the two and instructed her to put away her phone.

Asher looked around and wondered if he could slip away from the production set. His role was over, and he already had his marching orders for next week's filming of the Sunday dinner scenes. He desperately needed a shower, and he wanted to look nice for his anniversary dinner with Lauren.

He contemplated their life together. He'd never really envisioned them living anywhere else besides New York City. Yet, despite their decent incomes, they felt very much like the proverbial hamster on a wheel. Their earnings seemed to allow them to live in a decent building with a steady diet of take-out meals. However, they weren't really saving money.

What if Blue Bloods *gets cancelled or the show ends?* Asher would ask. Lauren would posit, *What if people stop buying books?*

There was a more likely chance of the former than the latter. Asher didn't like to think about it, but everyone associated with the production of *Blue Bloods* expected Tom Selleck to retire soon. *Could the show really carry on without him?*

For Lauren's part, she'd imagined living in the country. Asher always dreamed of writing a police procedural novel. With her professional help, of course. *Would they be able to adopt a simpler, less hectic lifestyle after spending the first thirty-some years of their lives in Gotham, the nickname made popular in the Batman comics?*

He knew this. Their life in rural America would certainly be safer than New York City, which was beginning to resemble the fictional version of Gotham City from the Batman comic books.

So he thought, anyway.

CHAPTER TWENTY-ONE

Friday
Cubbison's Farm
Harford, Pennsylvania

Emma Cubbison presided over nearly two hundred varieties of vegetables and herbs during peak growing season. John contributed to Cubbison's Farm's sustainability by tending to their pasture-fed beef cattle, dairy cows that fed on organic feed, and free-range chickens. Throw in the two streams that crossed their land, teeming with trout, and Cubbison's could hold its own with the best farm-to-table eateries in the nation.

Many business-minded acquaintances had suggested the family expand their food service operations because of their abundant resources and Emma's touch for creating ambience for their diners. Creating a garden dinner requires more than putting a quality meal on the table. Guests hoped for something different than what a brick-and-mortar restaurant offered. By the same token, a smattering of picnic tables with gingham placemats and a bud vase wasn't sufficient either.

Emma understood this, and she researched successful farm-to-table operations online, paying particular attention to the positive reviews they'd received. Uniformly, positive reviewers would write they weren't sure what single thing made the dining experience exceptional. However, she was able to discern a pattern of certain elements, which she adopted at Cubbison's.

Setting up for the Founder's Day gathering required more than pulling the teakwood tables and chairs out of a storage barn. Each of the tables had to be properly adorned with flowers and herbs from her gardens together with candlelight for ambience.

To add to the outdoor beauty, there were no electrical light fixtures whatsoever. Emma had designed a floor plan, if you will, that included battery-operated string lights hung through the canopy of the river birch trees she'd had John plant years ago. The soft glow of the light coupled with the birch trees' peeling white bark added texture and color to the carpet of green grass.

The guys were bringing in wooden farm crates to be set throughout the dining area. Emma thoughtfully placed plants and flowers in decorative pots on top. Adding place settings to the tables would be the last thing she'd do before preparing the food for the evening. Her biggest fear was bad weather moving in from the west. Today, it was sunny without a cloud in the sky. And it was hot.

John eased up behind Emma and gave her a bear hug. "Honey, this looks incredible. Why can't we call the whole thing off and enjoy it all by ourselves?"

Emma laughed as she melted in his arms. "You have no idea how tempting that sounds. John, you realize this is not a big moneymaker for us, especially considering the time and effort in the preparations."

"Think of the exposure," John said. "The *Times-Tribune* is sending a reporter from Scranton, and WNEP is gonna dispatch a news crew. It could boost our market sales."

"Of course it will. But we've talked about this so many times. We wanted to keep it small. You know, within the family. I've hired people in the past, and they didn't work out."

John took a deep breath and released his hug. "About that. Listen, the kids are getting older, and they'll be able to take on more responsibility. Wouldn't you like to step back a little? You know, spend more time on your real passion—gardening."

"Back at ya," said Emma as she continued setting up the tables.

"Huh?"

"Back at ya, John Cubbison. Are you ready to turn over the farm operations to Luke and Matthew?"

John laughed heartily. "Do you want us to starve? I'd be chasing our cattle down the highway and through the neighboring farms for months."

"Exactly. Let me get Cat through high school first. Plus, do not be surprised, Daddy, if she announces one day that she wants to go to college."

"Okay, that's fine. There are some good schools in Scranton, such as Lackawanna. My mother went to Marywood."

"What if she says Penn State? Or, like me, one of the California colleges."

John gulped. He couldn't imagine sending his daughter away from home at the tender age of seventeen, which was how old she'd be in September after she graduated from high school.

However, California? Never. Ever.

He decided to change the subject. "Are you comfortable with Dad and Cat being out so late in New York? I understand their hyping this aurora thing. I just don't know if I want them walking the streets late at night when it's time to return to the hotel."

"I agree, John. But I googled it, and Cat was telling the truth. It is literally less than a half-mile walk to the hotel. On major streets, too. No dark alleys. No subways. No Uber rides."

"I wish Dad had a gun with him."

"So he could get into a shoot-out with street thugs? That sort of thing doesn't happen where they're staying. It's probably full of tourists on a Friday night."

John grimaced but decided to let it go. He didn't want to unnecessarily worry his wife. "Okay. I trust their judgment. What can I do?"

"Kiss me, for starters." Emma puckered up, and John promptly obliged. She patted him on the chest and looked into his eyes. "Stop worrying about our kid. Figure out where to set up a bar for all of the wine that truck over there is bringing to us." She pointed to the panel van bearing the Saint Joe Winery logo. They'd promised to bring ice to chill the white, glasses appropriate for both types of wine, and servers to keep it all straight.

"How about the whiskey barrels from Catskill Provisions? I have those big, two-inch red oak slabs we cut for extra tables. I can lay them across four barrels and create a bar. Plus, it'll keep our illustrious guests from grabbing a bottle or two to swig behind the birches."

Emma laughed. She loved her husband for helping take the tension off her. "Okay, mister. Chop-chop about it."

As John hustled off toward the barn to enlist his sons' help, she shouted one further instruction. "Don't forget to grab a couple of bottles for us. We're gonna need it later!" John threw his arms up in the air, pumping his fists as if he'd just won a marathon. She loved her playful husband and his somewhat immature nature. She needed it to offset her anxiety.

CHAPTER TWENTY-TWO

Friday
30 Rockefeller Plaza
New York

The unplanned stop to watch the filming of *Blue Bloods* put Sam and Cat behind schedule. Cat, however, wasn't sweatin' it. Certainly, the respite in their hotel room with a change of clothing might have refreshed them for the evening activities. But the opportunity to watch a television production in person was too good to pass up. Especially since it gave her grandfather a little more pep in his step.

As they made their way down Fifth Avenue, Sam continued to chat on and on about the experience. "It's a good thing we didn't see that posting yesterday. I would've made us watch then, too."

"That's okay, I liked it. Well, up until that man made me stop filming. I understand, though."

Sam shrugged. "I guess they don't want anyone putting spoilers on the internet. I kinda thought he made a mountain out of a molehill."

The two paused for a moment to take selfies in front of Trump

Tower. The doorman proudly stood by the two of them under the polished brass façade. A giant United States flag proudly hung in the lobby and was visible through the three-story plate-glass windows. They took another photo beneath the Trump Tower clock located immediately outside the entrance on the sidewalk.

Sam and Cat slowed their pace as they approached Rockefeller Plaza. The large complex consisting of nineteen office buildings covered twenty-two acres in Midtown Manhattan. It was some of the most valuable real estate in the world. The centerpiece of the complex was the massive skyscraper known as 30 Rock. The sixty-six-story building made of limestone and granite included over six thousand windows to provide extraordinary views of the city.

In addition to housing the offices of the famed Rockefeller family and their philanthropic endeavors, a variety of professionals, including accountants, attorneys, and investment firms, filled each of the building's thirteen-thousand-square-foot floors.

However, it was the studios and headquarters of NBC that 30 Rock was best known for. Shows like *Saturday Night Live*, *The Tonight Show*, and *Late Night* were filmed there. It was not unusual to ride an elevator skyward while rubbing elbows with a comedian or guest of one of the nightly shows.

Cat led the way across the plaza surrounding 30 Rock when a sudden commotion near the entrance caused her to stop in her tracks. Sam instinctively rushed in front of her and held his arms wide to protect her from the men racing in their direction.

People could be heard shouting from near the entrance.

"Stop! Thief!"

"Call security!"

"Where are the cops?"

A large, elderly man in a fashionable suit was running directly for the Cubbisons. The younger men, dressed in expensive pin-striped suits, gave chase, their ties flying up and over their shoulders as they waved their arms to enlist the assistance of any onlookers. Also giving chase were three members of the 30 Rock security team, their burly bodies barely able to keep up.

Sam pushed Cat back and to the side of the intended path of the man being chased. He twisted his body to avoid a collision with the slightly younger Sam. The maneuver caused the fleeing man to slow and stumble. He was unable to regain his balance and suddenly fell forward, faceplanting in a grassy section of the plaza. Seconds later, the two men in pursuit caught up. Rather than pinning the alleged thief down, they were bent over with their hands on their knees, gasping for breath. The chase and the heat index had taken its toll on them.

Sam and Cat remained on the scene to watch it unfold. Several onlookers did the same as foot patrol officers from the NYPD finally arrived. Shockingly, they were on a first-name basis with the man being pursued.

"Come on, Gary. Get up. Are you ever gonna learn?"

The older man rose to his knee until one of the officers reached under his arm to assist.

"He stole my wallet!" said one of the men who'd recovered from the chase.

Two people standing behind Sam and Cat were talking about the events.

"That's old Gary Bosley," the man explained. "He's like a serial pickpocket, if there is such a thing. He's been arrested, like, thirty times."

His female companion asked, "Thirty times? Why isn't he in jail?"

"They kinda treat him like a small-town drunk. He spends the night in a holding cell, then they kick him out the next day. I read in the *Post* he never shows up for court, but the Manhattan prosecutors don't care. I guess they've got bigger fish to fry."

"The cops know his name?" the woman asked, surprised at how the criminal had been handled.

"Yeah. Everybody knows Gary. Listen, make no mistake. He's a pro who knows how to game the system. One time, plainclothes detectives waited for him to lift a wallet. Rather than chase him down, they followed him. They busted him at his storage locker full of stolen wallets, watches and stuff. Hell, he even kept a detailed record of every time he stole from someone, broken down by when, where, who, and what he got."

"Freakin' nuts!" the woman exclaimed.

Sam leaned into Cat. "I agree with her. He's like a wolf in sheep's clothing."

Cat shrugged and took her grandfather's hand. "Everybody knows him, too."

They sure did.

CHAPTER TWENTY-THREE

Friday
60th Floor
30 Rockefeller Plaza
New York

Dirk Kantor knew old Gary, too. In fact, he'd hired him to lift the wallet from the fancy-suit guy walking into 30 Rock. The consummate burglar, Kantor relied upon chaos and confusion at times to gain access to a building. He needed someone to initiate a chase by the building's security team. It was the perfect cover to enter the building without drawing undue scrutiny.

Not all heists occur at night. Not all burglars dress in black clothing with black paint on their faces to avoid detection as they sneak into buildings. Some, like Kantor, come right through the front door, on occasion as an invited guest. They take advantage of unsuspecting victims who are a little too comfortable in their surroundings.

Kantor had stolen secure financial data in the past although he usually employed hackers to do the work from afar. Bank and medical records were the most common request of his employers. Tax returns of a prominent politician, especially a sitting president, were a first. He imagined the penalty if he were to be caught would be severe. Then again, he could give up his employer and walk scot-free.

His vulnerability would lie in facial-recognition software that would use security images to identify him. However, he'd never been arrested and used multiple disguises when performing his heists. Today, he wore a long, blond wig with a ponytail and topped off with a New York Yankees ball cap. The pasted-on goatee and sunglasses finished off the ensemble.

He would abandon the props once inside the building in one of the many restrooms located throughout the retail shops located within. By the time he entered the accounting offices, through the front door just as the receptionist prepared to leave for the day, he'd lend the appearance of any businessman arriving for a late Friday meeting.

As for the team pushed upon him by his employers, they were already imbedded within 30 Rock. To their credit, they were ghosts. Kantor was assured they'd remain out of his way unless something went haywire. The information they sought was too valuable to compromise because Kantor failed in his mission. The backup squad would extract the accounting files by force if necessary.

He was given a communication earpiece for them to warn him in the event he was at risk of discovery. Also, if there was difficulty exiting the building, instructions could be given to him for alternate extraction means.

Kantor waited patiently in the lobby as people began to file out of the offices for the day. Many were discussing the spectacular aurora they expected to see that evening. Kantor appreciated the distraction from the heavens. The Night of the Northern Lights was just one more distraction to assist him with the heist.

His patience soon paid off. The front desk of the firm was abandoned. In a flash, he confidently entered the back offices of the accounting firm. The intelligence his employers provided was spot-on. Everything from the layout of the cubicles housing underlings to the locations of the top partners who represented the president.

Clearly, they had someone on the inside. As he made his way toward the corridor where the senior partners' officers were located, he tried to avoid eye contact although he wondered which set of eyes that bothered to assess him belonged to the insider on his employers' payroll.

Kantor had done this kind of work before on behalf of Mossad as a dark ops field operative. His ability to speak fluent, near-perfect Egyptian Arabic provided him the ability to move throughout the Middle East with ease. He would've remained there to continue his craft, but the money in America was too lucrative.

Kantor reached the supply storeroom adjacent to the entrance to the south corridor where the partners' offices were. He imagined they overlooked the plaza below. After a quick glance at the mostly empty offices and inattentive late workers, he dashed into the storeroom and found a place to hide away.

He steadied his breathing as he remained in a crouch in the far reaches of the storage room. In the hallway, muffled voices could be heard. Occasionally, the door would open as a member of the firm's staff dropped something off or searched for a needed office supply. When the door was open, he was better able to discern the topics of conversation. Some referenced the aurora display. Others talked baseball. A few discussed politics, as their very famous client was running for reelection.

Soon, one by one, the accountants and staff left the building. If the intel provided by his employer was correct, the cleaning crew would enter the floor around nine o'clock. Just more than an hour away. By his own estimation, he would need about that long to locate the proper office. Then the daunting task of rifling through the files to find the requested information would begin.

It would be impossible for him to carry out decades of tax returns and supporting documents. Fortunately, his employer was fairly specific. They knew what they were looking for in order to prove wrongdoing by the president and his family. They simply needed the documentary evidence to see the light of day.

Kantor eased to the storeroom door and opened it slightly. He closed his eyes to focus on his auditory senses. His brain searched out any sound of human activity. Typing on a keyboard. A conversation. Shuffling of heavy feet. A cough or sneeze.

Nothing. Quiet. It was time.

He eased into the hallway and began moving quietly from door to door, avoiding unnecessary sudden moves that might attract the attention of someone remaining in the offices. He searched for the senior partner's name until he found it.

Kantor ignored the brushed aluminum handle. Instead, he turned his attention to the deadbolt keyhole that remained locked after office hours. Picking locks had been part of his repertoire since he began covert operations. He had a touch like no other.

He pulled the skeleton key out of its zippered case and carefully inserted it into the lock. From the back of the specialized tool, an extended, telescoping cylinder protruded, revealing seven numbered hashmarks. He slid his free hand to the end of the cylinder. Applying gentle pressure, he pushed the cylinder forward, listening for the inner workings of the deadbolt to speak to him.

Methodical. Choreographed. Expertly from years of practice.

Kantor could visualize the three-dimensional picture of the lock's interior. He slowly coaxed the cylinder forward, making minor adjustments as the lock dictated. He manipulated the pins using the ridges of the skeleton key's cylinder. Then, with one final, forward push, the deadbolt clicked open.

He pressed the communication's earpiece in a little further as some perspiration loosened it. He slipped inside the senior partner's suite and gently closed the door behind him. He began his quest.

There were multiple file cabinets located in the outer offices where the accountant's staff worked as well as in two hallways, one that led to a conference room, and one parallel to the main hallway that led to a private break room.

Kantor sighed. He decided to start with the partner's office first. He couldn't imagine a more important client than the President of the United States. He guaranteed himself the files resided near the senior partner's desk. He was right.

He rifled through the files in the dim light provided by the city. It was dark outside now, but New York, as always, was lit up like the Rockefeller Center Christmas Tree. Using his penlight, he searched file after file in search of the year and corporate filings they sought. It was taking longer than he envisioned, but he presumed he would have all night if he could evade detection by the cleaning crew.

Then the words he dreaded to hear came in the form of a whisper through his earpiece.

"Possible compromise. Stand by."

Kantor closed the file drawers after hurriedly replacing the Pendaflex folders where he found them. He scanned the room in search of a hiding place. His only option was under the partner's desk.

The chatter increased on the radio.

"Guards have visual."

"Approaching now."

"Take from behind. Quietly."

"Roger that."

"On my go."

Kantor could visualize what was happening. He'd been part of a hit team lying in wait numerous times. He barely breathed in the dark office, waiting until he received the all clear.

Those words never came.

CHAPTER TWENTY-FOUR

Friday
Top of the Rock
30 Rockefeller Plaza
New York

Lauren and Asher enjoyed their dinner. As was typical on any given day, they shared what had happened at work and discussed news events that interested them both. Then, because of the sentimental nature of their tenth anniversary, they lovingly recalled momentous occasions during their lives together.

Unlike some couples, the Doyles had never had a conflict within their relationship relative to their personal finances. Certainly, like most families, they wondered where the money went. Many a conversation throughout their marriage began with the words *on paper*. On paper, we should only spend this, but we make that. *Where does the money go?*

During dinner, the same conversation took place right about the time they got the check from their waiter. Asher jokingly held it up for Lauren and wiggled it slightly. It was exhibit A, he said, of where the money goes.

Although they both agreed dining out took a sizable bite out of their monthly budget, neither was prepared to set aside the extravagance to take up cooking. For the Doyles, there was only one way out of their expensive lifestyle—leaving the city.

After assessing their first ten years of marriage, they envisioned their second. Children were not on the horizon. They enjoyed each other too much to add another tiny human being into their lives. One day, but not any time soon, they agreed.

The financial discussion led them to imagining life in the country again. It had been Lauren's dream although Asher was coming around to her way of thinking. They vowed to take day trips away from the city and not to Montauk, the easternmost tip of Long Island, where they enjoyed visiting. Not New Jersey, either. It was the same as New York, they concluded.

No. They wanted to travel into New England. Check out the coast of Maine. Maybe Woodstock in Vermont or the Poconos in Pennsylvania. Even upstate New York would be better than the city. There were lots of options open to them that didn't require the equivalent of life as a sardine with high rent.

Happily in love, they left the Rainbow Room and rode the elevator to the Top of the Rock to view the aurora. The attraction featured timed ticketing to avoid visitors waiting in long lines. It was a system that had worked for the observation deck and was later adopted by Disney for its theme parks.

They exited onto the seventieth-floor open-air roof deck and were immediately greeted with a warm gust of air. The higher altitude, eight-hundred fifty feet above sea level, did little to alleviate the heat of the day. Only the coming darkness would help but not at first. It would be near midnight before temperatures would start to modestly drop.

To maximize visitors' photo opportunities, the Top of the Rock had no metal or glass enclosures. The New York skyline could be used as a backdrop for photos of your group or selfies. That evening, the blistering heat cast a haze across the region. Coupled with the smog that sometimes set in when the air was stagnant, the customary views of the surroundings from the Statue of Liberty to the Hudson River were partly obscured. The tallest of the city's skyscrapers, like the Empire State Building and One World Trade Center, towered through the layers of haze, their illuminated windows sparkling in the last vestiges of daylight.

The excitement of the sightseers at the Top of the Rock created enough energy to light up the skies on their own. Like beachgoers counting down the sun's drop into the ocean, the aurora-viewers were anxiously waiting for daylight to give way to night.

Without any kind of clock as a guide, they seemingly found a way to count down the seconds until sunset.

Ten. Nine. Eight.

They counted until they reached zero and unanimously erupted into joyous applause.

CHAPTER TWENTY-FIVE

Friday
Top of the Rock
30 Rockefeller Plaza
New York

Overwhelmed by the emotion-filled moment, tears began to stream down Cat's face. Embarrassed, she tried in vain to turn off the waterworks. She came close once, but another young girl nearby was crying as well, resulting in Cat's tears flowing again. Even Sam felt the excitement as chills came over him in great anticipation.

"Grandpa, look around us. Have you ever seen anything like that? This is ten times better than last night. No. A hundred times. Right?"

"It is everything the newspeople said it would be. A spectacular achievement of Mother Nature."

"It's like God is painting us a picture, Grandpa Sam. Look at how the colors kind of float through the sky."

Wisps of blue and green filled the darkening sky. The highly charged particles from the Sun collided with the Earth's atmosphere, spreading rapidly around the Northern Hemisphere. The most common color, a pale greenish-yellow, began to take on an iridescent glow. As nitrogen particles collided with one another, hues of blue and purple permeated the sky, providing an entrancing, magical display for the world to see.

"This is amazing," Sam muttered as he took it all in.

Cat began to film the celestial event. Holding her arms high overhead to avoid being blocked by the adults, she slowly turned as she created a three-hundred-sixty-degree panoramic video of the sky in relation to New York.

When she finished her video, she noticed a man waving toward her.

"Hey! Come over here. You can get a great picture of the tallest buildings in the city."

Cat looked up at her grandfather, who nodded. He took her by the hand and walked over to the railing. The couple stood aside and allowed Cat to position herself for some unobstructed photography.

"Thank you, young man," said Sam. "That was nice of you both."

"Think nothing of it," he replied and then paused. "Sir, may I ask you a question?"

"Certainly. I gotta tell you, we're not from here, so I may not be much help."

"We are. And, um, actually I've seen you both today."

"Really?"

"I'm Asher Doyle, and this is my wife, Lauren." Asher extended his hand to Sam, who hesitated before reluctantly shaking hands. His nature was to be wary of anyone in New York.

He managed a smile. He placed his arm around Cat's shoulder. "Sam, and this is my granddaughter, Cat. We're in town from Pennsylvania. Um, you say you recognized us?"

"I'm a scriptwriter for the television series *Blue Bloods*. Today, I got roped into playing a nonspeaking part as a member of the SWAT team. I saw you and your granddaughter standing in the shade near the wardrobe tents."

Sam beamed with excitement. "You work on *Blue Bloods*? I mean, with Tom Selleck?"

"I do," replied Asher. "For quite a few years, in fact. So what did you think about our production?"

"Well, we couldn't see a whole lot, but Cat managed to take some pretty good pictures until, well, until they made her stop."

"Yeah, *das ist verboten*," said Asher with a laugh.

Sam furrowed his brow, as he didn't quite understand what Asher had said.

"That's forbidden," offered Lauren by way of explanation. "Asher was speaking just a few of maybe ten words he knows in German."

"Grandpa Sam, I just got the best snaps of the trip. Thank you for letting us into your spot."

"You're welcome, Cat," said Lauren. "I'm Lauren, and this is Asher. We live in the city, so we've seen the views from up here more than once. Although, never quite like this."

"Amazeballs, right?" Cat asked gleefully.

Lauren laughed. "I'm a book editor for Random House. I honestly believe amazeballs sums it up nicely."

"Look, Cat," said Sam. "As it gets darker, the aurora becomes much brighter. I even see some red coloring here and there."

"Is this the first time you've seen the northern lights?" asked Asher.

"Yes, sir," Cat replied loudly. The excitement on the rooftop observation deck had built to a pinnacle as chatter between the visitors grew.

The conversations became so loud that initially, nobody heard the sounds of transformers blowing up on the other side of the Hudson River. The canopy of haze and smog obscured their view beneath, where the cascading failure of the New Jersey power grid was underway.

Then it happened.

Some who'd experienced the devastation wrought by the terrorists on 9/11 believed New York was under attack once again. Others thought a fireworks display was occurring across the Hudson. However, when a substation exploded to the north of the five boroughs, followed by spontaneous blasts due to transformers failing around the Upper East Side of the city, the aurora-gazers realized that something was horribly wrong.

PART 4

Friday

It was the day the sun brought darkness.

CHAPTER TWENTY-SIX

Friday
Haleakala Observatory
Maui, Hawaii

At the airport, Professor Burgoyne had difficulty hailing a cab or an Uber. He hadn't made prior arrangements for a member of the DKIST staff to pick him up because he never expected cell phone communications to be disrupted in latitudes as low as Hawaii. The aurora borealis had only been visible to the naked eye in Hawaii on a couple of occasions in recorded history. Once, during the Carrington Event in 1859, and a second time, barely, during the biggest solar flare ever recorded by SOHO in April of 2001, when a powerful X-class geomagnetic storm delivered the Pacific Rim a glancing blow.

The lack of transportation was due to the huge influx of mainlanders fleeing the once-in-a-lifetime solar event. Those who understood the power of the storm knew to evacuate to the southernmost point in the U.S. They'd filled the flights out of Denver and the west coast with a sizable head start over the professor.

He finally negotiated a ride share with another visitor. After being dropped off at the observatory, he raced into the building, where he was greeted by the entire staff. They were unable to contain their enthusiasm and excitement.

"Professor! It's unbelievable!"

"You should see it through the telescope!"

"We can't wait until it's dark!"

Burgoyne swallowed hard at that last statement. He glanced at his watch, a windup Timex Men's Expedition he'd owned for years. It was immune to the powerful effects of a geomagnetic storm. It was still set for the eastern time zone.

"Darkness?" he muttered the question to himself without addressing his team's exuberance. He received his response with the next excited utterance.

"The power grid just collapsed across the entire lower forty-eight!" said Baxter. "Even Texas. Can you believe it?"

Baxter was quick to point out that the Texas grid had collapsed despite the fact it was independent from the Eastern and Western Interconnection power grids that covered much of North America. The fact Texas had lost power under the circumstances was a testament to the power of the perfect storm.

Burgoyne took a deep breath and exhaled. His face became dour as he raised his hands to encourage his charges to calm down. "Listen, we need to do our best to curb our enthusiasm. We are experiencing an event I've hypothesized about and imagined occurring. It is a solar storm unseen in nearly two hundred years." He paused to take another deep breath and to remove his hat. He ran his fingers through his graying hair and adjusted his ponytail.

"That said, most of the people residing in the Northern Hemisphere are about to face difficult times. Many will die as they run out of clean water, food, and as society begins to collapse around them."

One of the graduate students asked the question on many of their minds. "Professor, are we gonna have the same problems here? I mean, we still have power."

"That's true," replied Burgoyne. "However, over sixty percent of our electricity comes from oil. Oil that is shipped to us from abroad. Renewable resources—like solar, wind, and especially geothermal—produces about a quarter of our energy. If we properly marshal our resources, we can survive better than those with no power.

"There's another problem, however. Hawaii imports many food products and other essential supplies from the mainland. I suspect that will end abruptly. As in already. That will take its toll on us all."

"What are we gonna do?" asked Baxter.

A dozen young faces studied their professor. He was exhausted. Not just from the trip and his travel across many time zones. It was from worry. He'd contemplated all of these questions as his flight from Denver seemed to stay just ahead of the geomagnetic storms.

"First of all, we're going to do everything we can to prepare ourselves for some troubling times. I want all of you to do several things with the petty cash I'm about to retrieve from my office. Take each of your cars and fill up your tanks.

"Go to as many markets and convenience stores as you can. Buy nonperishable foods with long expiration dates. Think high-calorie, filling foods like beans, rice, pasta, and sauces. Peanut butter, honey, and crackers.

"Listen, just use common sense and move quickly. It's a matter of time before there is a run on the grocery shelves."

Baxter issued a reminder to the group. "Toilet paper? You know, like during the pandemic?" Many believe it was an article about grocers in Hawaii running out of toilet paper at the start of the COVID pandemic that had prompted America's shelves to empty as well.

"Absolutely. Other everyday items like toothpaste, soap, personal hygiene."

Burgoyne paused. He could tell he was overwhelming them. "Please take a breath. Now is not the time to panic. After you run your errands, I want you to stop by your homes and gather clothing, pets, food supplies. Anything of use. Bring it all here. We are going to hunker down and help one another through the next several weeks and months."

"Months?" asked one of the students.

Burgoyne nodded and replied, "Yes. Quite possibly. We are fortunate that Haleakala is in a very remote area of Maui. I don't believe we'll be bothered by anyone."

"I have a gun," said Baxter, almost apologetically. Among the students, guns were the bogeyman. "It's a handgun I bought from a friend who was short on cash."

"Do you have ammunition for it?" asked Burgoyne.

"Um, no."

"Buy some. All you can." He reached into his hip pocket and retrieved his wallet. He handed Baxter his VISA card. "Use this for all your purchases."

They all remained affixed in place. Stunned as the reality of the spectacular solar storm set in. It was about more than pretty auroras and scientific study. It was also about survival.

CHAPTER TWENTY-SEVEN

Friday
Cubbison's Farm
Harford, Pennsylvania

It was just after eight. Dinner was over. The wine had flowed. And the attendees of the first Founder's Day dinner hosted by Emma Cubbison had already declared this year's soiree as one to be remembered for years. There was even talk of hosting it there next year and the year after.

Emma, reinvigorated by the success of the event and the fact that it was nearing its conclusion, escorted her honored guests outside the tree canopy to a grassy area with an unobstructed view of the sunset. Everyone was in good spirits as they chatted among themselves, enjoying the sunset marking the end of the day turning to night. All were anxious to catch their first glimpse of the aurora borealis as it invaded the lower latitudes.

Matthew was the first person to notice the power outage. Between the battery-powered string lights that filled the tree branches and the candlelit tables, nobody had noticed the fact the light from the main house and the porch lights of the market were out.

Matthew was exchanging text messages with a friend when suddenly his screen went dark. He entered the house to charge his battery. When the lights didn't come on and the air conditioning wasn't working, he knew they'd experienced a power outage.

Admirably, when he alerted his father of the issue, he didn't make a fuss that might distract his mom. "Dad," he whispered into his father's ear, who was preparing the tables to be cleared of their dishes, "something's wrong. I think the power went out."

John immediately turned his attention toward the market and the main house. There was no sign of light. "Okay, don't trouble your mom with this. I'll go check it out. In the meantime, clear the tables and take the dishes into the house." John began to walk away when Matthew touched his arm.

"But, Dad, my phone stopped working."

"Maybe it needs to be charged?"

Matthew shrugged and said, "I thought I had."

John patted his hip pocket in search of his own phone. He'd left it inside. "Where's your brother?"

Matthew nodded across the dining area in response. Luke was chatting with an attractive young woman who came with the newspaper reporter. John waved at the tables as a reminder to Matthew as he walked toward Luke with a purpose.

He tried to be polite although he was slightly annoyed with his son for not staying focused on the cleanup.

"Excuse me," he said to the young woman. "May I borrow my son for a moment?"

"Sure," she replied with a shrug and a glance at Luke.

As John led his son away, Luke shouted back to the young woman, "I'll call you."

John whispered into his son's ear, "Gimme your phone."

"Um, sure, Dad. Is something wrong? Is it Cat and Grandpa Sam?"

"No." He took the phone from Luke and attempted to power it on.

Nothing.

"Did you charge your phone today?"

Luke took it back and pressed the power button and then tried a forced shutdown in the event an application on the device was hung. The screen remained black.

"I did, and I haven't even used it except for getting her number earlier," replied Luke. Bewildered, he stared at the screen. "I don't understand this. I made sure it was a hundred percent in case Cat wanted to text me something. She's been sending me pictures of their stops. Tonight, they were at 30 Rock. You know, it's the—"

"I know where they are," said John in a concerned, yet dismissive tone of voice.

Luke sensed his father's consternation. "Dad? What's going on?" He pointed toward the house. "I left the lights on when I left."

"Power's out," replied John. "Matthew's phone is dead, too."

As he slowly turned toward the dining area and the guests gathered beyond the trees, their voices could be heard over the dead silence.

"Hey! My phone stopped working!"

"Mine too. I wonder why."

"I can't get service."

"Does it even work?"

"Um, no."

"How does something like this happen?"

John delayed joining the group. He had instructions for Luke first. His first inclination was to power on the generators to the house and the market's refrigeration system.

"Luke, fire up the Generac for the house and then the gas-powered gennies for the coolers in the market. Go. Now!"

The excited voices heard across the field turned from irritation to panic. John wasn't sure what was happening, but he thought better of revealing his backup power systems.

"Luke!" he shouted to his son as he walked briskly toward him. He lowered his voice as he spoke. "Forget what I said. For now, anyway. Come back and help your brother."

Luke jogged back. "Are you sure? It's not a problem."

"Just a hunch, son. Listen, just do as I say, please. Clear the tables with Matthew, but I want you both to keep an eye on the house. Make sure none of these people wander in that direction, okay?"

Luke shrugged. "Um, okay."

"John!"

He recognized his wife's voice, and her tone reflected her concern.

"Coming!" he shouted back. He looked up, pausing to clear his head. The voices of the panicked group grew louder, rising to a crescendo as God dyed the skies with shades of blue and green with a slight tinge of red for good measure.

CHAPTER TWENTY-EIGHT

Friday
Top of the Rock
30 Rockefeller Plaza
New York

"We're under attack again!"

It was a logical conclusion for New Yorkers, who'd lived through the heinous terrorist attacks on 9/11. Any suspicious box on a street corner might be a dirty bomb. Every unmarked van parked near a skyscraper might be filled with explosives. Every crime committed by someone of Middle Eastern descent might be a precursor of a larger attack.

Just as every cough during a global pandemic could be deemed a sign of the contagion despite the fact we cleared our throats multiple times on any given day. Or a sneeze caused by the sensitive hairs in our nose being invaded by pollen or dust suddenly became a symptom of something far more sinister.

Eyes would grow wide. Mouths would fall agape. Mothers would pull their children closer to their hip.

When the transformers began to explode from the massive surge of energy finding its way to power lines, the planet's perfect antenna to attract the highly charged particles emitted in the solar storm, the minds of New Yorkers immediately deduced terrorism.

In a way, what was happening was far worse, and the ultimate death toll would prove it. Americans were about to be exposed to dehydration, starvation, and the depravity of their fellow man. It would be a steady, slow decline. A race where only the fittest would survive. A race that would take months and years to run. However, it was a race that would start out of the gate quickly.

"We have to get off the roof!"

"Yeah! This building might be a target!"

"Did you feel it shake? It may have been hit already!"

The rush for the exit came all at once. Chivalry was dead. Women and children need not apply.

Husbands dragged their wives by the arms as they pushed through the crowd in search of the stairwell. A few gullible souls repeatedly pressed the down button on the elevator, hoping for a miracle. Children cried. Women shrieked. Men shouted orders. Nobody attempted to help one another or work together. It was every man for himself.

Except for Grandpa Sam, Cat, Asher, and Lauren.

"We've got to stay calm, and we'll get out of this," said Asher as he dropped to a knee in front of Cat. Her face was filled with fright, but the tears did not flow. That would come later. For now, she was unsure of the threats they faced and was simply reacting to the emotions of the moment.

She nodded her head to indicate she understood. "What do we do?"

Asher gently patted her on the head and turned his attention to Sam. Lauren wrapped her arm through his for comfort.

"Sam, I don't know what is going on below us, but I do know this. That mob stampeding down the stairwell will join more panicked people like them. They're gonna trample one another. I think if we take it slow, avoid the mayhem, we'll make our way out of the building unharmed."

"Makes sense to me," said Sam as he looked past Asher toward the single emergency exit. People were elbowing and jockeying for position to squeeze through the doorway. He imagined them falling over each other as they forced their way into the stairwell. Cat would never stand a chance.

"Guys," began Lauren, "um, as an editor, I've read many novels about what can cause the power grid to collapse. A massive solar flare is one of them. There's a possibility that what we're seeing around the city is caused by that." She pointed toward the sky where the aurora continued its magnificent display while it masked its destructive power.

"What's blowing up?" asked Sam.

"Electrical transformers. Power substations. Anything that stores or transmits electricity. When the solar storm hits the planet surface, it's like a gigantic lightning strike that we can't see or feel. It's really hard to say exactly what effect it has because it's never happened in modern times."

"Until now," interjected Cat. She turned to her grandfather. "Do you remember the picture at the museum? It's like that."

In the darkness, Sam took a deep breath and exhaled. He had been afraid the depiction of the ways the planet could be destroyed might have a lasting effect on Cat.

"You know what, honey? The artist was wrong. The solar flare didn't kill all the people or burn up the ground. It just turned off the lights."

Asher had stepped away toward the exit and turned to the group. "I think we can go now. Remember, everybody stick together. Hold hands or lock arms. Give others plenty of space. Slow and steady."

They made their way across the rooftop observation deck. Each of them took one last look at the aurora from the building that nearly touched the sky.

Out of habit, Cat reached into her pocket to retrieve her phone.

She stared down at its dark screen. It was then she realized all of her photographic memories of the trip might be lost forever. She began to wonder if she could recall everything she'd experienced. Her mind wandered as they pulled her into the darkened stairwell. Would she be able to recall all of the memories she'd recorded since she'd received her first phone?

Tears began to stream down her face. Not out of fear or despair. But, rather, out of a sense of loss. As if part of her life had been stolen from her. She set her jaw and vowed to take the time to remember everything, including the precious moments with her family, whom she desperately longed to hug.

CHAPTER TWENTY-NINE

Friday
Top of the Rock
30 Rockefeller Plaza
New York

Calm turned to chaos. As Asher predicted, the pitch-black stairwell was full of fear-crazed people trying to exit the sixty-six stories that led to the ground floor. Inexplicably, for reasons they'd understand later, people were shoving their way upward toward the rooftop observation deck.

"Why isn't security trying to calm people down?" asked Lauren.

"Those two guys on the roof bolted as soon as the explosions began," replied Asher. "Despicable."

Another explosion caused the building to shudder, sending shock waves of panic through the fleeing visitors.

"Out of my way!"

"Move, dammit!"

Asher carefully led them past the sixty-fourth-floor entrance when several people decided to reverse course in an attempt to flee the concussive sound of the explosions from within the building. He turned to his group.

"Hug the wall," he said, his voice remarkably calm. Perhaps he'd lived in the fictional world of crime dramas enough to know that panic was contagious, especially when nothing is known. The characters on *Blue Bloods* were forced to portray themselves in a variety of scenarios. Oftentimes, unlike the viewer, the character doesn't know what's coming. Asher understood the psychology behind the panic of the unknown, as he was responsible for writing it into a story.

They descended several more floors, allowing people to rush past. Many stumbled and fell. Skin was ripped open on the concrete floor. Bones were broken as they braced their fall. Faces were battered in the dark, leaving blood-splattered walls and steps.

Cat felt the warm, gooey substance as she used the wall to guide her descent through the darkness. She was placed between Lauren and Sam, who kept a death grip on her hand. Lauren's hand was soft and comforting. Like her mom's.

Before long, they'd reached the fifty-ninth floor, where they encountered a pileup of bodies. Everything had come to a stop.

"Keep moving!" Asher shouted uncharacteristically after nearly a minute.

More people pushed their way upward, away from the blockage of bodies. A man answered his question.

"There's a fire in the building!" he exclaimed as he pushed off Lauren and rounded the corner to ascend.

Sam tried to slow the man's progress and asked, "Where? Did you see it?"

"I don't know. They just said there was a fire."

He disappeared into the darkness, cursing a few stragglers along the way. For the most part, the group of four was behind the rest of the evacuees.

"I don't hear any alarms," said Lauren. She had worked in high-rise buildings for her entire career. Fire drills were part of the security protocols the City of New York and insurance companies insisted upon since 9/11.

"Maybe they're down because of the power outage," offered Sam.

"They should be battery operated," said Lauren. "The same should apply to the emergency lighting system. None of this makes any sense unless the solar flare was strong enough to destroy them as well."

"Regardless," said Sam. "People believe there is a fire somewhere below, and they're not moving. They're even retreating for some reason."

"Asher, what should we do?" she asked.

Asher tried to make sense of the frantic voices speaking in unison below them. He expected that 30 Rock had more than one emergency stairwell.

"Maybe they're wrong about the fire," he replied. "Everyone is repeating the claim up and down this stairwell. Let's go inside the building and try to find another exit."

"I'll lead the way," said Sam, who gently tugged on Cat's hand. The young girl had remained remarkably calm throughout the ordeal.

Sam entered the darkened hallway on the sixtieth floor. A rush of cool air that had remained undisturbed in the front office struck him in the face. *This may not be the right way to go*, he thought to himself, *but at least I can breathe again.*

Seconds later, all four of them had escaped the hysterical people in the fire escape. Asher once again took the lead, ensuring everyone held each other's hand. He found his way into the foyer of the office suite near the elevator. There was no ambient light to assist him in navigating through the dark space. Twice he bumped into furniture, bruising his shins. He held his breath and fought the urge to let out a string of expletives.

He ran his hands along the wall and began to feel metal lettering that had been affixed to it. He muttered the letters aloud as he crossed through the foyer. "D-E-L-O-I-T-T-E ..." His voice trailed off.

Accountants. They probably leased the entire floor. He stopped the group when he reached the reception desk.

"Wait here," he said. The group remained by the elevated desk while Asher felt his way along the curved top until he reached the double doors leading into the offices. He felt for the handle, hoping it wasn't locked. A huge grin came across his face as their first obstacle was hurdled when he reached the opening. What Asher didn't notice was that it had been kicked open, breaking the locking mechanism.

They were not alone.

CHAPTER THIRTY

Friday
60th Floor
30 Rockefeller Plaza
New York City

Dirk Kantor, the consummate professional thief, finished locating the files on the list he'd been provided by his employer. Undeterred by the sudden darkness, he crammed the documents into his backpack and prepared to leave. The sporadic explosions outside puzzled him, but he focused on the task at hand. Then the chatter in his comms roared to life again after a brief period of silence.

"Fire in the hole!"

"Extract!"

"Roger. Extract the asset."

Whatever was happening in the world around him had resulted in a change of plans as far as the team of mercenaries in the building was concerned. The sudden outage and the presence of a fire in the building would create more than enough of a distraction for him to make his escape undetected.

He slowly opened the door to the senior partner's office and closed his eyes, forcing his ears to do the work. He could hear muffled voices as well as the sounds of heavy footsteps. Shoe soles clapped on concrete flooring, not the plush carpet adorning the accounting firm's offices.

He risked detection and stuck his head and shoulders through the door opening. He was having difficulty discerning the direction the activity was coming from although he presumed it was the fire escape. Perhaps there was a fire.

Where were the alarms? Was it set by the men assigned to protect him? Was it related to the power outage?

Kantor forcibly shook himself back into the present. Now was not the time to speculate. He needed to go, with or without his extraction team.

He carefully retraced his steps back toward the front entrance of the sixtieth floor near the bank of elevators. He recalled seeing an emergency exit sign above a door in the reception area. He slowly felt his way along, perplexed as to why the offices had no emergency lighting. He exited the executive suite of offices and entered the vast, open space full of cubicles.

Wham!

A thunderous crash was heard ahead of him as someone kicked open the locked door entering the reception area. He instinctively ducked behind a desk, pressing the earpiece into his ear to listen for radio chatter from the extraction team. There was nothing.

"Move," a man whispered, barely audible to Kantor from his location.

"Moving."

"Clear."

Suddenly, Kantor felt uneasy. These professional killers were working in unison to sweep the offices in search of him, he presumed. They had the ability to contact him through their communications. Yet they hadn't advised him of a rendezvous point or provided any form of instructions. And now they were maintaining radio silence.

The voices he just heard should've been audible through his earpiece. They were not.

They're not here to pull me out. They need to provide a scapegoat for the FBI. A dead one, most likely.

The recesses of Kantor's mind took over. He was being hunted by trained killers. He had no weapon, and even if he did, he was wholly incapable of defending himself against the mercenaries. His predicament triggered only one possible response in the fight-or-flight scenario—escape the threat.

There were a couple of things that were in his favor. He knew the layout of the office suite very well. He'd studied it repeatedly in preparation for the heist. Second, the power outage appeared to have caught the mercenaries off guard just as much as he was. He assumed they didn't have any form of night optics. Otherwise, they'd be moving into the offices faster. Kantor believed he'd have the edge of moving in darkness.

He remained in a crouch behind the desk. Waiting. Listening. Peering under the desk, hoping he could catch a glimpse of a shadow. Legs moving through the cubicles, bodies pivoting from side to side as short-barreled weapons sought a target.

Kantor focused his thoughts on his recollection of the floor plan. The muffled voices and shuffling feet only served to confuse him. Then he remembered. There was a break room behind the storeroom's location.

He broke cover to crawl on his hands and knees along the walls. He couldn't see, so when he crawled headfirst into a steel planter, he groaned in agony. The pointed end of the planter cut a sizable gash in his forehead, causing blood to gush down his face. He was temporarily blinded as it flooded his eyes.

"This way." He'd been discovered. Or at least, they'd confirmed he was still there.

"Check the beacon," one of the men whispered a little too loudly.

Dammit! Kantor screamed in his head as he grabbed the earpiece and flung it across the room into the center of the cubicles. The plastic earpiece hit a particle-board partition and landed on the desk before rolling to a stop.

"He pulled it," the man whispered. Then he raised his voice. "Kantor, we're here to get you out."

Screw you! the master thief replied internally. He wiped the blood onto his sleeves and scrambled on all floors around the planter. He moved faster now in his attempt to escape.

Suddenly, a man's voice came from the reception area. "Okay, everybody. The door's open. Let's stick together and follow the walls so we don't trip over furniture."

He spoke in a barely audible whisper. "What? Are you kidding me?" A group of people had unknowingly followed the mercenaries into the offices. They had no idea what was lying in wait. *Their loss*, he thought.

His pursuers no longer attempted to hide their position. They couldn't afford to lose Kantor. Flashlights were illuminated, and the shriek of a young girl filled the air. A trigger-happy killer overreacted.

He let out a quick burst from his automatic weapon. Even the silenced gunfire, although muted, created an explosive sound as the bullets ripped through the cubicles and stitched the wall above the newcomers.

"Find Kantor!" ordered one of the mercenaries, breaking their silence. "I'll take care of these others."

"Roger!"

Flashlights were turned on, and they began scanning every cubicle.

"Please don't hurt us," an older man begged.

Begging never dissuaded a killer. Another burst of gunfire pierced the air, shooting out wall sconce fixtures and tearing through more sheetrock.

Kantor could now count four voices begging for their lives. They were not his problem. He rose and ran along the wall in a low crouch as the beams of flashlights illuminated the carpet where he'd rammed the planter. They were close. He had to take the risk.

He stood and raced forward as he caught a glimpse of the emergency exit door as a flashlight swept across it. He remained laser-focused on escaping. He rammed into the door with his hip, shoving the push bar to open the steel door.

His timing was less than a second too late. The men pursuing him began shooting. Their silenced weapons rained hellfire upon him. The bullets tore through his body and the backpack full of documents he'd stolen. Some ricocheted off the steel door into the concrete stairwell beyond.

Dirk Kantor was killed instantly, and the mercenaries quickly closed on his body to recover the real asset—a sitting president's tax records. Then they turned their attention to eliminating any witnesses.

CHAPTER THIRTY-ONE

Friday
Cubbison's Farm
Harford, Pennsylvania

Naturally, the Founder's Day dinner brought out the local politicians. All three Susquehanna County commissioners were in attendance. Chairman Michael Paul was the first to speak up in an effort to calm everyone's nerves. He pushed past the group until he was between them and the dining area, where the candles and string lights continued to brighten the space.

"Okay, folks. I don't think there's any reason for alarm. These things happen, especially in the country. It's part of our rural charm."

"I don't know, Mike," countered one of the guests. "What's up with the cell phones?"

"Yeah! I've never seen anything like it," added another.

"It's probably just a cell tower gone down because of the power outage," opined the chairman.

Emma moved next to the commissioner's side, her eyes searching for her husband. She was relieved when she saw John making his way through the dining area.

Paul continued his efforts to calm the group. "Listen, I don't have all the answers. I do know that it's best to remain calm in any unusual circumstance. Needless to say, however, I think we need to call an end to the wonderful evening. Your travels home might be a little more complicated without traffic signals and such."

"Geez, Mike, we've only got three or four in the whole dang county."

Paul shook his head in disbelief. "Okay, maybe so. Just be careful. Now, can we please thank our hosts before we depart for the evening. First, how about a round of applause for Saint Joe Winery for the delicious wines!"

Without hesitation, the group responded by clapping their hands. Some were still hesitant to assuage the concerns that screamed inside their minds, but they politely applauded, nonetheless.

"And, of course, a hearty thanks to our hostess, Emma Cubbison. And yes, there he is. John, join us, would you, please?"

All the attendees enthusiastically applauded the Cubbisons' efforts, with a few throwing in a hoot and holler to drive the point home.

"Thank you, everyone," said Emma. She desperately wanted to pull John aside and get his take on what was going on. She shook hands with Paul and the other two commissioners. Most of the rest of the guests stopped by to personally thank her and heap praise on the family for their efforts.

However, soon, the throngs of people were making their way to the darkened parking lot of Cubbison's Market, where a surprise awaited them.

"John, nobody's cell phone works, and I'm not buying the downed-cell-tower explanation. I'm guessing the lights don't work on the property, either."

He wrapped his arm around her and led her back toward the lit dining area, where the crew manning the wine bar were dutifully cleaning up after themselves.

"Emma, I don't want to jump to conclusions. Okay?"

"What?"

"The power is out, and the cell phones won't function. The only thing that I know of that would do that is a massive pulse of energy like the kind nuclear bombs release when they're detonated."

"What about the solar flare?" she asked.

John grimaced and nodded. "It's the only explanation I've got. The same enormous power that generated the aurora could've knocked out the electricity."

"Why the phones?" Emma looked around at the string lights. She pointed upward as she asked, "And why not these things?"

John shrugged. "The phones are basically minicomputers run by tiny circuits and wiring. The string lights don't require any complex electronics since they're battery operated."

"Wouldn't a power surge blow the bulbs?" asked Emma.

"I dunno. Maybe, you know, if the lights were plugged into an outlet and, therefore, the power grid. They seemed to have avoided—"

John's explanation was interrupted by shouting coming from the parking lot. Doors were slamming, and the questions came immediately.

"What the hell is going on?" was shouted more than once.

"My car won't start!"

"Heck, I can't even unlock mine!"

John grabbed Emma by the hand and began to walk briskly toward the parking lot. He stopped briefly by the back door of the market to ensure it was locked before rounding the side. His suspicions were correct. None of the vehicles were operable.

He leaned over to whisper to his wife, "The solar flare did this. The same delicate circuitry that powers the cell phones also runs throughout these cars. Think about it. Everything is connected to a computer. They wouldn't have been able to withstand the enormous energy."

"Why didn't we feel something?" she whispered back.

"We're not wired."

"John!" shouted one of their guests. "Whadya make of this? I've never seen anything like it."

John wasn't sure how he wanted to approach the situation. He suddenly realized he had sixty-some people who were stranded at their home. He and Emma walked toward the crowd that gathered in the center of the gravel parking lot. As he did, he glanced toward Old Jimmy surrounded by a dozen bales of hay stacked neatly with potted plants perched on top. His eyes darted back to the group as his mind raced. *What if?*

He considered the plight of their guests. Susquehanna County contained thirty-eight thousand residents located mostly in the countryside. The largest towns had a combined population of ten percent of that number. The county was also a large one bordered on the east by large mountains and smaller, hill-like mountains to the west. Some of the folks would have a long trek home in the dark.

He stopped just short of the group, feeling the eyes of the stranded people upon him. He leaned over to Emma and whispered, "They're gonna expect us to put them up for the night. I don't know that we have a choice."

"Geez. You're right. Some of them will have to sleep in the barn. And we have strangers from Scranton. What about them?"

"It's not a good situation, but we gotta figure it out. Might as well get started."

John stepped ahead of Emma. Within seconds, the crowd had gathered around and encircled him.

"Hey, everybody. I wish I had answers for you, but I don't. Let's just talk about what we know for certain."

Commissioner Paul read off the obvious. "No power. No cell phone service. No cars."

"All true," said John. "What we don't know is why and how widespread this situation is. For now, I think we need to focus on getting settled in for the night. Unfortunately, we only have a couple of beds available, and I suggest they be reserved for the elderly among us."

"I have a bad sciatic and need a bed!"

"I've got a crick," said one older man. "The doc warned me not to sleep in my easy chair. I need a bed."

"I need to stay near a toilet. You know, on account of, you know, unexpected leaks."

"I've gotta pee right now. Am I supposed to go behind the hay bales somewhere?"

Seconds later, an argument broke out as to who was most deserving or most incontinent. John closed his eyes and shook his head from side to side. It was gonna be a long night.

CHAPTER THIRTY-TWO

Friday
30 Rock
New York

The New York City Emergency Management Department formed by Mayor Rudy Giuliani in 1996 was considered one of the most well-prepared agencies in America to deal with the myriad crises a large city might face. They'd been tested many times in the past, but the unmitigated disaster caused by the back-to-back coronal mass ejections was the greatest.

Any agency or individual who undertook to prepare for an emergency addressed five basic protocols—prevention, mitigation, preparedness, response, and recovery. No governmental agency was fully prepared for the absolute destruction of the power grid. Especially for an entire nation.

The operations center for the emergency management agency was powered by generators, enabling the team to work. However, they had no means of receiving information from throughout the city. All lines of communication were down. Response vehicles were rendered inoperable by the powerful solar storm. The mass hysteria in the street hindered officers on horseback or bicycle from moving about the city.

It was impossible to mount a coordinated response to any distress calls, however delivered. New Yorkers were finding their way to fire halls and police precincts. They in turn would send someone, typically on foot, to notify the Emergency Management team.

Looting was a given. Since the sixties, when New York experienced power outages, even for a temporary, short period of time, looting was rampant. There weren't enough law enforcement officers in New York to police petty crimes on an ordinary day much less during a grid-down scenario.

Fires were a bigger issue. When the power was down, especially in the winter months, residents would burn kerosene heaters in their homes to stay warm. Some would negligently start fires in vacant buildings to keep warm. It was inevitable that structure fires would break out, capable of consuming entire city blocks.

To prepare for fires in the event of an outage, New York relied upon fire engines that contained pumps capable of pulling water from hydrants or even nearby ponds. Tankers might accompany the engines if the fire was large enough. During a power outage, backup batteries or generators allowed computers to trigger response protocols. Water resources ran on computerized generators designed to respond to the fire department's needs. Even the gas-powered generators required computer-controlled mechanisms to divert resources where the city needed them most.

When the perfect storm hit, all of these contingency plans were for naught. Police and fire response was akin to the late nineteenth century, a time when word of mouth together with horse-led wagons constituted the emergency response team.

"We've got fires throughout the city," the deputy commissioner for response said to his management team. "Frankly, we can't put them out. The best we can possibly do is assist those trapped in burning buildings to find safety. Then, again to the best of our capability, rescue teams can turn over any of the injured to paramedics."

"Deputy Commissioner, it's not safe for our people out there," began one of the fire chiefs in attendance. "The 33rd on the Upper East Side was overrun by a pack of thugs. We'd been notified of an apartment building on fire, so we responded on foot. Even our paramedics toted their gear on their shoulders. While our people pulled out the victims, the looters overwhelmed the paramedics and stole their pain medications. Well, actually, they stole everything and ran into the night."

"We can't stand down, Chief," said a representative of the NYPD.

"I don't disagree. I'm just saying my people are exposed out there without somebody to watch their backs."

The deputy commissioner was about to respond when the fire chief added, "I am not exaggerating. If we don't keep these fires under control, in this heat, they're gonna jump from structure to structure. And if it gets windy ..." His voice trailed off, allowing his words to hang in the air.

The deputy commissioner looked grim. "There are many issues to address, but I see fire as the highest priority. Frankly, we cannot stop the crimes of opportunity that will take over this city in the next several hours. Until the power is restored, lawlessness will be a fact of life, sadly. I have no way of reaching the governor although I'm sure she is aware of our situation just by using common sense. Hopefully, the National Guard can assist us.

"In the meantime, we need to focus on these fires and helping people. Let's talk about—" The deputy commissioner was abruptly interrupted by a uniformed police officer who entered the command center unannounced.

"We've just confirmed a major high-rise fire at 30 Rockefeller Center. At the moment, it's spread through the forty-sixth and forty-seventh floors."

"Are you sure?" asked the deputy commissioner. "Not in the belowground levels near the maintenance and utility rooms?"

"That's correct. There were reports of multiple explosions that coincided with glass blowing out of the west façade. The on-site security personnel are helping with the evacuations, but apparently there are people on the upper levels who've become trapped."

The veteran of the New York City Fire Department took a deep breath of air, filling his chest to its maximum before letting go of a deep exhale.

"We have to take them as they come. Let's get the word out to save those folks and evacuate Rockefeller Plaza before the fire spreads between buildings. Let's go!"

CHAPTER THIRTY-THREE

Friday
30 Rock
New York

Cat's little heart wanted to beat out of her chest. Her eyes were wide, never blinking, searching for movement. Begging God to help her find Grandpa Sam. Fearful of what was yet to come. Curled up in the fetal position to protect herself, her rapid breathing threatened to give her away. She wanted desperately to scream. *Help! Go away! Please leave me alone!*

Cat fought all of these urges because her survival instinct told her calling out would lead to her death. She forced herself to slow her breathing. She willed her eyes shut, for just a moment, to regain her composure.

And to think.

Seconds mattered. In minutes, it would be over. She needed God to intervene to save their lives. She just wished He would hurry it up. She drew upon her life's experiences, few that they were. Not times when she was in peril, which was only once that she could recall. The fun times. The games she'd played on the farm.

Like hide-and-seek.

Years ago, when she was six or seven, before her brothers graduated from high school and became too important to play with her, the kids would play their version of hide-and-seek. Well, it was more like barn cat and field mouse, as they called it. The boys were the barn cats stalking their prey, Cat, the field mouse, through the hay bales.

She'd created a maze of hay bales, some stacked tall with her brothers' help and others short, which included tunnels for her to crawl through. It was the highlight of her day when they played, and the guys were good sports about it. They could easily find her but made it seem like she was elusive.

Cat was suddenly calm and clearheaded. She could escape these bad guys and their guns by leading them through the maze of cubicles in the dark. Just like when she played with her brothers, she'd use what was available to create diversions. She might throw a steel pail over a stack of hay bales while scampering off at the same time. By the time they heard the sound, she'd be thirty feet away on the other side of the barn. *Maybe it would work for real,* she thought to herself.

Their flashlights were sweeping the floor. Back and forth, washing the carpet, searching for them. When the first shots had torn open the wall and ceiling over their heads, Asher had forcibly pulled her to the floor. All three had held their breath for several seconds, waiting for the next attempt to kill them.

When the second round of gunfire had let out its blast in the office space, each of them had panicked, rushing in different directions in search of cover. She tried to recall that moment. It seemed Asher and Lauren had moved back toward the door. Sam had scrambled forward and reached for her hand. However, Cat had lurched to the right, falling on her belly. She'd slithered along the carpet until she could shimmy under a cubicle.

As the flashlights washed the open office space, she was able to see the vast number of cubicles that surrounded her. They were no different than the hay bales in the family's barn.

A beam of light lit up the floor just two feet away from where she was hidden. It was time for a diversion.

She slowly reached on top of the desk and ran her hand along the top in search of anything solid. She bumped into a pencil holder and nearly knocked it over. However, her quick reflexes stopped it from tipping, which would've most certainly resulted in the game being over.

She dipped her fingers inside and slowly pulled it over the edge of the desk. She thought about how the boys used to play army in the fields, picking up rocks to act as a pretend grenade. They'd throw them over their heads like a basketball player making a hook shot.

She slid into the aisle between the first and second row of cubicles. She hurled the filled pencil cup toward the back of the room and quickly crawled a dozen feet or more before ducking under another cubicle. By the time the pencils crashed into a computer monitor, she'd expanded the distance between her and her pursuers.

However, she didn't rest on her laurels. The beams emanating from their flashlights converged on the noise. She moved again, rushing down the aisle between the second and third row of cubicles, once again diving under a desk. She was closer to the center of the room now, much farther away from her pursuers.

Suddenly, from outside the office in the reception area, she heard loud talking.

A man shouted in a deep, booming voice, "Come on, everybody! The door's open."

A woman responded, "Okay. Pass it down the line. Tell the others in the stairwell to come this way!"

"Okay!" a soft-spoken man responded.

Emma furrowed her brow. There was something about—

Her thoughts were interrupted by loud whispers between her pursuers.

"We got more coming."

"Yeah, we've got the asset. The more time we waste, the more likely it is that we'll burn up."

"Move."

"Roger that."

The man in the reception area shouted again, "Through this door, everyone. Hurry!"

Cat wanted to warn them. She risked standing so she could see the flashlights of the shooters. They were pointed at a partially open door toward the back of the cubicles. They each hopped over something as they stealthily entered the stairwell. Within seconds, they were gone.

She took a moment to breathe a sigh of relief. Then she got up her nerve to find Grandpa Sam. She hoped, no, prayed, that the shooters weren't tricking her.

"Grandpa Sam," she said in a loud whisper, "are you okay?"

She heard a loud thump.

"Ugh."

"Grandpa?"

"Yeah, over here. I'm fine. Where are you?"

"I'll come to you." Cat stood and stumbled through the cubicles, her hearing being so attuned to her surroundings that she was certain where he was located. A chair swiveled and then rolled into the aisle in front of her. Her grandfather crawled out. As she reached him, she almost slipped on a dozen or more pencils on the carpet.

"Come here, Cat. My God, you're okay!" Tears flowed down Sam's face as the two crashed into one another. They held each other, making no attempt to restrain their emotions.

"Guys? Are you both all right?" Lauren's voice startled them at first.

"Yes," replied Sam. "We're over here. In the middle."

"I think there are others in here, too. You know, from the stairs."

Asher responded, "No, that was us. We needed to create a diversion and had nothing to work with. So we pretended there were a bunch of people coming into the office."

"We hoped the shooters would leave to avoid more witnesses to whatever they were up to in here," added Lauren.

"Great thinking," praised Sam. As the Doyles joined them, they all hugged one another and gathered their wits about them. First, Sam asked, "Who threw the cup of pencils? They almost hit me in the head."

Cat gasped. Her diversion had led the shooters straight to her grandfather.

"I'm sorry, Grandpa. I was trying to lead them away from me." She began to cry again as she realized she'd saved herself while putting her grandfather at great risk.

"Listen, what you did was brilliant," said Sam as he consoled her. In the darkness, he tried to look into Asher's and Lauren's faces. "Same for you two. Brilliant moves that saved all of our lives. However, I think we might have another problem ahead of us."

CHAPTER THIRTY-FOUR

Friday
30 Rock
New York

Abby Baker and Danny Marino had been partners on Engine 23 for seven years, an extraordinary length of time in an age when firefighters were underpaid and seeking early retirement. The two were childhood friends growing up in the Bronx just a few houses from one another. After high school, Marino spent a few years in the Army while Baker became a firefighter. She'd recruited him into the FDNY when he returned stateside.

Engine 23 was a close-knit group who'd dedicated their lives to saving others and protecting New York from burning out of control. The company itself was one of the FDNY's oldest, having been organized in 1865. The small firehouse located on West Fifty-Eight Street near Central Park was dwarfed amidst the high-rises that filled Billionaires' Row.

Tonight, they'd face a challenge like no other. Captain Delroy Duffy, their incident commander, had gathered everyone at the firehouse to bring them up to speed. He likened their task to the Marines who stormed the beaches of Normandy during World War II. It would be no different than hand-to-hand combat with the enemy.

Their primary goal, with the assistance of the NYPD, was to evacuate people from 30 Rock. Secondarily, to the extent they could without being harmed or risking their lives, was to work to contain the fires to the upper floors. The firefighters didn't have to question this directive. They knew, at best, they could slow the rate the fire burned and moved throughout the building. Without water, it would be damned near impossible to contain it.

Baker's nickname was Cookie, a moniker she'd earned early in her career as she endeared herself to her fellow firefighters at Engine Company 23 by baking cookies. Marino, nicknamed Q-B in honor of the famed Miami Dolphins quarterback of the same name, had taken his moniker to heart, as he frequently led the Engine 23 team to fight structure fires.

Baker and Marino led the charge down Seventh Avenue toward 30 Rock. Fully outfitted in their gear and carrying more in their arms, the contingent managed to jog the three-quarters of a mile to respond to the fire in ten minutes. Ordinarily, they would've already sprung into action, dousing the building with water and saving lives. However, word of the fire had been slow to reach them due to the power outage.

Once they arrived at the entrance to the building, they immediately realized their first obstacle would be to clear the area of onlookers and those who'd already been evacuated. The NYPD was doing their best but advised her that without horseback patrol officers, the task was daunting.

Instead, Baker and Marino moved inside and left pedestrian traffic control to the police. A police captain was standing atop the reception desk with a bullhorn and a flashlight, bellowing at people to clear the building immediately. Marino approached him first.

"Whadya got, Captain?"

"All I've been able to confirm is that we've got a blaze on the upper forties into the lower fifties. People fleeing the building report loud explosions maybe coupled with some type of incendiary device. You know, I haven't stopped to conduct interviews."

He pulled his bullhorn to his mouth and shouted at a group of people who were hugging one another. Most likely coworkers who'd been reunited, they were clogging up the exit to the building.

The captain continued. "We've got windows blown out on forty-nine and fifty. Smoke is billowing out of the north and west sides of the structure."

"Have you deployed any firefighters?" asked Marino.

"Yeah, up the north stairwell. That was about thirty minutes ago. They were off-duty, they said."

"Did they have any gear?" asked Baker.

"Only what the building security had in their lockers. A couple of Halligans and axes. They gave them N95 masks to protect them from smoke inhalation. That's it."

"You said they went up the north stairwell. Any particular reason why?" asked Marino.

"That's where the smoke was coming out," replied the police captain before he returned to the task of herding people acting liked frightened cats out of the burning building.

Marino turned to Baker and the other firefighters from Engine 23. "Follow me. We're gonna have to hoof it up fifty stories."

The group huddled near the bank of elevators, the only part of the spacious entrance unoccupied by frightened people. They readied their gear. They pulled their hoods over their heads. They Velcro'd and buckled their jackets and affixed their oxygen tanks to their backs. Those who accomplished their dress out first assisted the others. They were a team.

With their Halligan bars in hand, and flashlights in another, they moved single file toward the emergency stairwell on the south side of the building. A Halligan was a tool used to pry open doors as well as any task requiring twisting, punching, or striking. It had been designed by an FDNY deputy chief named Hugh Halligan in 1948.

Marino led the way. They reached the stairwell and had to force evacuees to make way. "Fire department! Please move against the wall!"

They ignored his pleas. He tried again. "Out of the way. Fire department. Move against the wall, now!"

The people descending the stairs slowed, giving Marino and the others the opportunity to move into the stairwell. Soon, they were single file walking slowly but deliberately upward. In between Marino instructing people to move out of the way, Baker sought information.

"We're firefighters. Tell us what you know."

Her first request for information resulted in half a dozen people shouting their responses in unison. It was hard to discern what they were saying, so Baker tried again.

"One at a time, please! Do you know where the fire started?"

"Forty-nine!"

"Fifty!"

"No, it was forty-nine. I'm sure of it!"

Another voice yelled, "Fifty. But it was moving up to fifty-one and fifty-two when I passed them."

As they continued to march up the stairs, the heated air coupled with lack of ventilation and heavy equipment began taking its toll. The team began to slow with the exception of Marino and Baker, who were the youngest and in the best physical condition. As a group, they made the decision to split up. Marino and Baker would continue up to the fiftieth floor, and the rest of the firefighters would handle forty-nine.

Baker continued to seek information. "Are there people trapped?"

"Upper floors."

"Definitely, upper floors. Beyond fifty-two. I was in fifty-three."

The higher they climbed, the fewer people they encountered. At one point, a group of men crashed into Marino, sending him backwards into Baker. The two fought to hold onto the rail in order to maintain their balance as the men rudely rushed past.

"Hey! Careful! There are more firefighters coming up behind us. Stay against the wall!"

The men didn't respond, and Marino doubted they'd make way for his comrades. He shook his head in disappointment and continued. By the time they reached the forty-fifth floor, the number of people coming down became a trickle.

Plus, they were all injured in some way. Superficial burns and smoke inhalation were the most common injuries sustained. Marino and Baker performed triage in the stairwell. Mostly, they advised the people fleeing the fire that the first-degree burns, while painful, would heal with basic first aid. They were advised to avoid touching their burned skin and to keep it covered if possible until treated. For those who'd inhaled too much smoke, Baker and Marino shared quick hits from their oxygen tanks. It seemed to breathe new life into the evacuees, giving them the strength to continue their hasty exit.

The process of treating these individuals as they descended the stairwell slowed them down. Soon, the other firefighters could be heard catching up to them. He shouted to them, confirming the information they already knew.

"The fire started on forty-nine. Some kind of explosive devices were involved. The fire is moving upward toward fifty-two. We have people trapped at fifty-three or higher. We'll move upward to fifty-one. You clear forty-nine and fifty."

"Got it!" one of the firefighters responded.

Minutes later, the two friends reached the forty-ninth floor. The heat was stifling as black smoke puffed out the cracked door. Baker stopped to look inside and saw that the space appeared to be fully engulfed in flames with black smoke billowing against the drop ceiling, parts of which were fully ablaze while the rest was not.

"Accelerant," she mumbled to herself. Baker knew the physical evidence indicating the presence of accelerants included black smoke and overhead damage inconsistent with the naturally available fuel like papers and furniture. The fact that certain parts of the drop ceiling were burning while the rest was not was consistent with the reports of explosions. Possibly from an incendiary device.

"Keep moving!" She had to shout to her partner because of the noise from the blaze.

The two slowly climbed up to the fiftieth floor. They were no longer encountering people descending the stairs.

"Do you think it's emptied out?" asked Marino.

Baker looked into the fiftieth-floor office suite. It, too, was filled with fire and black smoke. "I doubt it. Let's go find out." She pointed upward with her flashlight. The light beam was diffused by the smoke. As they ascended one more flight of stairs, they became increasingly blinded to their surroundings.

CHAPTER THIRTY-FIVE

Friday
30 Rock
New York

"What are we gonna do? We can't go down there!" Cat feared the fire and the prospect of walking through the black smoke in the already darkened stairwell more than the gunmen they'd just encountered.

"We could try to cut across the building to the other side," shouted Sam in response.

"What floor are we on?" asked Lauren.

Asher, who'd led the way, had lost track of their location in relation to the sixtieth floor where they'd entered the stairwell. "Fifty-two. Maybe fifty-one. I'm not sure."

"I don't think going forward is a good idea," said Sam. "The fire must be down there somewhere."

"I can feel the heat on my face," added Cat.

Lauren moved closer to her husband. "People heading for the roof assumed choppers would be sent to rescue them. Are we sure they can't fly?"

Asher took a deep breath out of habit. It caused him to have a coughing fit. After it passed, he talked it through aloud. "I doubt it. At least not within the city's emergency management capability. Now, I suppose the military might have them. I mean, supposedly, in the event of a nuclear attack, we'd still have operating trucks and machinery like helicopters."

"Should we go back?" Lauren repeated her question.

"We can, or we could explore our options. Something tells me the few military choppers capable of withstanding a solar storm like this one might also be a little busy."

Lauren touched his sweaty, soot-covered face, then touched her own. She could only imagine what they all looked like.

"I say we try to go down first," offered Sam. "We know what this stairwell looks like. Maybe the other side is better."

Asher reached out until he was able to touch everyone. "Okay, listen up. Pull your shirts over your nose and mouth as much as you can. Stay as low to the floor as possible, even if it means we have to crawl. The freshest air will be there, while this toxic, black smoke will follow the heated air to the ceiling."

"Okay," the other three said in unison.

"Stand against the wall behind me," instructed Asher. "I need to see if the door is hot."

First, he dropped down to a knee and tried to determine if any smoke was seeping through the tight seal the steel door provided. Then with his hand covered by his untucked shirt, he tapped the door. Quickly at first and then a little longer. While it was not cool to the touch, it certainly wasn't holding back a raging fire.

"Okay, stand against the wall and turn your head away."

They did so, and Asher slowly opened the steel door. Inside, he could barely make out the smoke that filled the office. However, he saw no evidence of flames, as they would've certainly illuminated the space.

"Here we go," he began. "Follow me along the wall. Sam, close the door behind us once we're inside. We can walk at a low crouch, but if you feel me drop down, don't hesitate to do so."

They held each other's hands a little tighter than before. The group had bonded during the experience, and all were comfortable in allowing Asher to lead them to safety. For his part, Asher only knew what to do in the event of a building fire from conducting research as part of his scriptwriting duties. He recalled that most people died because the flames consumed most of the available oxygen during the burning process. This resulted in deadly carbon monoxide being released into the air. Then there was the fuel causing the fire to spread. Many burning objects might emit toxic gases harmful to humans. These killing fumes were widely considered to be more dangerous than the fire itself.

The space they entered was different from the cavernous bullpen holding the cubicles in the accounting office. They were in an extra-wide hallway lined with cushioned benches and numerous doors. Some of the doors were ajar, and Asher had the others wait while he explored their interior. He was never sure if an entryway led to the center of 30 Rock and the elevator foyer.

Each office was filled with simple furniture consisting of a desk, a credenza and two chairs facing the desk. He imagined some kind of employment firm or administrative function.

Back in the hallway, he led them deeper into the offices. There was no sign of the fire. But the air was not clear. Soot and smoke permeated their nostrils.

And it was hot. Like a sauna. A dry heat that seemed to rise and fall as they moved toward the center.

In the dark, the maze of hallways made the cubicles in the accounting firm seem like an easy puzzle to solve. At one point, Asher wasn't certain they hadn't gone in a complete circle or perhaps got turned around. He pushed through the self-doubt until the heat seemed to grow stronger.

Asher slowed their progress. Something had changed. The smoke-filled air seemed to fill the hallway, but it simply lingered around them. Then, suddenly, but with increased speed, the smoke began to blow away from them in the direction they were moving. It was if it was being sucked by a vacuum of some sort.

The hallway opened up into a larger space. They could hear hissing and a flapping sound.

"What is that?" asked Cat.

Before anyone could answer, a door was flung open in front of them, and a ghostly figure raced toward them. A ghost dressed in rags. A ghost that was less spirit-like and more of a human fireball.

"Arrrrggggghhhh!" the woman screamed as she rushed through the door, chased by flames. The vacuum that seemed to suck the smoke toward the opening suddenly reversed itself. As the door opened wider, a ball of fire roared directly toward them.

"Get down!" shouted Asher. "Cover your heads."

They couldn't hear his last words as the flames shot past with the roar of a huge beast. The woman on fire made it a few feet past them before falling forward in a heap, her burnt flesh filling the air with the rancid stench of death. Her clothing immediately caused the carpet to catch on fire along with the seat cushions of benches nearby.

Asher rose to a low crouch to see if he could help her.

BAM!

The impact was so quick and hard he was knocked off his feet, his body tumbling down to the floor. With the air punched out of his lungs, his vision blurred as he tried to regain full consciousness.

The raging fire behind the door had sucked the smoke-filled oxygen toward it. When the door opened, the new source of fuel fed the flames, drawing the fire in the direction of the oxygen source. The result was Asher's body being swept down the hallway by the blaze. He writhed in pain as the exposed skin on the back of his neck and arms singed from the flames.

"Asher!" shouted Lauren, who began to crawl on all fours to help her husband.

"Stay low," cautioned Sam, who was already by Asher's side. He calmed his nerves and spoke close to Asher's ear. "Where are you burned? I can't see."

"Arms. Neck." Asher's response was filled with gasps for fresh air.

"Ash, baby, are you okay? Please talk to me."

"Stunned. Burnt, but not too bad. I'll feel it in the morning, though."

Lauren laughed and gently stroked the back of his head. The singed hair had left a noticeable bald spot. She loved her husband and was thankful he wasn't more injured. The jokes about the bald spot would have to wait.

The sound of glass breaking caused them all to jerk. Suddenly, the smoke reversed itself again and was sucked rapidly toward the other side of the building. Doors to offices left open were being slammed shut. One after another, the hollow-core doors were sucked inward by the pressure of the fire and smoke that was now billowing out of the north side of the building.

With a groan, Asher rolled over and got back up to vertical. He took advantage of the slightly cleaner air and took a deep breath. The searing pain on the back of his head and arms was immaterial. He was alive.

He pivoted on his butt to look in both directions, desperately trying to see in the dark. He needed to make a decision. Then the inferno made it for him.

CHAPTER THIRTY-SIX

Friday
30 Rock
New York

The explosion was deafening. So much so, Cat's ears lacked the ability to absorb the massive amount of energy as sound. All that registered was the pain caused by the concussive effect of the blast below them. She covered her head and curled into a ball, a maneuver that was instinctual and somewhat logical. Cat wanted to urge the others to do so, but it was too late. Within a second, the floor disappeared, dropping downward to the offices beneath them. Carrying bodies with it like they were on a frightening, malfunctioning ride on the Tower of Terror at Disney World.

Their screams were primal. Guttural. Induced by the most fear any of them had ever experienced. In their minds, they were being sucked into hell.

The floor's collapse was as unexpected as it was stunningly fast. Debris from concrete, sheetrock, electrical wiring, and pieces of drop ceiling cascaded on top of them. They were slowly buried in an avalanche consisting of parts of the fiftieth and fifty-first floors of 30 Rock. Their bodies were battered as the building materials rained blow after blow upon them until it finally stopped.

And then fire surrounded them. In all directions, flames dashed and darted from floor to ceiling. Mesmerizing. Yet deadly.

Crushed under the debris, pinned to the concrete floor, Cat had only one thought. All her short life, she'd longed to see the world. Visit the places she learned about online. Now, none of those things mattered. Her eyes slowly closed as she visualized the faces of her family. In her mind, she repeated the phrase, *There's no place like home. There's no place like home.*

"Fire department. Call out!"

"Fire department. Call out! Is anybody here?"

Baker and Marino moved methodically through the fiftieth floor in search of people trapped in the blaze. More than once, they considered retreating to the emergency exit to evade the flames that were spreading throughout the floor. Just as they were about to turn back, the ceiling collapsed near the center of the offices and came crashing down.

Both firefighters were knocked backwards and instinctively rolled over to shield their faces. Marino crawled on top of Baker's head to shield her. Her helmet had been dislodged by flying debris. His fire coat protected her from the flames that washed over them.

"Jesus, Q-B," she said breathlessly. "That was close. What the hell?"

He lifted his body off hers with an eye toward the huge pile of debris that had come crashing down from the fifty-first floor. "Yeah. That's exactly what it is. Hell."

"This is a lost cause. Way too dangerous, especially without comms or backup. Let's go up a floor."

Marino rose to his knees and helped her up. He used his gloves to brush off glowing embers that covered her back and were caught in her jet-black hair, made more so by the soot. After they checked their gear, they rose to a low crouch and began moving away from the collapse toward the emergency exit leading to the south stairwell.

Ping! Ping! Ping!

Baker grabbed Marino's coat sleeve and tugged him to a stop.

"Did you hear that?"

"What?"

"Just wait. Listen."

Ping! Ping! Ping!

The metal-on-metal sound repeated, followed by a loud groan.

The two firefighters directed their lights in each other's faces. Somebody had fallen through from the upper floors.

Ignoring the flames that darted up the walls together with its toxic smoke, they raced back into the offices.

"Fire department! Call out!"

"Is there somebody here?"

Ping! Ping! Ping!

"My god!" shouted Baker.

Marino reached the debris first. He dropped to his knees and carefully began to remove parts of the ceiling and hunks of concrete.

"Can you hear us? We're here!"

"Yes," came the reply from a weak, raspy voice.

"Ma'am? Ma'am? What's your name?"

"Lauren. Four of us."

Baker turned around and shined her flashlight down the corridor toward the emergency exit. Marino asked, "Are you thinking about getting help?"

The fire was beginning to consume the hallway's walls. "No time, Q-B. We've gotta hurry. Seriously."

Frantically now, they began grabbing debris and throwing it behind them. They worked together to remove larger pieces of concrete, careful not to get cut on the protruding pieces of steel rebar.

Throughout their extraction effort, the pinging sound continued. Until it abruptly stopped.

Baker was the first to notice. "Lauren! Lauren! Can you hear me?"

"I'm here. I can see your flashlights."

"Okay. Good," said Baker. Marino, however, became concerned.

"Lauren, were you pulling on a pipe or hitting something metallic?"

"Um, no."

Marino slapped his thigh. "Shit! Lauren! What are their names? Your friends. Who are they?" He turned to Baker and motioned for her to make her way to the other side of the avalanche of debris.

Lauren's voice was weak, but she responded, "My husband, Asher. Two friends. Cat, a young girl. Her grandfather, um, Sam."

Both Marino and Baker began calling out their names, hoping to elicit a response. None of them responded, and the pinging of the pipe never continued.

Marino focused on rescuing Lauren first. She was alive. While he cleared enough space for her to wriggle out of confinement, Baker was doing the same on the other side. Searching frantically for any sign of life. A leg. An arm. Anything she could find before the approaching flames reached the debris.

Lauren was sitting upright next to Marino, who continued to dig through the rubble. She found her voice. "Asher Doyle! Can you hear me? Asher!"

Her voice increased in intensity as she called out for Sam and Cat. Then she found her strength. Now, all three of them were digging into the pile, tossing pieces of concrete around like they were pebbles. Once the upper floor was removed, they were able to see the bottom of the pile.

Baker suddenly shouted, "I've got a hand! A child!"

"Lauren, go help her," ordered Marino.

The two women frantically dug through the pile, revealing more of Cat's battered body.

"She's unconscious!" shouted Baker over the roar of the strengthening fire.

"Get her out of here!" yelled Marino before adding, "I've got an arm. Left. Wait. There's a wedding ring."

"Asher!" shouted Lauren, who almost left Baker's side but caught herself. "Please help him!"

"On it!" Marino carefully began to tear the pieces of the pile away. More and more of Asher's body was revealed. His face was bloodied, but he was breathing. Marino reached into his pocket and retrieved an ammonium inhalant ampule. Victims were easier to help when awake rather than unconscious.

Asher responded immediately with a loud groan.

"He's alive!" Marino hollered exuberantly. He knelt over Asher and spoke directly into his ear. "Where does it hurt?"

Asher began to cough violently until he cleared his throat. "It's easier to say where it doesn't." Laughing at his own humor, he began coughing again.

"Yeah, I've felt that way myself, my friend. Let's get you out of this mess."

"My wife? Lauren?" whispered Asher.

"She's fine. They found the young girl. Cat, right?"

Asher nodded. "Sam?"

"Not yet. He's in the middle, I guess."

Just as Marino finished pulling Asher free, Lauren appeared by their side, sobbing.

"Thank god you're alive. I could never live without you, Ash. Please, are you okay?"

Asher managed a smile and lifted his hand to her face. He could barely see her in the light provided by the approaching fire.

Marino rose to a crouch as Baker appeared with Cat in her arms. "She's alive, but barely. I can't revive her."

"Go," ordered Marino. "Lead these two down with you. I'll find the fourth person."

"They call him Grandpa Sam," said Lauren.

Marino stuck out his jaw and adjusted his jacket. "I'll find him. All of you, go. Hurry!"

Lauren helped Asher to his feet and draped his arm over her shoulders. Baker gave them instructions, and she wrapped her fire jacket around Cat's body. Lowering herself as much as she could, she led the way, moving toward the narrowing corridor between the walls that were starting to disintegrate from the fire.

Marino turned his flashlight onto the debris pile. "Where are you, Grandpa Sam?"

CHAPTER THIRTY-SEVEN

Friday
30 Rock
New York

To pick up the pace, Baker paused to strip off some of her gear after they'd cleared the floors where the fire raged. Asher insisted he was up to the task of carrying Cat down the stairwell, but Baker knew better. A quick review of his physical responses to basic coordination tests told a different story. He and Lauren were both able to assist by carrying her gear, which helped lighten the load.

One of the things she noticed as they made their way out of the building was she did not come across any firefighters along the way. No police, either. It was if they were the only ones left in the high-rise, which led her to wonder if the fire had spread to the lower floors.

The situation became even more surreal when Asher opened the ground-floor door to allow Baker to lead the way into the lobby. It was empty. As in, not a single soul empty. The police captain shouting orders was gone. The people hustling to safety had been evacuated.

All that was left was trash on the floor that they stumbled over as they shuffled toward the exit.

"I don't understand," said Baker. "Where is everybody?"

Asher moved ahead of her and gently pressed his body against the heavy glass door. The eerie silence within the lobby was immediately replaced with the loud roar of mayhem outside.

The three of them emerged onto Rockefeller Plaza to the sounds of screaming, shouting, and agonizing pleas for mercy.

"Come on, people, get away from the building!" ordered a uniformed NYPD officer.

"Why isn't anyone—?" Baker began to ask as she walked toward him, but he ignored her question.

"If you've been injured, triage and paramedics are that way." He pointed his flashlight toward several white tents set up more than a hundred yards away from the building. Temporary lighting towers had been set up around them.

"But ..." Her voice trailed off as she turned back to 30 Rock. She looked upward and saw the difference from earlier. At least seven floors were fully involved with a raging fire that poured through the broken windows. Black smoke spiraled into the sky, partially obscuring the aurora New Yorkers had been enjoying just hours earlier.

The police officer brought her back to the present. "Move it! The building's structural integrity has been compromised. We have to move everyone back. Now!"

"My partner's still in there," she said, spinning around with an unconscious Cat in her arms.

"You'd better tend to that girl and let your partner do whatever it is he's doing." The officer shuffled his flashlight back and forth as if it were a broom capable of sweeping away the dirt.

"Come on, um ..." began Asher.

"Baker. Abigail Baker."

Asher's recognition of her name was immediate. "Seriously? Abigail Baker."

"Yeah. Like on *Blue Bloods*."

Asher managed a cough-filled laugh. "Yeah, I know. Thank you, Baker. Follow me; I'll try to clear a path."

Asher led the way, pushing through the crowd of people, who either stood in place dumbfounded or ran in one direction or another, aimlessly seeking loved ones or safety. On either side of the plaza, the sound of glass breaking could be heard as looters were having their way with the high-end retail stores.

"Almost there," announced Asher as the tops of the white tents came into view. People were crowded around the entrance in an attempt to see a paramedic or doctor. Asher immediately noticed they didn't have any visible wounds. To be sure, they appeared distraught and weary. But they weren't knocked unconscious like Cat.

"Stay in line," he said to Baker, who had Lauren tucked close to her side. The two comforted Cat, hoping that somehow, she could hear them.

Minutes later, Asher returned. "I talked to a head nurse in charge of triage. She knew my dad. She's gonna meet us at the back of the tent so we can get Cat some help without causing a riot."

They left the line and peeled off toward the back. Periodically, Asher glanced over his shoulder to make sure nobody followed them. Satisfied their cutting in line wasn't going to draw the ire of anyone, he led Baker by the elbow to the back of the tents, where an elderly nurse greeted them.

"Please, through here. Let's get this young lady some help."

Baker followed the nurse while the Doyles lagged behind to allow the professionals some room to work. Baker returned immediately, her arms still in the same position they had been in as she'd cradled Cat down the stairwell.

"I need your help with something."

"Sure. Anything."

Baker took a deep breath. "Um, will you help me with my arms? I can't move them."

From her shoulders to her wrists, Baker had held Cat so tight that her muscles were swollen and the joints became stiff as if locked in place. Together, Asher and Lauren gently massaged her arms and straightened them until they fell by her sides. Baker tried to reach up and rub them herself. She was unable to.

Instead, she turned her attention back to the burning building as a sudden explosion blew out the windows of another floor above where they'd come across one another. She appeared sullen, prompting Lauren to move in front of her.

"Are you gonna go back up to find the other firefighter?"

"Marino. Danny Marino. We've been friends since we were kids. I can't believe I left him alone."

Asher and Lauren were unsure as to what they should say. Cat needed to be saved, and Sam was still missing. Finally, Asher had a suggestion.

"I feel better now. Let's go back up together. We'll find them both. I promise."

Lauren's eyes grew wide at the thought of her husband going back into the inferno. "No. I wasn't hurt or buried as bad as you were. Let me go with Baker."

"Excuse me, Mr. Doyle?" the triage nurse approached them. "The young lady is awake. Would you like to speak with her?"

"Is she okay?" asked Lauren.

"She'll have quite a bit of bruising. Her midsection is tender, so internal bleeding is always a concern. You'll need to monitor her for the next few days. I'll provide you some notes on what to watch for."

"Shouldn't we take her to a hospital?" asked Asher.

The nurse responded with a cynical laugh. "I'm sorry, Mr. Doyle. There are no functioning hospitals in the five boroughs. There are makeshift trauma and treatment tents like this one, but that's about it. The best we can offer is initial diagnosis and treatment, followed by a pat on the head together with a wish of good luck."

Asher ran his fingers through his soot-covered hair. That was when he discovered for the first time that the flames had singed a bald spot in the back. He abruptly pulled his hand away and examined it, half-expecting to find a handful of hair in it.

He glanced at Lauren and responded, "Okay, we'll come see her for a moment, but then we have to go back and find her partner and the young girl's grandfather, who are trapped inside."

"They're not gonna allow you in, Mr. Doyle. Nobody, even firefighters. I'm sorry to tell you this, but they're on their own."

Her words hung in the air as a woman began to wail in despair over the loss of a loved one. Her cries of agony at her husband's untimely demise didn't make Baker feel any better. She turned to stare at the flames shooting out of 30 Rock, making no attempt to hide her tears.

Marino was utterly dumbfounded. The bottom line was this—Sam wasn't there. He'd simply vanished. With the flames closing in, Marino used his flashlight to surveil his surroundings for the fourth or fifth time. He thought perhaps the man had crawled off into another office as the debris fell downward. However, there were no doors near the pile. And now, the flames were inching forward, steadily consuming the walls at both ends of the corridor. Marino's window of opportunity to escape the raging fire was shrinking.

More debris fell from above and pelted his helmet, knocking it slightly askew. When the dusty concrete and sheetrock stopped, he glanced upward and shined his light into the fifty-first floor. That was when he saw it.

"I'll be damned!" he shouted as he stood and stretched the flashlight as high as he could toward the opening. An arm. Sam's arm, he presumed, was dangling over the edge of the brittle concrete and steel separating the two floors.

"Sam! Can you hear me? I'm a firefighter! Sam!"

Marino had lost focus on his own plight. A flame shot through the wall to his left, touching the sleeve of his jacket. He instinctively jumped away and almost lost his footing.

"Grandpa Sam! Hey! Can you hear me?"

Marino looked around. The ceiling was ten feet high. He'd need to stack up desks or find a ladder. There was no time for that. He needed to try to wake Sam as a last-ditch effort before he fought through the flames and entered the fifty-first floor.

He picked up baseball-sized pieces of debris and threw them upward with an underhand motion. After several tries, he made contact with Sam's limp arm.

"Sam! Did you feel that? Come on, buddy. Wake up!"

Marino tried again. The previous attempts had helped him find his mark. On the second try, he made solid contact, actually drawing blood from Sam's knuckles.

"Ow."

Marino heard it. He was sure of it. Sam said *ow*. He began to jump up and down in his gear. "Sam! Sam! Did you feel that? Hey!"

Sam didn't respond verbally. However, he did move his arm, drawing it out of the opening and out of sight.

Marino was screaming at Sam now. Telling him the others were safe and that they needed to go. Sam still didn't respond.

More debris began to fall from the opening, causing Marino to duck for cover. He knew the building was becoming unstable, and it was a matter of time before it was reduced to rubble. He wiped the dirt from his face and began to look upward. He directed his light into the opening, and there he was.

Sam had crawled on his belly to stick his head over the edge. His blood-soaked hands had a death grip on two pieces of rebar sticking out from the side of the floor.

"Where's Cat?"

"They took her outside. Lauren, Asher, and my partner are with her. She's alive."

"Great," said Sam, who began to cough.

Marino thought he detected blood spray coming out of his mouth, but he wasn't sure. It could've been dripping from the wounds on his hands. He had to stay calm although he needed to instill a sense of urgency in the older man.

"Sam, listen. We've gotta get out of here. This floor is almost covered in fire. What's it like up there?"

Sam rose, and his head disappeared for a moment. He returned to the prone position to answer the question. He pointed forward, toward the north side of the building.

"There's a lot of fire over there. Nothing behind me but smoke."

Marino nodded up and down rapidly. "Okay. Okay. Can you walk? Or crawling is better."

"Either one. My chest hurts, and my head. I got hit by something."

"Okay, Sam. Here's what we're gonna do. I need you to make your way back to the fire escape. You know, the concrete stairwell. Can you do that?"

"Yeah, but there's a lot of smoke in there."

"I understand, Sam. But I'm gonna roast if I don't get out of here. Can you meet me?"

"On my way."

Sam disappeared from view. Marino turned toward the south side of the building. The entire hallway was engulfed in flames. He tried to remember what he'd observed as they'd entered the space. Office after office. Small, sparsely furnished. Doors were closed.

He'd give it a shot. He had no other option.

Lauren and Baker stood arm in arm behind the cordoned-off area in front of 30 Rock. There were several people awaiting loved ones to exit the skyscraper. Some were distraught and others angry at the fact they couldn't help.

Asher stood slightly behind the two women, allowing Cat to lean against him. The young girl had been through a lot and was still having difficulty taking a deep breath. The nurse had given Asher some antibiotics and inhalers to help her recover. She admonished him to be judicious about the use of the antibiotics. The infection needed to be completely eliminated. There were no hospitals to help her, the nurse had reminded him.

"It's been too long," muttered Baker.

"Where is he? I can't lose Grandpa Sam!" Cat began to cough as she sobbed.

"Hang in there, guys," encouraged Asher. "Give Marino time to—"

Two silhouettes appeared against the backdrop of the entrance. One had his arm slung over the other.

"That's Marino!"

"Grandpa Sam!"

It was a jailbreak the officers responsible for containment couldn't stop. All four of them pushed the police tape over their heads and began racing toward Marino and Sam. Even Cat, whose chest was heaving as she gasped for air, couldn't be deterred.

In the shadows of the once mighty 30 Rock aflame and near destruction, a joyous reunion took place between the group who'd come together to survive.

CHAPTER THIRTY-EIGHT

Friday
Cubbison's Farm
Harford, Pennsylvania

Eventually, the three county commissioners stepped in to tamp down the potential riot over sleeping accommodations. John was within seconds of telling them all to get the hell off his property. However, he thought better of it.

After the group calmed down and cleared their heads, several farmers who lived within an hour's walk offered to take some of the stranded guests home with them. John instructed Luke and Matthew to hitch an old wagon to a horse to provide transportation.

With the first successful run to the nearest farm, they did it again. For hours, the boys led families and their guests away from Cubbison's Farm. As a result, half the group of visitors was sent away. The rest lived near Montrose or New Milford, both ten miles away as the crow flies. John found accommodations for them on the property with the assurances the boys would take them home by horseback and wagon at first light. *I'll make sure of it,* he thought to himself.

On John's instructions, they'd refrained from starting the generators. His plan was to evict all the overnight guests as soon as possible in the morning before the stored foods became too warm. However, confident that the dozen or so refugees of the solar storm weren't a threat to his family or property, John deployed his alternative power. The summer heat was overwhelming and would quickly cause the refrigerated foods to spoil. He'd suggest to Emma that she consolidate as many of the perishables into the house as possible. He had to consider preserving their fuel resources.

Meanwhile, Emma kept busy preparing bedding for those who stayed in her home. Everyone was appreciative and naturally offered to help. She considered them her guests, and the trepidation on their faces brought out Emma's compassion.

As midnight approached, the evening wound down, and Emma finally found herself alone in their bedroom. She kicked off her shoes and sat on the edge of the bed. That was where she broke down crying. She tried to control her sobbing, but the best she could do was stifle it. Under the unusually quiet conditions, every voice carried throughout the farmhouse.

John slowly opened the door and closed it behind him, turning the knob to avoid the loud click of the latch. He was done for the evening and needed some quiet time with his wife. He heard her sniffles before he entered the room. It broke his heart to see her so distraught.

John peeled off his sweaty shirt and took off his boots. He sat on the bed next to her and playfully raised his elbow to expose his armpit. "I hope this doesn't scare you off, ma'am."

Emma leaned her shoulder into him, ramming his body hard enough to make him tilt to the side. She was grinning and wiping away the tears as she spoke.

"You can't make me laugh when I'm crying. That's bad form."

"Worked, didn't it?" asked John as he eased back up next to her.

"Maybe. Just the same, you can keep your arm by your side and your smelly pits to yourself."

"I know. I know. If I can't take a shower in the mornin', I'll find a spot in the creek."

Emma leaned away from him and retrieved a battery-powered lantern off the nightstand. She handed it to him. "Why wait?"

John studied her face and saw the sweet smile that caused him to fall in love with her. He also looked into her soul, prodding behind her eyes in search of answers. Although, he already suspected the cause of her despair. He'd been suppressing the same feelings all night. Until now.

He dropped his chin to his chest and sighed. He began nervously rubbing his knees as he thought of the best way to broach the subject without sending his wife into an emotional tailspin. However, the strong woman that she was, Emma broke the silence.

"She's okay, right? I mean, even if they were on that rooftop when everything went bad, it's only a short walk to their hotel. I checked it myself on Google."

John swallowed hard. He didn't want to give her false hope, but he certainly had no intention of dashing them either. "Dad's a pretty smart old codger. Safe, too. He'll get to the hotel. Know that."

"Then what? John, they're a hundred fifty miles away. Do you think New York got hit with this, too? Grandpa Sam's truck won't run. Are they supposed to walk back to the farm? Stay put? I mean, there's no way to speak to them."

Emma started crying again, rocking back and forth, looking for solace. John patted her knee reassuringly and took her hands in his.

"I've thought about this off and on during the last few hours while I concentrated on getting as many people off the farm as possible. First of all, I didn't want to show them we had multiple generators that ran on our farm diesel. That would make our home an inviting place to ride out the storm or to come back to at some point. You know?"

Emma nodded without responding verbally. She was trying to keep it together. Her kids were her greatest emotional weakness.

John continued. "We also have the truck. I don't know for certain, and I wish Dad were here to talk to. However, that old truck doesn't have any kind of electronics. Heck, everything is operated by toggles and knobs."

"What are you saying?"

"I don't really know yet. It's possible Old Jimmy will run, unlike all the modern cars that are stalled in our parking lot. If it can, I might be able to take it to New York City to get Cat and my father."

"Go try it!" Emma was suddenly excited about the prospect of rescuing her daughter from the evil clutches of the Big Apple.

"Honey, if I start it now, the whole world will hear it. You can hear a pin drop around this place. If these people heard the truck run, they'd want me to drive them all over the county. I have no interest in doing that."

Emma stood up and began pacing the floor. She rubbed her hands together and then stopped with her hands on her hips.

"John, what if they're in danger? Minutes may matter right now."

He stood with plans of hugging her, but she pulled away slightly. "I understand that. If I start up the truck and leave here, these restless natives will be pounding on your bedroom door, demanding an explanation. I have to believe Dad will keep her safe. And I need to think through all of the ramifications of what I have in mind."

"Such as?" she asked. Emma was still somewhat perturbed. She wanted desperately to tuck her daughter into bed.

"I can only assume the blackout conditions apply to New York City, too. If so, they don't have transportation. What if they decide to leave the hotel? Or the city? You know, because they're anxious to get home to us." *Or because it's too dangerous to stay*, John thought to himself. He was not going to say it aloud.

"So?" Emma didn't understand his point.

"Well, we could end up missing each other. New York City is a big place, and the routes from there to here provide a lot of opportunities for us to be like two ships passing in the night."

She flopped back onto the bed, turning her back to him slightly. "Are you gonna let them fend for themselves?"

"No, not necessarily. I just want to see what the morning brings and make sure I'm not missing something. That's all."

Emma slipped under the covers and curled up in a ball. She'd retrieved a stuffed lamb off Cat's bed with a purple ribbon affixed to its neck. It was the first prize she'd earned as an entry in a baby contest when she was two and a half years old. Emma held it tight as the tears flowed again.

"I understand," she whispered, choosing to trust in her husband's unemotional judgment. For a few minutes, she stared at the window overlooking the outdoor dining area. The string lights continued to brighten up the darkness. She smiled as she mentally patted herself on the back. She'd done a great job pulling the event together. However, now all that mattered was getting Cat home.

PART 5

Saturday
From Lights to Looting

CHAPTER THIRTY-NINE

Saturday
Haleakala Observatory
Maui, Hawaii

Sunrise brought an end to Burgoyne's all-night vigil admiring the skies over Hawaii. After he'd given instructions to his young staff to hustle around and gather anything they thought might be useful to survive the coming weeks and months, he'd retrieved his bank account information from his modest apartment. He'd driven off the dormant volcano into the small community of Pukalani to the First Hawaiian Bank branch before it closed. He withdrew the entirety of his checking and savings accounts, in cash, to the astonishment of the tellers and the branch manager, who had to approve the transaction. It took nearly ten minutes to fill out the paperwork required by the IRS and the Department of Homeland Security, and to gather the thousands of dollars.

The branch manager, who knew Burgoyne personally, questioned him more than once as to whether he was sure he wanted to withdraw such large amounts. He questioned Burgoyne's plans for the cash. Then, as Burgoyne was leaving, the news reports hit Hawaii of the massive power outages across the Continental U.S. Burgoyne was walking toward the bank's exit just as dozens of people could be seen walking briskly toward the ATM and the front door. He smiled slightly, pleased with himself for beating the rush.

His next stop was Long's Pharmacy, where he got six-month refills on his prescription medication. Burgoyne was in decent health despite his lack of exercise. Like so many Americans, he fought a tendency to have high blood sugar with metformin. Also, he took a variety of cardiovascular medications to control blood pressure and to keep his arteries clean. While there, he stocked up on many first aid basics.

As the sun set in Hawaii, it was already after midnight in New York. Some of his students were glued to the television in the break room as the BBC managed to stream via satellite some video from New York City. Burgoyne credited them for having the foresight to protect their portable video and satellite equipment from an electromagnetic pulse.

He lost interest in the broadcast as the night went on. Although not surprised at how quickly society in the city collapsed, it saddened him at the same time. Yet, deep down, didn't he expect the same in Hawaii? His first inclination as soon as he returned to the observatory had been to send everyone on errands to prepare for a long-term power outage.

No, he didn't expect the solar flare to be strong enough that far south to affect their grid. However, he'd learned the importance of keeping America's supply chain operating. Hence, the shopping spree and the bank withdrawal had been done out of an abundance of caution.

The sun warmed his skin as it began to rise over the Pacific. At ten thousand feet above sea level, the nights became chilly, even in August. The sun glistened on the volcanic rock surrounding DKIST. Burgoyne often referred to their peak as being like the moon. There was little or no vegetation until the lower elevations.

Burgoyne had had a conversation at the end of Friday with some of the other administrators at DKIST. None of them shared his concern about food and supply shortages. Although, they did plan on taking a long weekend away from the observatory to see how things played out.

Burgoyne was going to observe the way Hawaiians handled the crisis from afar. In his opinion, if he waited to *see how things played out,* as his colleague said, it would be too late. His experiences at the bank and drugstore proved that.

Baxter appeared unexpectedly and startled the tired professor, who hadn't been that deep in thought since the day he was offered the position in Hawaii. It was a strange world compared to his former home in upstate New York. He missed the rural living and the change of seasons. However, he felt like he had a calling to study the Sun from the new state-of-the-art facility. In this moment, he was very glad to be standing atop this dormant volcano, Haleakala, a Hawaiian word that meant house of the sun.

"Professor, the reports from the BBC are beyond comprehension. Especially in New York City. It's hard to fathom."

Burgoyne nodded. He slowly turned completely around, taking in a three-hundred-sixty-degree view. Below the clouds, he wondered how long it would take for Hawaii to come apart at the seams.

CHAPTER FORTY

Saturday
Rockefeller Plaza
New York

It was Cat who insisted that Grandpa Sam get checked out by the paramedics who'd set up tents at Rockefeller Plaza. She really liked the nurses, and they seemed to have taken a shine to her because of her bravery under the circumstances. Besides, she explained, she'd told them all about her grandfather and had promised to introduce them. She was, after all, a woman of her word.

Other than his body having been battered like the others', Sam's biggest issues related to the amount of toxic smoke he'd inhaled. Because he'd been entrapped in the enclosed space with the smoke and fumes, he'd breathed in the toxins. Sam had soot around his nose and mouth as well as singed nasal hairs. His breathing was labored and noisy. Because of his incessant coughing, his voice was becoming hoarse.

Otherwise, the symptoms that would've concerned them most, such as a change in his mental condition or edema in his airways, were not present. They insisted he spend fifteen minutes in a portable oxygen tent. The pure oxygen helped clean out his lungs. He was also given an inhaler in case he had difficulty later, along with some antibiotics.

An hour later, the group was reunited, and they found a part of the plaza where they could speak without being interrupted by people milling about. They sipped water provided by the medics and took in their surroundings.

"These people have lost their minds," said Sam as he slowly drank the water, pacing himself per his doctor's orders. "I mean, you can see it in their faces. Some are panicked. Others determined to get from one place to another. But mostly, they look lost."

Lauren, who was administering first aid to the back of Asher's head and neck, managed a laugh. "I know the feeling. I've never experienced anything like this in my lifetime. I guess I don't go to work on Monday. Duh, that's a given, right?"

"Yeah," added Asher, who winced as she applied burn gel to his neck. "We're all creatures of routine. Next week, we had a full schedule filming the Sunday dinners. Now, nothing. Does this mean I don't have to pay the rent? You can bet I'm not paying ConEd."

Lauren laughed, but Sam and Cat didn't know that ConEd was the shortened name for the New York City power company. Cat tried to relate.

"No more school, I guess," she said in a dejected tone of voice. "I like school and my friends."

Sam tried to console her. "You know, Cat, life in the country might be different than this. I'll bet they'll find a schoolhouse for you kids like the old days."

"What about church?" she asked.

Sam laughed. "Do you think God is gonna give us a break because the power is out? He's been around a lot longer than electricity."

The four of them made small talk until the sound of gunfire filled the air. It frightened many of the people in the plaza, but Asher kept the group calm. "That was probably off in the distance. Even with the sounds of people talking and milling about, this is the quietest I've ever experienced in the city. Sounds will carry farther and echo off the buildings."

"It's becoming less safe," said Lauren. "They were looting these stores before everyone emptied out of 30 Rock. Can you imagine other parts of the city?"

"Times Square is probably mayhem," began Asher before he caught himself. Sam and Cat's hotel was in the midst of said mayhem. He tried to imagine what they would have to face in the mile-long walk back.

Lauren picked up on his concern. She had an idea although she hadn't broached the subject with Asher. However, she knew her kindhearted husband would be on board.

"Listen, I know the Marriott Marquis is a nice place. However, we'd love to have you guys stay with us until this passes over. We have a guest bedroom that nobody ever uses. We don't have a lot of food in our kitchen because we eat out all the time, but it's more than the minibar at the hotel. Whadya think?" She looked at Asher for approval after the fact.

He winked and smiled. He apparently had the same suggestion on his mind.

"We could never impose, especially under the circumstances," said Sam. "Besides, our car and clothes are at the hotel."

"I don't think your car is going to run, Sam," said Asher. "Have you noticed that there is no traffic on the streets. You'd think everyone would be trying to drive out of the city."

"If they could," added Lauren. "Some of the apocalyptic books I've edited included subplots about vehicles ceasing to function. I think there are exceptions, you know, related to old cars because they don't have computers or lots of wiring."

"How are we gonna get home, Grandpa?"

Sam looked down into Cat's face. He lovingly licked his thumb and wiped a smudge of soot off her cheek that the paramedics had missed.

"I don't know, honey. I think Lauren's right about the car. After we rest and heal a little, I suppose we could walk."

"How far is home, Sam?" asked Lauren.

He shook his head vigorously from side to side. He didn't want to say the answer out loud in front of Cat. One hundred fifty miles was a long way, even to a child. "It's a healthy walk."

"All the more reason you should stay with us," insisted Asher. "We can all get some rest. First, we'll eat up all the food in the refrigerator."

"Ice cream first!" exclaimed Lauren.

"What kind?" Cat asked, genuinely excited about the prospect of sitting around by candlelight, eating ice cream before it melts.

"Okay, don't judge," she replied. "I love Ben and Jerry's ice cream. I buy a lot of different flavors for variety. Chocolate Chip Cookie Dough. Strawberry Cheesecake. Brownie Batter. Chunky Monkey."

"The list is long," added Asher with a laugh. "Personally, I'm a straight-up, keep-it-simple, Hershey's chocolate lover."

"You'd like Pennsylvania, then," said Sam. "We're all about our homegrown Hershey's chocolate."

Lauren knelt down in front of Cat. "Whadya think? Are you up for a slumber party? I've got a neighbor your age who might give us some clothes for you to wear."

"You know, our building is like many others on the Upper West Side. We have gravity-filled water storage on the roof. We might even be able to take a shower. It might be cold, though."

"I'd swim in the lake to get this smell off me," said Sam jokingly. Then he became serious. "If you are sure we won't be imposing. Resources are, um, you know."

"They're not worth anything if we can't help our friends," said Lauren, cutting off the debate. She took Cat by the hand. "Come on. We've got a long walk ahead of us."

CHAPTER FORTY-ONE

Friday
Central Park
New York

Initially, the three-mile walk to the Doyles' condominium was uneventful although slow going. Asher and Lauren had walked the route many times, even at night. What struck them as odd considering it was three in the morning was the number of people in the streets. Whether the normal homeless souls or the late-night partiers, on any given night in New York, the sidewalks were occupied. Even at this hour, the sidewalks were shoulder to shoulder in many areas. Oddly, people still couldn't bring themselves to walk on the street despite the sea of stalled vehicles.

The short route to their home would've entailed a walk through Central Park, much along the same route Cat and Sam had taken to visit the Museum of Natural History. That was a risky proposition at three in the morning during normal times. Prostitutes, drug addicts, and mentally unstable homeless people roamed at night without the threat of police intervention. There was no way Asher would subject his wife and new friends to what might lie in wait amidst the chaos.

They stuck to the main streets near landmarks like the New York Athletic Club and Columbus Circle. Even as they zigzagged along West Fifty-Seventh over to West Fifty-Ninth Street, the southern edge of Central Park, Asher urged the group to stay close together and remain focused on their surroundings.

He led them down the middle of Central Park West, a heavily traveled connector between the high-rise office buildings of Manhattan and the residential areas on the Upper West Side. Buses, taxis, and all other manner of vehicles were left where they'd died at the time the perfect storm hit. Doors were flung open and trunk lids popped as people retrieved their belongings to walk home. Delivery vans were looted, the locks on the roll-up doors pried open and the goods inside strewn about in search of anything of value.

Fortunately, during the hour-and-a-half walk, they weren't accosted by anyone. Certainly, they could all feel the eyes peering at them from the shadows of the buildings. An NYPD police car blocked the intersection near the Doyles' condo. The cops had been working a fender-bender caused by someone driving a Jeep with Virginia license plates the wrong way on a one-way street. The patrol car had its windows broken and the dashboard vandalized. The Jeep's top had been torn open with a knife and its interior rifled through by looters.

Nothing was off-limits to those who took advantage of the power outage and lack of law enforcement protection for the innocent. In the early hours following the peak of the solar storm, opportunists ransacked businesses and stole anything of perceived value. *This is just the beginning*, thought Asher as he led the group through the wrought-iron fence toward the courtyard at the front of their building.

His eyes searched the darkness, hoping to see the twenty-four-hour doormen who prevented people from wandering into the building. They were gone.

Lauren noticed, too. "I'm surprised there's nobody here. Even if the security guards took off, shouldn't the homeowners be watching the entrance?"

"Especially with all the looting going on," added Asher. "Be careful, everyone. It's gonna be really dark in the lobby."

Lauren squeezed Asher's hand. The anxiety shooting through her body forced perspiration to pour out of her palms. She could sense his trepidation as well.

Sam and Cat followed close behind, with Cat periodically reaching out to touch the back of Asher's shirt. They were in an unfamiliar place and had to rely entirely upon the Doyles for their decision-making. Sam hoped he'd made the right choice in not going back to the hotel. Their condo was three times farther to walk than the Marriott. It had also been uneventful. Perhaps, he thought, he'd overreacted to the possibility of threats on the streets of the city. His ponderings were interrupted by a sound very familiar to the old country boy—someone racking a shell into their shotgun.

It's been said that the best deterrent to a home invasion was to fend off the attackers with a shotgun. It was the most forgiving firearm for the untrained. Its ability to scatter shot, whether small amounts in the slugger shell or a hundred or more in birdshot, could help an untrained shooter take down an assailant. Even the distinctive sound the gun makes when the shell is loaded into the chamber generally sends the bad guys running.

It startled Asher at first; then he regained his composure. He'd worked around weapons on the set of *Blue Bloods* his entire career. It was always safety first on the set thanks to an excellent armorer and actors who were trained in the proper handling of their assigned firearm.

"Hey! Easy. I'm Asher Doyle. I live here with my wife, Lauren."

"Twenty-three-B," she added.

A penlight was illuminated from behind several large pieces of furniture that had been turned on their sides and arranged haphazardly in the lobby. The once pristine lobby of 455 CPW, as it was known, was the hallmark of the historic conversion of the original New York Cancer Hospital. The converted building consisted of seventeen high-end units while the newer, twenty-six-story high-rise tower behind it was more affordable for families like the Doyles.

"Do you have ID?" one of the men asked as the other let his shotgun be seen in the dim glow provided by the penlight.

"No," replied Asher. "We lost it in the fire."

"What fire?"

"We were on the observation deck at 30 Rock when the lights went out. The building caught on fire."

"We almost died," said Cat in a meek voice.

The man with the shotgun grew stiff and swung the barrel back and forth as the other guard flashed the penlight in Asher's face.

"Wait a minute," began the man with the penlight, who was flipping through a binder. "This roster says only two occupants in the unit. There are no children registered to you."

Asher gulped. "Um, these are our friends who are in town from Pennsylvania. They joined us to watch the aurora."

"You're renters, right?"

"Yeah."

"Did you register your guests with the association office?"

"No." Asher had to think fast. After all they'd been through, he never expected this. "They just got into town. I was going to speak with the concierge and security when we got home this evening."

The two men whispered back and forth.

Lauren inched closer to Asher and whispered in his ear, "This is ridiculous. Do we look like looters?"

Sam heard her. "Listen, we can go. I'm sure it won't take us long to—"

"No," objected Asher, a little too loudly. The two men, who were debating whether to let them into the building, stopped their conversation.

"What's the problem?" they asked.

Asher was tired, sore, and now, incredulous. "You two peon

power security wannabes are the problem. Lauren and I live here, and these people are our guests. Both of them almost lost their lives in the fire, as did we. None of us have time to convince you idiots that we are who we say we are.

"So here's what. We're comin' in. If you're gonna shoot anyone, you can start with me or get the hell out of the way!"

He tugged Lauren's arm, who in turn reached for Cat's. They held hands and maneuvered through the toppled furniture directly toward the two men despite the shotgun pointed directly at Asher's chest.

As they got closer, the penlight was able to illuminate Asher's face. The man moved it rapidly from Asher to Lauren and then to the Cubbisons. He then shined it directly in Asher's face.

"All right, pal. I'm gonna go out on a limb and let you pass. But know this, all of this will be recorded, and the association will be notified. They have a zero-exceptions and zero-tolerance policy in effect."

"I'm sure they do," said Asher in a snarky tone. He walked a little faster as he cleared the obstacles and headed for the far end of the lobby where the double doors leading to the high-rise units were located.

"You can expect a visit from Mrs. Santore in the morning. She will not be happy about your caustic attitude, pal."

Asher kept walking in the dark but raised his right hand to give the middle finger. Lauren couldn't see what he did, but she knew her husband.

She giggled. "You're so bad."

"They're assholes."

CHAPTER FORTY-TWO

Friday
455 Central Park West Condominiums
New York

Ambient light from the aurora mixed with the orangish glow of fires across the city invaded the spacious living room of the Doyles' condo. The corner unit provided views west toward the Hudson River just six blocks away.

When the Doyles were married, their limited incomes prevented them from buying a unit at prestigious 455 CPW. They liked the security and feel of the historic complex, so they started out on a lower-floor, inline unit. Over time, as rentals became available, they moved higher in the twenty-five-story building and into a larger corner unit. Next on their wish list was a coveted view of Central Park.

Asher walked them into the living room. "Welcome to our home, be it ever so humble. Sorry about the power. I forgot to pay the bill."

"Very funny, Mr. Doyle," said Cat, who actually thought it was funny. "Um, do you have a bathroom?"

The wording of her question was childlike, naturally, but it also allowed Asher an opportunity to keep the mood light. As they had been walking up the stairwell, he'd promised Lauren he wouldn't dwell on the encounter with the two volunteer guards in the foyer. They were just doing their job, and she was actually glad someone was doing it.

"Young lady," said Asher, adopting an Irish dialect he'd learned from his grandfather, "we have an upgraded unit. Would you believe we have three bathrooms?"

"Just like our house," said Cat.

Lauren fumbled through the dark kitchen and lit two candles on the kitchen bar pass-through out to the combined dining and living room. She picked up one of the jar candles and motioned for Cat to follow her.

"Let me show you the guest bedroom. I'm sure Grandpa Sam won't mind the couch." She led Cat down a short hallway as Sam shouted, "He's already not minding it! It's so soft I'm not sure I can get my old bones out of it."

"Sam, Lauren and I aren't really drinkers, or I'd offer you a beer or something. There are probably a couple of bottles of wine, if you'd like."

"No, thanks, Asher. I haven't had a drink in years. Back in the day, I used to like it too much."

Asher understood. He grew up in a family of Irishmen in which alcohol was a part of their daily nourishment.

"Hey, Ash! We have water. The toilet flushed!"

Asher moved into the kitchen. Just because the toilet initially flushed didn't mean it would refill. But, as he'd hoped, the gravity-filled reservoirs on the roof of the building would keep them supplied for a while.

Cat and Lauren emerged from their bathroom breaks. "We can probably shower, don't you think?" asked Lauren.

"Absolutely," Asher replied as he shut off the kitchen faucet. "In fact, I would encourage everyone to do so immediately. I'm not sure how long the water supply will hold out."

"I smell," said Cat, lifting her shirt to her nose.

The front of Sam's shirt was covered in blood, as was Asher's. Lauren assumed the role of hostess by issuing orders to everyone.

"Sam, if you would, take the first shower in the guest bath. You'll find everything you need in there, from soap to shampoo to shaving gear. I'll find some clothes that I'm sure will fit you."

Sam hoisted himself off the plush sofa with a groan. "Good idea. I have a feeling once I find my next seat, I'll be there for the duration of our stay."

He made his way to the guest bedroom, and Asher followed him down the hall to take his shower. Cat helped gather clothes for Sam from Asher's closet while Lauren picked out something for Cat to sleep in. Tomorrow, as promised, she'd touch base with her neighbor to find something to replace Cat's torn outfit.

After the girls showered, everyone gathered in the living room. Lauren passed out the ice cream and found a couple of bags of Pecan Sandies to share with everyone. Refreshed and hyped up from the events of the last eight hours, the group blew out the candles in order to take in the views of the aurora.

"Guys, excuse me for a moment," said Asher, interrupting the silence. "I just had a thought."

"What is it, Ash?"

"Well, since we're all cleaned up, I think, just out of precaution, I'm gonna fill up the two bathtubs and all the sinks with water. If others in the building get the same idea or use up a lot of water in the next few days, the rooftop reservoir will run out. This will give us over a hundred gallons of drinking water."

"Very smart, Asher," said Sam. "Can I help?" He began to groan in an effort to get out of the chair he'd picked for easier ingress and egress. His body had never been this sore.

"I got it, thanks."

Moments later, Asher rejoined them, and Sam asked, "Say, you mentioned that you were filming the Sunday dinner scenes next week. Those are my favorite. Would you mind telling me about the process? And what's it like working with Tom Selleck?"

Asher was thankful for the question. His mind had been racing since the encounter in the lobby. Other than the frustration associated with the difficulty getting inside the building, the entire grid-down scenario was getting very real for him. He thought about the importance of having shelter and water. Security was obviously on everybody's minds, including the condo association's. Then there was food. This was a real problem for their group, one that he'd have to address with Lauren in private.

"Well, as a screenwriter, I was certainly qualified to join the script team at CBS to produce *Blue Bloods*. I had another item on my résumé that helped, and that was my father, who was once the police commissioner's liaison with the media. Since you know the show, think of Garrett's role with Commissioner Reagan."

"That's cool. I bet you can lend some real-life experiences to that part of the show."

"For sure," said Asher before continuing. "Then there were the intangibles. I come from a Catholic family although I'm not a practicing Catholic. As a kid, I learned everything about the church from attending Catholic school. One of my contributions to the show is that I'm able to lend that knowledge since the Reagan characters are devout Catholics.

"As for the Sunday scenes, it's really pretty interesting. First of all, the actors love them. You'd think the action scenes in the streets would be their favorite, but it's not even close. They love the interaction around the Sunday dinner table at Frank's house.

"Tom knows the dinner scenes are very important to the *Blue Bloods* fan base. He and I work closely together to get it right. We all like it, especially the actors, because, believe it or not, it's one of the rare occasions when they are on the same set together. It takes a lot of coordination to bring them all into town for that purpose." Asher was enjoying himself, so he really provided the production details.

"Now, this week, we were going to film five dinner scenes. One per day. It takes us six to eight hours to get our final cut. And, without exaggeration, it requires the actors to eat and eat and eat. Literally, the same food all day long.

"Oh, yeah. Here's something viewers don't know. Years ago, we quit using real silverware at the dinner table scenes. You know all that clinking the forks make when it hits the plate, for example? The highly sensitive microphones on set amplify it to the point it ruined the quality of the sound. The decision was made to ditch the silverware in favor of plastic. We dub in audio of silverware during the final production edits." He paused to laugh.

"The family dinner scenes are what we all looked forward to filming. The camaraderie between the main cast members is like a rowdy family at any dining table in America. They laugh. They joke. They intentionally screw up lines to aggravate one another. They throw food and dinner rolls. And, although their antics make for some long shooting days, every minute is worth it. I have to say, I'm gonna miss it."

Asher grew solemn and choked back his tears. Lauren, who sat in a chair next to him, reached over and squeezed his hand. He waited for Sam to ask questions about the filming or Tom Selleck, but none came.

Sam had fallen asleep in his chair, and Cat had curled up with a pillow on the sofa, blissfully dreaming about something other than raging infernos and power outages.

Asher leaned over and kissed his wife. If nothing else, he was good at bedtime stories.

CHAPTER FORTY-THREE

Saturday
Cubbison's Farm
Harford, Pennsylvania

Emma's biological clock woke her up before sunrise, just like always. Her state of exhaustion had kept her asleep. As was often the case, her mind kicked into hyper overdrive as she stirred awake.

Her days had always been filled with tasks around the farm or caring for her family. Since her days in college, during which her well-organized schedule enabled her to graduate in three years rather than four, Emma would wake up and visualize her to-do list as well as her appointment calendar for the day.

This day was no different except for the fact there was only one item on the schedule. Bring Cat home. She lay in bed, staring up at the ceiling, her eyes occasionally searching the nightstand for the LED clock that no longer functioned. She chuckled to herself as she thought about how she could easily be labeled a creature of habit. Her life was full of routines. Yet when there was turmoil within the family, she could easily be thrown off course.

She rolled over slightly toward her husband. She looked past him through the bedroom windows. The eerie, bluish-green glow of the aurora continued to enter the room. She couldn't decide whether to admire its beauty or curse what it had done to divide her family.

Emma desperately wanted to wake her husband and ask him to leave for New York. Now. She'd go with him. The boys would be fine. Who cared about the guests? She wanted her daughter back.

Feeling compelled to do something, she slid out of bed and got dressed. She went to the bathroom and flushed the toilet afterwards. The gurgling sound in the tank and the sudden silence was a reminder that the power outage impacted their water availability.

She remembered Grandpa Sam talking about how excited the family had been when they got *city water*, as folks in the country called it. They had been tapped into the municipal water supply, bringing them into the twenty-first century. Now, that modern convenience they so relied upon had been taken away.

In the dark, Emma pulled off the lid to the toilet tank. She felt inside with her hand until she reached a small amount of water for the next flush.

"Not enough," she muttered to herself. Then she had an idea.

She quietly moved through the farmhouse, listening to the strange snores and deep sleeping of the guests who'd remained overnight. She went through the back door to a concrete trough they kept for their horses on the occasions they tied them off at the house. After filling a pail, she made her way back upstairs. She emptied half the pail of water into the toilet tank until she could feel it reach the overflow pipe. Then, like a scientist holding her breath to see if an experiment worked, she flushed the toilet.

The result was not magical nor was it novel. However, for Emma, it was a reminder that there were ways to adapt to a powerless world. It brought a smile to her face and lifted her spirits. She filled the tank again and hustled outside, quietly, of course, to fetch another pail of water.

This was a lighthearted, pivotal moment for Emma. She now

understood how their lives would change. However, she was not afraid, nor would she be deterred from protecting her family.

"Honey? Are you all right?" John Cubbison's sleepy voice startled her somewhat. Gathering herself, she found her way back to bed and slid in next to him.

"Good morning," she said softly, kissing her husband on the cheek. "Guess what?"

"It's a little early to be guessin'," he mumbled.

"Guess what I did? I flushed the toilet."

Emma was clearly proud of herself for accomplishing such a simple task.

"I'm so glad you're finally potty-trained, Mrs. Cubbison." John's attempt at humor earned him a playful shove and another kiss.

"Don't you realize what this means? We can do this. We can live our lives without all of the things that make it easy like water and electricity. We can find a way."

John was fully awake now. He slid up in bed and rested his back against the headboard. He wrapped his arm around Emma and pulled her close.

"I have no doubt this family can pull together to deal with this. First, we need to get these people out of here so we can be alone, as a family, to talk about what's next. It's more than getting Dad and Cat home. There's so much to consider."

"I understand, and I want you to know, John, I love them very much. That said, I love you, too. We need to make sure you're safe. It's like the guy who tried to save someone drowning. Too often, the victim takes the rescuer down with them. I can't bear the thought of losing all of you."

"I get it," said John.

"Plus, you can't go alone. It's too dangerous. You'll need to take one of the boys or me."

John took a deep breath and exhaled. His mind raced as he began to consider the arduous task he was about to undertake. He also thought about preparing the farm for when he was away. There was a reason, when the power grid first went down, that he began to think about their security.

Beautiful auroras don't kill people. People kill people.

CHAPTER FORTY-FOUR

Saturday
Cubbison's Farm
Harford, Pennsylvania

John grabbed a flashlight and headed off for the storage barn in search of their camping supplies. Namely, the graniteware porcelain coffee pot. Both of them required coffee to start their day. Black. No frills. Unspoiled by creamer or sugar. Full octane with caffeine guaranteed to brighten anybody's sleepy eyes.

Years ago, when the boys were in grade school, they went through a phase when they wanted to camp out. The family farm had an abundance of unique places to pitch a tent, from a ridge overlooking the creek to woods to grassy knolls in the middle of the pasture amidst the livestock.

There was a girls' tent for Emma and Cat as well as a larger boys' tent for the four guys. Sam assumed the cooking duties. He fashioned himself somewhat of a chuckwagon, cowboy cook. He had a cast-iron grate that he laid over the fire, capable of holding the coffee pot and two other pots for oatmeal or stew. The Cubbison family had handed down cast-iron cookware through the years, and soon the campouts became the family's version of a getaway.

There were no trips to Walt Disney World or beach trips to the Jersey shore. Their farming operation didn't take a week off so they could go see Mickey Mouse. Instead, they found ways to create a respite from the daily chores, and camping was one of the family's favorites.

By the time John returned to the backyard, lugging the cooking gear, Emma had a fire going using the seasoned oak they'd cut in the early spring. As the sun began to peek over the horizon, they were pouring their first mugs of coffee. John was the first to bring up the subject of retrieving Sam and Cat from New York.

"Honey, you have to know that those two are on my mind constantly. I mean, there are a lot of weighty things like what our future holds, but they're my priority."

"What are you thinking?" she asked.

"Okay, first, I have to assume that old truck will make it. Face it, the most it's traveled in the past ten years were the occasional trips into Montrose for a parade. Twenty-some miles is a far cry from a three-hundred-mile round trip to New York."

"Is there any reason it wouldn't?" she asked.

"We have enough gasoline to get there and back. The engine and transmission would be my biggest concerns. First of all, I want to change all the fluids. It's been July 4 a year ago that we took it to Montrose. Condensation can mess with the oil. The moving parts can get stuck, and corrosion sets in."

"You guys start it from time to time, right?"

John nodded as he took another sip of coffee. "Yes, that helps. I still wanna change the fluids, just to be sure."

"What about the fact you're gonna stick out like a sore thumb?" she asked. Emma had warmed some leftover dinner rolls from the night before and handed one to John together with a small bowl full of melted butter. He dipped a roll in and eagerly gobbled it up.

"We don't have a choice," he replied as he munched on the bread.

"Here's the way I see it. Well, in the country anyway, which is most of the trip, we should be all right. I'm gonna drive the back roads through the mountains."

"I assumed the interstates would be a mess," Emma interjected.

"For a lot of reasons. Stalled cars and trucks. People walking in all directions. Plus, I don't want to go anywhere near Scranton."

"Once you cross into New Jersey, you're gonna have to deal with a lot of population."

John's chin dropped to his chest. He knew what he was trying to accomplish was near impossible. He'd have to study a map to determine how to cross the Hudson River and get to their hotel in Times Square. He did know that Secaucus and Hoboken were very urban, densely populated cities.

"I'm thinking about hiding the truck in the suburbs. You know, on the outskirts of the cities. From there, Matthew and I can ride the boys' bicycles into New York."

"Wait, Matthew? Have you already decided to take him and not me?"

John sighed. "Honey, I know you want to go, but we need you here to watch over the farm. This will be dangerous enough without one or both of us getting hurt and leaving the kids to fend for themselves."

Emma didn't like the thought of that happening. It would be easy for her to counter his argument by saying it would be all right. However, she knew it might not be.

"Okay, I agree. Why Matthew?"

John gulped and stood from the cut tree stump he'd been perched on. He topped off his coffee and did the same for Emma.

"This is hard to say because I love our boys equally. Face it, Luke is more responsible and reliable."

"Which is all the more reason he should go with you," said Emma.

"Honey, if something happens, and I pray it doesn't, Luke is better capable of handling things here while I'm away. Matthew can't. All I need on this trip is a warm body to be another set of eyes."

"You won't have to worry about him burying his head in his phone on social media."

"Exactly," said John. He sighed as he took another sip of coffee. "I regret not training him more with our guns."

Emma shook her head and buried her face in her hands. They needed guns to defend themselves on the road. She wondered what it might be like in the city.

"A shotgun? They're pretty forgiving."

"You also can't hide it. I think we might be inviting trouble if we waltz into New York totin' long guns. We can conceal pistols better. Remember that Christmas when Dad bought us all Ruger .44 Magnum revolvers?"

Emma chuckled. "How could I forget the look of glee on our eight-year-old daughter's face?" she asked sarcastically. Emma shook her head as she recalled everyone unwrapping their special gift. Since then, only Grandpa Sam and John occasionally carried the powerful handgun when out on the farm. Primarily to deal with feral hogs.

"Well, we have six matching weapons with plenty of ammo for each. Matthew has never fired it, but neither has Luke, for that matter. I'll teach them both the basics before we leave."

"They make sense because you can hide them under your shirt."

"I've got leather paddle holsters for our jeans. We'll both tuck one on each side."

"Aren't you the cowboy?" she said jokingly. As a mother, she was concerned about her husband. Then she thought about his prior statement. "You said both?"

"Well, all of us, actually. Honey, we've got to protect ourselves now. That means carrying a weapon at all times. Handguns and rifles when out on the farm. A handgun around the house. It doesn't have to be the .44 Magnum. We have lighter, easier-to-handle pistols, too."

"Really? Do you think this is necessary? We live in the country, for Pete's sake."

"That's true. But, honey, desperate people do desperate things. If you really give it some thought, we have a lot of resources to survive this whole mess as long as we can protect ourselves and our way of life.

"Remember this, though. If we can't protect it, it isn't ours. There may come a time when somebody tries to take advantage of our generosity or, worse, our perceived weakness. We have to be able to turn away people, by force if necessary, any threat."

Suddenly they were interrupted by two of their uninvited guests who'd emerged from the house.

"Hey, got any more of that coffee?"

"Yeah, we're hungry, too. What's for breakfast?"

In that brief encounter, Emma was beginning to see where John was coming from.

CHAPTER FORTY-FIVE

Saturday
455 Central Park West
New York

Befitting their experience in New York City, Cat and Sam were rudely awakened by pounding on the Doyles' door. Because the condo unit faced the west, the sun didn't wake them like other tenants. Their mental and physical fatigue would've kept them asleep for many more hours.

It took Sam a moment to get his bearings. Waking up in a strange place was difficult enough to comprehend. The incessant knocking jolting him awake made it worse.

"Grandpa?"

"Stay here, Cat," he replied, patting her on the head as he slowly walked past her. Before Sam could get to the door, Asher hustled out of the bedroom, wearing nothing but his boxer shorts.

"Sam," he said in a loud whisper. He motioned for his guest to move back into the living area. "Stay out of sight and be quiet."

Sam was beginning to remember the events of last evening and the unwelcome reception they'd received upon their arrival at 455 CPW. He wondered if this early morning visit related to their presence in the Doyles' condo.

Asher reached the door as the knocking began again. Much louder this time. He turned to confirm that the Cubbisons were out of sight before responding to the knock.

"Who is it?"

A gruff voice responded, "Doyle! Open up! Bart Patterson here."

Asher knew who the young man was. He was the son of a prominent resident in the building. Asher considered the young man to be friendly, so his demeanor was certainly out of character. His family had been longtime residents and were close to the association's president, Jesse Santore. Some in the building had cried nepotism when Patterson was hired as Santore's special assistant and liaison to the maintenance and security personnel at 455 CPW. Asher thought it seemed like a waste of money, but he didn't care as long as their rent didn't go up.

Asher opened the door slowly, allowing only a small crack. A flashlight was immediately shined in his eyes, temporarily blinding him.

"Come on, Bart! Is this necessary? We've had a rough night."

The young man had changed. "We've called a mandatory meeting of all residents in the courtyard outside. There are no exceptions except, of course, your unauthorized guests."

News travels fast, Asher thought to himself. He wanted to snap back at Bart but didn't. He tried to keep his cool.

"Bart, can't you give me a summary of what it's all about? We've been through hell and back."

"Mandatory, Doyle. Just you and your wife. But be prepared to address the other matter with Mrs. Santore."

That's Mrs. Mistress, to you, pal. Asher had heard the rumor of the woman, twice Patterson's age, initiating an affair with him years ago. Not that it mattered. Asher had avoided both of them.

"What time?" asked Asher without engaging Santore's *do-boy* any further.

"Thirty minutes. Mrs. Santore will want to speak with you immediately afterwards."

Without saying goodbye, Patterson marched off to pound on the next resident's door. Asher slowly closed his door and turned the bolt lock, a symbolic gesture to block the encounter with the man out of his mind.

Asher turned to find Lauren peering around the corner at the hallway and Sam holding Cat close to him in the living room.

"Did you hear all of that?"

"Yes," they replied in unison before Lauren added, "Bart's got a lot of nerve. He's always been a little prick."

"Easy," said Asher as he approached her. He nodded toward the tender ears attached to Cat. "Obviously, he's got peon power."

"What's that mean?" asked Cat.

Asher shook his head and took a long tee shirt from his wife to cover his half-naked body. "Cat, that's when a person, like Patterson, who doesn't have much control over anybody, has been suddenly elevated to a position of power over others. If it weren't for this whole solar-flare mess, he could never talk to me that way. Mrs. Santore has apparently given him more authority than he can handle or deserves."

"She sounds like a piece of work, too," said Sam.

"You have no idea," said Lauren. "Her husband was abusive, so we all felt sorry for her. When he died, under suspicious circumstances, everything changed. She became a tyrant."

"A very wealthy tyrant," added Asher.

Lauren placed her hand on his back. "What are we gonna do?"

Asher sighed. "Let's get dressed and hear them out. Then we'll speak to the tyrant."

Sam stepped forward. He glanced back at Cat's concerned face and looked Asher in the eyes. "Listen, we don't want to be any trouble. I feel a lot better, inside and out. Sure, I'm sore, but I'm rested. With the daylight, Cat and I can walk down—"

Asher raised his hand to cut Sam off. "Listen, my position hasn't changed since last night. I really believe you're both better off here than anywhere on the streets."

"Yes, absolutely," said Lauren. "Forget about that bully. They can't prevent you from being here. We all need each other. No matter what, we will stick together."

Cat reached forward and took her grandfather's hand. She offered him a reassuring smile. "It'll be okay. Let's wait and see."

After getting ready, Lauren and Asher went through their kitchen cabinets and placed all the food they had on the countertops. It wasn't much. They didn't do it to remind Sam and Cat they were extra mouths to feed. Asher presumed the association was going to ask everyone to pool their resources. It was the logical thing to do. Admittedly, if their pantry had been full of nonperishables, he'd refuse to give up their means of survival.

"You guys help yourself," said Lauren. "We'll be back in a little while."

The couple slipped out the door, leaving Sam and Cat alone to talk.

"Grandpa, there's not much to eat."

Sam studied the boxes and cans strewn about the kitchen. He tried to imagine the four of them dividing up the snacks and canned foods. He looked at the boxes of rice and pasta. They were worthless because they had no means of cooking it. He dared not open the refrigerator for fear of letting valuable cold air escape. He could only imagine that it was equally bare.

He wandered out of the small kitchen to the windows overlooking the river. The sun was shining, and the heat could be seen floating off the tar and gravel rooftops below them. After seeing their food supply, he came to realize staying there was not an option.

For any of them.

CHAPTER FORTY-SIX

Saturday
455 Central Park West
New York

"Everyone! Hey! Everyone settle down. We need to get started," Patterson bellowed at the residents. He was enjoying his role as Mrs. Santore's right-hand man. Asher and Lauren stood off to the side in order to observe the eighty to ninety people who were clustered together in front of the steps leading to the high-rise building. The diverse group was made up of people from many nationalities. It was impossible to differentiate between those who lived in the large, multimillion-dollar condo suites and those like the Doyles who leased their space.

The chatter died down, and the group started to tighten their semicircle where Mrs. Santore stood looking down upon them. Asher noticed a few of the other young couples in the complex standing off to the side, arms folded, skeptical of what was going on.

"Thank you all for joining us under these most dire of circumstances. For those who don't know me, I am Jesse Santore, the president of the four-fifty-five Central Park West community.

"We have a five-member board of directors, which is charged with the responsibility of administering the rules and regulations of our historic residential complex. As of this time, three members are either missing or known to be out of town. That leaves only our treasurer, Jacob Stanfield, myself, and available staff to handle administrative matters.

"Here's what we've been able to discern from police reports and insider information thanks to several of you in the know. The planet was struck by a major solar flare or possibly two. Apparently, this perfect storm, as they call it, may be one of the largest in modern history.

"The result has been uniformly catastrophic across the entire Northern Hemisphere from western Europe to our west coast. The power grids have collapsed, causing communications to be disrupted and electricity to stop flowing. I can't tell you what this means for our way of life. Many of you have experienced the chaos outside this beautiful residential complex.

"We have been unwillingly thrust into a survival situation like no other. And the only way to persevere is by working together as a community. It is incumbent upon me, as the association president, in conjunction with the board of directors, consisting of Jacob and myself, to establish a path forward."

Santore reached into her pocket and retrieved a small notepad. She licked her thumb and flipped through the pages until she found what she was looking for.

"Before we get into the details of how we will be governed, I feel compelled to mention some ground rules. A moment ago, I mentioned the word community. Community is not defined as the Upper West Side where four-five-five Central Park West is located. Community does not include the homeless or the displaced. We can only protect and take care of our residents, nobody else."

She paused for effect without looking up from her notes. Then she did something extraordinary that completely infuriated Asher and Lauren. She called out people like them in front of their neighbors.

"Following our discussion, I will need to speak directly with the following tenants," said Santore, who proceeded to list half a dozen names, including the Doyles'. "Please note that I specifically referenced tenants. Unit owners will receive greater deference in these matters than those who reside here temporarily by virtue of their lease contract."

"Screw you, lady," muttered Lauren under her breath.

Asher glanced around the crowd and noticed several people nervously shifting their weight from foot to foot. It was obvious who else had been exposed as harboring unsavory guests.

"As for the rest of the members of our community, we need to do everything possible to ensure our health and well-being for as long as possible until ConEd and the government can make the necessary repairs. I'm told this can take as long as two weeks, possibly three, before the power comes back on.

"Toward that end, we have to do a couple of things. First, please conserve our water." She pointed upward to the top of the high-rise where the reservoir was located, not that anyone could see it from the ground. "Drinking only what is minimally necessary and toilet flushing once a day. No showers or baths."

"We broke the rules and didn't even know it," whispered Lauren to Asher.

He nodded. "At least twice so far."

Santore continued. "Also, we will ask that you voluntarily bring all food products to the central lobby by noon today. We will be pooling our resources to give us all an equal opportunity to get through this."

Asher leaned into Lauren. "Told you."

"This is crazy," she said. "What are we gonna do?"

"About which part?" he asked in response.

"All of it. Okay, we don't have much food," she replied as she sneered at Santore. "Take it, you tyrant. I can skip a shower or two. But what about Sam and Cat? I can't kick a grandpa and that young girl out into the streets of New York."

Asher nodded. "I agree." He thought for a moment as Santore droned on about half a dozen other rules she'd come up with. He imagined that condo associations around the city were taking the same approach. He shook his head and said, "This is a waste. Do you wanna go back upstairs?"

"What are we gonna tell them?" she asked.

"I don't know. They're good people. We'll figure it out."

Lauren took him by the hand, and they started toward the emergency stairwell door that had been propped open with a concrete planter. Their early departure drew the attention of many residents, and Bart Patterson in particular. Lauren noticed their stares.

"Wait. Should we play the game and listen to the tyrant kick us while we're down?"

"Screw her. I don't wanna give her the satisfaction."

Asher led the way, surreptitiously scratching his sideburn with his middle finger as he walked past Patterson.

CHAPTER FORTY-SEVEN

Saturday
Cubbison's Farm
Harford, Pennsylvania

For hours, the Cubbison men ferried their overnight stragglers to points closer to their homes. Luke was glad to drop off the news crews at the interstate, where he earned a kiss on the cheek from the reporter's assistant. The horse and wagon took most as far away as Montrose. John took a few people cross-country on horseback. Riding a few miles directly across the landscape saved seven or eight miles of walking on the roads. By late morning, they had the house to themselves.

All of their guests seemed genuinely appreciative although most asked a lot of pointed questions about the Cubbisons' farm and how much food they produced. While there were much larger livestock operations in Susquehanna County, very few combined livestock, chickens, and an extensive gardening operation like Emma's. The Cubbisons had built a brand around their farm that was well known throughout the region.

Prior to the collapse of the grid, this was a blessing for the family's business. Now, it might turn out to be a curse. With the family gathered in the kitchen, Emma started the process of serving her family the foods most likely to spoil the fastest. While the generators were capable of maintaining the frozen foods the longest, vegetable and dairy products would be the first to go.

She whipped up a bowl of egg salad served on leftover bread from the night before. Neither boy complained as they, too, were now seeing the challenge they faced in the near future. After they each fixed up a paper plate of sandwiches and potato chips, John opened the discussion regarding the trip to New York.

"Guys, we have lots to discuss and prepare for, but we need to talk about bringing Grandpa Sam and your sister home."

"How will we find them, Dad?" asked Luke, whose eyes glanced from his mom to his dad. He'd noticed the worry on his mother's face since he'd emerged from his bedroom that morning.

"I want to believe they would've gone back to their hotel and waited."

"Maybe the lights didn't go out in New York?" questioned Matthew. "I mean, that's a big city, and they're probably ready for these things."

"While there's a lot we don't know," John began in reply, "I have to presume the power outage was widespread and not just in rural Pennsylvania."

Matthew scowled. "Maybe we should wait a few days. You know, until we have more information."

"We can't leave them out there alone," said Emma with a hint of anger in her voice. She was glad Matthew wasn't the final decision-maker. "If the solar activity knocked out electricity throughout the region, including New York, they might be in great danger."

"Mom's right," said Luke. "When she won the trip that day, my first thought was New York was no place for my sister."

John swallowed hard. Luke's statement stung although he didn't mean it that way. John had felt the same way. However, he didn't want to prevent her from having the learning experience.

"That's why we've made the decision to go find them," he said.

"Talk about a needle in the haystack," argued Matthew. "What if they're not at the hotel? What if they started driving home already?"

"Cars aren't working," said Luke, who gave his brother a dirty look.

John added, "Besides, Grandpa Sam knows his way around our part of Pennsylvania. I bet I can show how they'd find their way home."

"I know where to look," said Luke. "Route 6. Right, Dad?"

John nodded. "He hates the interstates anyway, and I'm sure, after what he probably witnessed last night, he'd choose a less-congested route."

Matthew shrugged and looked outside. He instinctively felt for his cell phone. He'd become addicted to his social media accounts and game apps. Anytime he became bored or disinterested in a family discussion, he turned to his phone.

"How many miles is it, Dad?" asked Luke.

"Roughly a hundred fifty miles. I haven't had the chance to map it out in our old atlas. That thing's probably from the nineties."

"Nothing's changed since then," said Emma, who was staring at Matthew. She was growing concerned about how much help he'd be to John on this dangerous endeavor.

Luke, who continued to be positive about their prospects of finding Cat and Grandpa Sam, turned to his dad and asked, "When are we leaving?"

Emma reached out and touched John's arm before answering the question for him. "We're not sure yet. There are benefits to traveling at night versus the day."

Luke asked, "Are we taking Old Jimmy? Will it make it?"

"Are we all going or just you and Mom?" asked Matthew.

John sensed his wife's concern. He processed the boys' questions while reassessing whether he was making the right decision. Protection of his wife and farm was still a priority.

"Okay," he began, his eyes darting from one family member to the next. "Matthew will be going with me. Luke, I need you to tend to the farm while your mom handles, um, everything else."

"I'm going?" asked Matthew, surprised at the revelation. "Really, I don't know how I can help."

"You'll be a big help, and I'll explain it to you while we change all the fluids in the truck and move the dead cars out of the parking lot with the dozer."

"Dad, I can be a big help to you on the road," said Luke.

"I know, son. Both of you will need to step up as we face this dang mess. Luke, you're better suited to handling the livestock."

Matthew shook his head and stared at his empty plate. He let his displeasure with the decision be readily apparent through his demeanor.

"John, have you decided between traveling at night or day?" asked Emma.

"It's gonna take us a few hours because of stalled cars and the roundabout trip through the countryside," he explained further, for the benefit of the boys. "As of now, and I'll play it by ear as we approach. I plan on hiding Old Jimmy before we get to the densely populated areas. We'll switch to bicycles for the last twenty miles or so.

"As for timeframe, I wanna pull out of here at three in the morning. People will follow their same sleep patterns for a while. We'll be on the road when they're not out and about. And, if New York is chaotic, as I expect it might be, they might be burned out by the early morning hours."

"Dad, you know I'd like to go with you," insisted Luke. "Even if I can't, I think you have a solid plan."

CHAPTER FORTY-EIGHT

Saturday
Cubbison's Farm
Harford, Pennsylvania

The rest of the day was spent preparing the farm for as many contingencies as they could imagine. The family worked together with John being the one spearheading the effort. He and the boys worked on the truck and cleared the parking area by towing the disabled vehicles with the bulldozer. The decades-old dozer, devoid of electronics, was unaffected by the solar flare. Everyone was in good spirits as they went about their day. Even Matthew began to warm up to his role. As the afternoon progressed, John tried to remind Matthew of the strengths he possessed that would help them. Despite the dogged heat, the family worked together without complaint.

They gathered under the canopy of trees where just the night before a large party had taken place. The string lights were still in place, as were the tables and chairs. All of the wine was left behind as well except for several bottles pilfered by guests when they left that morning.

John took the opportunity to discuss a few things. "Let's talk about our security. We need to shrink the size of our farm in order to patrol its perimeter. Luke, tomorrow, drive the cattle to the fields adjacent to the house next to Mom's garden."

"All of them?" asked Luke. "They'll overgraze it in no time."

"Just for now, son. When Matthew and I return, we'll have four of us capable of protecting our land on horseback."

Luke had a thought. "Dad, whadya think about that old Cushman with the dump bed in the barn. Do you think it runs?"

John laughed. "Your grandfather refused to get rid of that old thing. I really don't know, son. We pulled the battery out years ago. The batteries from our new Kawasaki Mules might work in it."

"It's got a dump bed, which will let me take hay to the cattle. I'll try to fix it in the morning."

Emma volunteered. "I'll help you get the cattle shuffled around. If you can drive them toward the gate, I'll pen them in. Also, Luke, before we leave the subject of security, your dad has suggested we carry pistols at all times inside the house while carrying a rifle as well when outside. Also, I think one of us should always be awake."

"I'll take the late shift," offered Luke. "You get up early anyway."

"Your mom is right," added John. "Stay around the house, the store, and the outbuildings. Avoid standing around in the open. You should be fine. However, we have to remember, if Cat and your grandpa can walk here from New York City, so can desperate people willing to do anything to take what is ours."

"Hell, Dad, there are people in Scranton who'll shoot you for a can of beer," added Matthew. He'd never told his parents about the Friday night he and buddies drove down to Scranton to party. They had no particular place to go other than they were drinking beer and bored. They made a wrong turn, and suddenly bullets came flying in their direction. It was the last time Mathew planned on going there at night.

"Good, we all understand one another. We have to keep our eyes wide open now. A neighbor who used to be a friendly acquaintance may come up our driveway to ask for food. The first time, they'll ask nicely. Unfortunately, we have to turn them away."

"Wait. Why?" asked Matthew.

"Because, son, we can't feed the whole county," replied John. "This may seem harsh, but we don't know how long this is gonna last. We can't give away food that we might need for ourselves."

"They're not gonna take it well," said Luke.

"Exactly, son. They won't. Which means you have to be prepared that the next time they come asking, they may not be as nice. If there is a third time, it'll be at three in the morning with guns and a few of their equally desperate friends."

"John, do you really think it will get that bad?" asked Emma.

"Sadly, honey, I know it will. I want all of us to adopt the mindset of being polite to our friends and strangers alike. However, as much as I hate to say this, we may need to shoot at people to run them off."

Matthew wandered away from the group but asked in a loud tone of voice, "Geez, Dad. Seriously?"

"Yes, son. Seriously. I suspect you and I will see things tomorrow that look straight out of an apocalyptic movie. Our world has changed now."

"Are we gonna shoot somebody because they're hungry?" Matthew asked.

"No. Only if they threaten us. Listen. There is no law enforcement to speak of. We can't dial 9-1-1. They couldn't respond if they wanted to. Besides, they probably have their hands full in Montrose. We are on our own out here, and for the next several days, Luke and Mom will have to be vigilant around the clock."

"This sucks," muttered Matthew.

John grimaced and nodded. "Yes, son. It does."

CHAPTER FORTY-NINE

Saturday
455 Central Park West
New York

The bolt lock clicked open, startling Sam and Cat, who'd been nervously awaiting their hosts' return. Sam had no way of keeping time, but it seemed to go faster than he expected. Once they were safely inside with the lock snapped into place, Asher and Lauren joined them in the living room. Their faces told the story.

"That didn't take long," said Sam with trepidation in his voice. Their sour moods were an indication that his and Cat's time in the building was coming to an end.

"We didn't stay for the whole thing," said Asher without making eye contact.

"Yeah, we bailed before that Santore woman was finished," added Lauren. "And before she could give us a hard time about you guys."

"I kind of figured," said Sam. "Listen. Cat and I have talked about it. We think we can make it back to our hotel on our own. Or maybe across the river toward home." Sam's voice trailed off as he wandered toward the tall windows. The morning sun was just getting high enough to reflect off the murky waters of the Hudson River. It was unusually still because all the traffic had stalled.

"Did you guys get something to eat?" asked Lauren, ignoring his statement. She exchanged glances with Asher.

Cat shook her head. "We wanted to wait until you got back. You know, just in case."

"In case of what?" asked Lauren as Cat welled up with tears in her eyes. Lauren immediately moved by her side to comfort her.

"In case we have to give up the food so we can stay."

Anger built up inside Asher. This young girl shouldn't have to think of such things. He needed to have a conversation with Sam and wondered if they should take a walk outside their condo. But then he remembered the look Patterson had given him as they exited the community gathering. He needed to stay close to home with the door locked and a chair crammed under the handle to prevent it from being opened.

"Sam," he began, glancing between Cat and her grandfather, "we have a pretty good idea of what is expected of us if we stay here, and none of it is good."

"Or acceptable to us," added Lauren. "We need to talk about it. I think I'll take Cat in my room to show her—"

"I can stay," she insisted. "I'm sorry I started crying. I'm not a baby or even a child. Right, Grandpa?"

Sam laughed and fought back his own tears. They all wanted to cry, ages notwithstanding.

"That's right, Cat. Asher, please tell us what you know."

"Basically, Lauren and I are second-class citizens here because we rent. You guys are supposed to leave because you're not a guest of a, quote, homeowner. They want all of our food by noon. And there are several other ridiculous requirements that we heard on the way out."

"We were the first to leave, even before it was over," added

Lauren. "We think all of this is ridiculous, and we don't want any part of it."

"What are you thinkin'?" asked Sam.

"Lauren and I have agreed. If you have to leave, we're going with you."

"To the hotel?" asked Cat.

Asher gathered his courage. He walked along the back of the sofa and looked toward the west. Toward New Jersey and Pennsylvania beyond that.

"Sam, would there be a place at your farm where we could live temporarily? A barn or hayloft? Even a tent?"

Sam started laughing and turned to Cat. "What do you think? Do you think the horses and barn cats would share a stall with these two?"

She hugged Lauren again. "They could have my room. I'd sleep in the barn. I like it out there."

Sam addressed Asher with a huge smile. The tears in his eyes gave away his emotions. Sam wasn't sure he and Cat could survive the trip alone. Now they had a chance. "Let's sit down and talk this through."

"Okay," said Lauren. "Let me put together something for us to eat that doesn't travel well. If we're gonna do something like this, we'll need food for the road."

Even though she was in the kitchen, she could listen to the conversation through the pass-through opening.

Asher became serious. "Sam, this is a big ask on our behalf. I mean, you don't know us, and your family might object."

"You listen to me, Asher. You two saved our lives in that burning skyscraper. You took us in when you didn't have to. I guarantee my son and daughter-in-law will forever be in your debt."

"We'll pull our weight, I swear," said Lauren from the kitchen. "Well, we know nothing about farming, but we're willing to learn. Whatever it takes to stay alive."

"I think it's a great idea!" exclaimed Cat. "When do we leave?"

The loud pounding on the door bore the unmistakable signature of Bart Patterson. His bellowing voice confirmed it.

"Open up, Asher. You two are expected downstairs to speak with Mrs. Santore."

"We're a little busy right now, Bart," shouted Asher as he stuck his hand in a bowl of Doritos. "We'll catch up with you later."

They could hear Patterson jiggling the door handle in an attempt to get inside. Lauren turned to Asher and mouthed the words, "Does he have a key?"

Asher shrugged. "Maybe? Probably?"

Lauren responded, "Bart, we're getting our food together to bring to the lobby. Our friends are gonna help us drop it off on their way out." She grabbed a chair from the dinette set and quickly, but carefully, slid the back under the handle to deter Patterson's entry.

"They're leaving, correct?" Patterson bellowed.

"Yes, sir. They sure are," Asher replied with a hint of spite. "Give us some time to explain, and then they'll be on their way."

"Good to know," Patterson grumbled.

The group sat still for a moment. When the pounding ceased and the bellicose Patterson shut up, they presumed he'd bought the Doyles' ruse.

"Okay, back to the plan," said Asher, dismissing Patterson's interruption. "We thought about the Marriot, but I'm sure their resources are limited, and there are a lot of mouths there to feed. They might be out of food already."

"Clearly, the biggest issue is transportation," began Lauren, turning to Sam. "How far is it to your place?"

"One-fifty," he replied. "While you were downstairs, I was thinking about the route I'd take and how long we could walk in a day."

"Good, good," said Asher as he scooched up to the edge of the sofa. He studied Sam's face. "Um, Sam, are you okay trying to undertake a trip like this?"

Sam suspected this issue might come up. He'd asked himself the same question. "Age is just a number. I'm in good health and spend most of the day on my feet whether it's walking the pastures or tending to the livestock. I'm good for eight hours, maybe more."

Asher made some quick calculations. It would take a week, if not more. "It would be risky with a lot of variables to consider. Obviously, we'd have to watch out for people who might cause trouble. We'd have to find a place to stay every night. There's this hella-hot weather to endure. Are you sure you're up for it?"

Although he was addressing Sam, Cat readily replied, "I'm ready. How 'bout you, Grandpa?"

"The two of us don't really have a choice. Asher and Lauren do. You guys could ride it out here. You know, without us."

"No," said Lauren emphatically. "If you're sure there's room for us at the farm, then that's what we'll do. I mean, we want to do it."

"Okay, let me ask this," said Sam. "Is it better to wait? Maybe things will calm down in the city?"

Lauren replied, "I don't think Santore and good old Bart will let us wait it out. They are on a serious power trip."

"Plus, they have a key to the unit," added Asher. "It's standard practice in the event of a security issue or fire. If we don't turn over our food and escort you guys out, they'll be up here to force us all out."

PART 6

Sunday
Checkout time

CHAPTER FIFTY

Sunday
Cubbison's Farm
Hartford, Pennsylvania

Both John and Emma tossed and turned that night. They talked until near midnight, well past the time they'd normally doze off. As they slept, one of them might roll over to change sides from left to right, slightly nudging the other in the process. That was followed by a whisper. *Are you awake?* And a brief conversation would ensue about the arduous task John and Matthew were about to undertake. Emma was fraught with worry for Cat as well as the guys seeking to rescue her. John still had his doubts as to whether he could find them. He'd resigned himself to leaving it to fate.

Well before dawn, Emma, as usual, was the first to rise. She fixed the family a lumberjack breakfast, as Grandpa Sam liked to call it. Scrambled eggs, ground sausage from a feral hog slaughtered weeks ago, and skillet biscuits. She made sausage, egg, and cheese sandwiches for the road, lovingly wrapping them in aluminum foil.

Throughout those early morning hours, Emma's mind was on

their trip but also on their day-to-day life. She found an unused spiral notebook in Cat's room and began to make lists. She had no illusions as to whether she'd be able to procure these items, as the nearest grocery store was miles away and most likely emptied by now.

No, Emma was thinking ahead. In the coming days and weeks when others would be hungry, they'd be looking to the Cubbison family to feed them. Offering worthless dollars in exchange for a bushel of string beans. Whipping out the plastic credit card as they'd grown accustomed to doing. Emma was beginning to realize that she'd like to stock her shelves with backups of essentials. Flour and yeast for making bread. More canning supplies. The ingredients to cure meat. First aid supplies in the event someone got hurt.

Ammunition, Emma wrote at the top of its own page.

Guns were John's thing. He was an accomplished hunter, as was Sam. Luke was a natural, priding himself on his long-range marksmanship. Since the power outage, John seemed obsessed with their security. He wasn't explicit, but his thoughts continually came back to the threat their family would face from their fellow man. Whether it be for hunting or defense, ammunition was a precious commodity. *You just can't run down to the nearest Walmart or New Milford Hardware to pick up a few boxes*, she thought to herself. Would people trade their own weapons and ammo for food to sustain themselves another week? How much would the local corporate farmers who relied upon GMO seeds to satisfy their bosses at Koch Industries give for Emma's heirloom seeds?

Emma was sure she was on the right track. As she prepared her lists to supplement what she had and to acquire what she didn't, she began to consider a new enterprise. One that was not dissimilar to the market she already ran. Only, the currency would change from cash or credit card to goods and services. A barter market.

John's plan of leaving by three in the morning became more like four. The breakfast the family shared and long goodbyes pushed their schedule back. He took the time to provide Luke some last-minute instructions on taking care of the livestock and chickens. He jotted down a list of priorities for his son to consider throughout the day. Not surprisingly, security was at the top of the list.

"It's all about situational awareness," he began by using a term he'd picked up reading a novel. He motioned for Matthew to pay attention. "Bear with me while I explain."

"I'm listening, too," said Emma as she prepared food for the guys' road trip.

"Most of the time, our minds are tuned out. As you go through the routine of your day, like feeding the cattle or cleaning out the barn, your mind wanders. Sometimes, I've driven into town and realized I couldn't recall what I'd seen for the last ten miles.

"Now, if I lived in Scranton or Binghamton, I'd be more careful about my driving because there are a lot more cars. My level of awareness is subconsciously raised from being tuned out, like Matthew right now, to a relaxed frame of mind, which allows me to comfortably drive while watching out for some idiot to run into me."

"I'm listening," protested Matthew.

John laughed and said half-jokingly, "I know, buddy. Listening is different from awareness. Listening is hearing me talk. Relaxed awareness involves absorbing my words while being mindful of what your mother is doing or whether someone is standing outside the window with a gun."

Matthew's head turned to look at the window. Now he was paying attention.

John continued. "Suppose it's raining outside or there's snow on the road, you may be confident driving, but you stay focused on your every action behind the wheel. Don't brake too hard. Watch your speed. Slow down in plenty of time to stop without skidding into the car in front of you. They call that focused awareness.

"Here is the most important level, the fourth of five."

Matthew interrupted him. "Shouldn't the fifth level be the most important?"

"A good question, and the answer is sort of," replied his dad. "The fourth level, and most important for the situation we're in right now, is what most people would call high alert. Using my driving analogy, suppose you have the green light at an intersection, but out of the corner of your eye, you see a car speeding toward you from the right. You know he's not gonna stop, so you have to make a defensive maneuver to protect yourself. Your adrenaline is pumping. You might pray for help from God. You might be breathing heavily. Your body is on high alert for the danger, and it responds accordingly to protect itself from harm."

John caught his breath as he told them about the fifth level of awareness. "Number five is comatose. In the above scenario, that's when you literally freeze at the steering wheel and brace for impact. Your mind doesn't think you can react, so it shuts down. You become hyperaware of what is happening but paralyzed to do anything about it. We don't want this to happen. Ever."

Luke appeared concerned. "Dad, will you be up front with us? Are we going to have to go through life worrying if we're gonna get shot at or burned out of our house?"

John grimaced. Perhaps it was too early for this conversation, but really, it was not. Especially since Emma and Luke were going to be left alone.

"Son, what I am saying is that we have to find the right level of situational awareness to fit the times. Two days ago, we didn't have to be concerned with a scenario where people, or groups of people, came here to cause us harm. The threat is real now.

"We have to find a way to let our bodies and minds rest while being aware of our surroundings. Situational awareness doesn't mean being paranoid or obsessively concerned about security, which is where my mind is right now. However, until we're all together again and we've established routines and security measures, I will be obsessed about our safety. You should be, too."

Emma finished packing the soft-sided cooler with their food. She eased over to her spiral notebook, where she turned to the page titled *Ammunition*. She drew a star next to it and underlined the word three times for emphasis. Now she understood.

CHAPTER FIFTY-ONE

Sunday
455 Central Park West
New York

"Help!"

Cat's bloodcurdling scream was preceded by the plate-glass window in the guest bedroom exploding inward. Shards of glass flew throughout the space, crashing off the walls and ceilings before settling on top of her bed. Her restless sleep and quick reaction might have saved her from further harm as she turned away from the window and covered her face with her arm at the moment of impact.

Seconds later, the cavalry came running, led by Asher, who burst into the room. Without thought, he repeatedly slapped at the rocker-style light switch on the wall to turn on the lights. Then, in the panic, once he recalled that the power was out, he blindly moved into the room and immediately cut both feet when he stepped on the glass.

After screaming in pain, he found his way to the bed. "Are you okay, Cat? Talk to me!"

"My arm hurts," she mumbled from under the covers. "It stings."

Lauren caught up with Asher and illuminated the room with a flashlight. "Asher, don't move. There's glass everywhere."

"Cat! Cat! Are you okay?" Sam shouted from the hallway as his momentum caused him to bump into Lauren.

"I think so," she replied after removing her covers.

"What happened?" asked Lauren.

With Asher remaining still like his feet were stuck in concrete, Lauren scanned the room to find the cause of the breakage. In the drywall ceiling above the closet door, she saw a round hole with parts of the sheetrock pushed in around it.

Leaving the light trained on the indentation, she asked, "Is that a bullet hole?"

Sam leaned in to look. He replied calmly, "I think so. Let's get these two out of here and tend to their wounds." The reflective light showed blood around Asher's bare feet oozing onto the rug.

Lauren and Sam put on their shoes. Using Sam for balance, Asher carefully removed several pieces of glass from his feet. He carefully retraced his steps with the aid of the flashlight to exit the room. Cat's wounds were minor thanks to her quick reaction.

It was just after three in the morning. As they bandaged up the wounded, Sam stood on a chair and, with the aid of a steak knife, dug the bullet out of the ceiling. He returned to the living room, where candlelight lit up the space.

"If I were to guess, this is a .223 caliber. We use them in some of our hunting rifles. It's also the round commonly used in AR-15 rifles."

"How did it get up here?" asked Asher.

"Believe it or not, some bullets can travel straight up nearly ten thousand feet. Heck, there are sniper rounds that can record a kill shot over two miles away. This is either a stray or some idiot deciding to shoot up the building."

"It scared me," said Cat.

"I know, honey," said Sam. "The good news is that the angle from the ground to this floor never put you in danger from the bullet unless you were standing at the window." He casually walked away from the window where he stood.

"Either way, this is an example of why New York is too dangerous to stay," added Lauren. "Santore, Patterson, and their cop wannabes can't protect us from this."

Asher stood to test his feet. They'd be sore and would have difficulty healing if he walked for miles every day, but it was necessary. He vocalized his thoughts.

"Those people left us alone last night. Maybe they forgot about us or they had more pressing issues to address. Nonetheless, we insulted Santore and Patterson by walking out on their little meeting. When everyone gets their day started, I expect they'll be banging on the door again."

"I agree," said Sam. "Let's start gathering our things and prepare to hit the streets at sunup. Should we tell them we're leaving?"

"I'll leave a box with the food we can't carry at the front door along with a note," replied Lauren. "There's no sense in initiating a confrontation. The fire exit doors we need to take are on the west side of the building away from the guarded entrance."

After eating a canned-goods breakfast consisting of corn, kidney, and garbanzo beans in a bowl topped with Cholula hot sauce, they loaded up the rest of the food in soft-sided luggage or backpacks that could be slung over their shoulders. The priorities were bottled water, protein powder, and the Doyles' varied brands of energy bars.

The afternoon before, Lauren had introduced Cat to their neighbor down the hall who had a young girl about Cat's size. After Lauren explained what had happened to Cat, the family generously provided her shoes, clothing, a backpack, and an unused journal with some pens if Cat chose to keep a diary. The two girls hit it off, and as a result, the adults took a moment to rethink their decision to leave. In the end, it was Cat's insistence on going home that kept them on track.

Lauren, with Cat's help, hastily removed her wedding photos

from albums. Other pictures were on her Apple devices, most likely lost forever. Certainly, she could retrieve them from the so-called Cloud, if there still was one.

As they left, Asher and Lauren said goodbye to their belongings. They wondered aloud whether they'd be able to return one day to retrieve them. Asher was pessimistic. If the grid collapse stretched into many months, eventually Santore would order her underlings to enter their condo and empty it out for distribution to others.

It was around six that morning when the foursome exited onto the streets of the Upper West Side. After being cooped up inside, they hoped to breathe some fresh air. Instead, their nostrils were infiltrated by the smell of smoke resulting from out-of-control fires. The wind that morning was nonexistent, causing the smoke to linger in the city.

"Everybody ready?" asked Asher, trying to adopt a cheery tone.

"I am!" exclaimed Cat, the most exuberant of the responses.

Lauren asked, "What are you thinking? Take Columbus all the way down, or make our way over to the Hudson River Greenway?"

"Along the river would be safest, but I have an idea I'd like to run past Sam."

They began walking at a steady pace toward the river. At that hour, the streets were mostly free of pedestrian traffic although, once they came to the Columbus Avenue intersection, they met people traveling south toward the tunnel as well. Asher spoke to Sam as they walked.

"Are you pretty good with cars? You know classics from the sixties or so."

Sam slapped the younger man on the back. "I'm a farm boy. When I wasn't feeding cattle or mending fences, I had the hood up on a car or truck, fiddlin' with the engine. Why?"

Asher took a deep breath and studied Sam's face. "Um, how do you feel about stealing cars?"

Sam's head snapped toward Asher. He paused for a moment.

"I'm not much for stealin' anything, but these are unusual times. Whadya have in mind?"

Asher pointed toward the intersection at West 100th Street. "Let's turn here. I wanna check on something. Then I'll explain."

CHAPTER FIFTY-TWO

Sunday
Cubbison's Farm
Harford, Pennsylvania

It took Emma a few minutes to overcome her emotions after she saw the guys off. She stood alone in the gravel driveway in front of the market, watching the taillights as the old truck puttered onto the road. She forced herself to focus on the day ahead of them. She and Luke had their regular chores to do in addition to continuing their preparations around the farm. Earlier, John had come up with a list of priorities that she hoped to adhere to.

She'd gone into Sam's bedroom and retrieved his old pocket watch that had belonged to his father. The self-winding watch kept perfect time. Without electricity, it was impossible for them to determine the precise time although Emma knew sunrise was around six. She set the pocket watch accordingly, vowing to keep it wound.

For what it was worth, she retrieved the John Deere wall calendar from the barn and tacked it to the kitchen wall. She thought it was important to keep up with the days and dates. Her gardens were designed for the plants to mature at certain times of the year. Clearly, her expert eye was able to determine when a vegetable was ready for harvest. The calendar would assist her in meal planning and storage. She needed to prepare as if this power outage would last for many months, even into the next year.

She and John had discussed their refrigeration needs and gasoline supply. They determined that if they ran the generators for one hour followed by a three-hour break, they could maintain the temperatures in the refrigerators and freezers in both the house and the market. During that one-hour time frame, she'd charge batteries to be used in flashlights and lanterns, while Luke would be responsible for recharging the lithium batteries for their power tools.

And, thanks to Luke's thinking outside the box, the battery for the Cushman. As expected, the battery from the four-wheelers fit the old utility cart that had been mothballed when the farm was stocked with a Polaris and a couple of Kawasaki Mule side-by-sides. The Cushman would be a huge benefit to Emma, as her organic gardens relied heavily upon manure and compost for fertilizer.

Emma was proficient at canning fruits and vegetables. In fact, the market's shelves were packed with Ball jars featuring the Cubbison's label, each of which had been prepared by Emma. Canning was already a part of her daily routine, and she kept a storage building full of the supplies.

That morning, she was going to try bringing the pressure cooker up to temperature over an open fire. It was a reminder of how much firewood they'd need year-round, not just to heat their home during the winter. Throughout the farm, fallen trees had been cut, split and stacked for future use. She suggested to Luke that every trip he made into the fields to haul hay to the cattle should result in a return trip full of firewood.

There were outbuildings scattered around the property, containing farm implements, tools, and pesticides. Throughout the day, as Luke went about his chores, he systematically emptied the outbuildings and brought these farming essentials closer to the farmhouse. They hoped they wouldn't be the victim of petty theft, but John had raised sufficient concern about others to warrant the extra effort.

It was midafternoon, and the two had worked at a frenzied pace to accomplish everything on their mental to-do list in one day. Emma forced Luke to take a break and join her for lunch consisting of Founder's Day dinner leftovers. They sat around the fire despite the unbearable summer heat as Emma's canning operation continued.

"I saw you having a serious conversation with your brother before they left this morning." Emma opened the conversation, curious about what had been said. Luke and Matthew were dissimilar considering they were twins and had very little in common on a social level. Their brief talk had ended in a hug with slaps on the back, so she assumed it was amicable.

Luke took a sip of sun tea brewed by adding six tea bags to a gallon glass container. He poured some sugar in his red Solo cup and stirred it to create sweet tea. The family planned on using up their plasticware and paper plates from the food service side of the business to avoid wasting water on washing dishes. Luke would gather up the trash bags and take them to the back side of the farm to toss in a small limestone quarry for burning at night to obscure the smoke.

"Listen, Mom. I get it. Matthew's kind of a screwup. But you've gotta understand. He feels like he's constantly being compared to me."

"Son, it's not like that. I swear."

Luke smiled. "Mom, you may believe what you're saying, but the favoritism shows itself sometimes. If I see it, Matthew sure as heck sees it." He paused for a moment before he continued. He and his mother were about to have a serious, adult conversation about their family dynamic. He didn't want to upset her considering they were split apart right now.

"For whatever reason, years ago when we were kids, I took one direction, and Matthew took another. I wanted to be out on the farm, messin' with the cattle or huntin' hogs. Mathew wanted to play video games on his Xbox. While he was shooting bad guys on *Halo*, I was practicing shooting bottles off a fence post at a thousand yards."

"*Halo*?" she asked, completely oblivious to the games her son had been playing.

"It's kind of an army game featuring this character, Master Chief, who hunts down his enemies. Or something like that. I don't know, I've never played it, which is my point. Matthew was into things I wasn't. He had friends that I didn't. He listened to hard rock music. I love country. See?"

Emma nodded. Before she spoke, the astute young man continued while he had the opportunity to reveal both his and his brother's inner feelings.

"You realize our life revolves around this farm, right? We don't get in the car and go see the Phillies or Eagles play. We don't do amusement parks or go to the beach. For me, that's great. I believe Cat is the same way. For Matthew, it leaves him out because his interests are elsewhere."

"How did this happen?" asked Emma. "Don't get me wrong. I love Matthew like I love you. I just don't see how you two followed different paths."

"Mom, it might be a growing-up thing," he replied. "Here's what I know. Matthew questions everything. It may seem like he's arguing, but really, he has an intuition about him that's different from the rest of us."

"Are you referring to our conversation yesterday about whether or not to retrieve your sister and grandpa from the city?"

"Well, sort of, I guess. That's a good example, though. Matthew didn't think it was a mistake. He just saw it from a different perspective is all."

Emma laughed. "Your dad was thinking along those lines, too. He just didn't say it out loud because he knew I'd start crying again, and he'd vowed to never knowingly make me cry."

"Do you see what I'm saying?" he asked rhetorically before taking a deep breath. "Here's what I told him this morning. I mean, not exactly, but pretty close.

"I told him to always just keep being himself, no matter what he believes others think of him. As I said to him, if everybody in this family thought exactly alike, we wouldn't be able to deal with those who don't. Make sense?"

"Contrarian," muttered Emma.

"What?"

"Contrarian. Fancy word that I think applies to Matthew. The popular opinion was to go rescue Cat and Sam from the clutches of the city. Matthew just wanted to look at it from a different perspective."

"Exactly! You may not know it, but it happens around the farm all the time. Dad gets frustrated with him because he thinks Matthew is being argumentative or just wants to avoid working. He has ideas, too. They may not be the same as Dad's, but most times, they're worth considering. I just think we need to listen instead of shutting him down. That's all."

Emma felt terrible. She'd never taken the time to understand why Matthew was different. Instead, it was a consistent source of division within the family. She fell silent as she processed what Luke had told her. He was not done.

"Mom, can I make you feel better?"

"Please. At the moment, I feel like a horrible mother."

"Don't. Matthew is more mature than he lets on. He's what I call a deep thinker. Those times when he seems reclusive, like he doesn't care about what the rest of the family is doing, he's thinking.

"He knows that he turned out different from me, and he's accepted it. But not in a man-in-jail-for-life kinda way. It's just allowed him to be at peace with his uniqueness. When he left with Dad this morning, he was like a different person. He was like me. He was strong, confident and ready to do whatever it takes to bring them all home safely."

Emma began to cry. Partly because she'd misread Matthew for years. Partly out of a sense of relief that he would be more of an asset to John than a hinderance. She couldn't wait to hug her other son when he got home.

CHAPTER FIFTY-THREE

Sunday
Upper West Side
New York

Asher hoped to stop by the NYPD's 24th Precinct to gather information. Mostly, he was concerned about the safety of the streets in the four miles between here and the Lincoln Tunnel. However, he was searching for a glimmer of hope that perhaps the power outage wasn't widespread. The closer they got to the four-story, mostly concrete building, the more his hopes were dashed.

The parking lot in front of the entrance of the 24th was littered with dead bodies. As they came into view, Lauren steered Cat aside and pulled her head close to shield her from the carnage. Asher and Sam slowed to take in the scene.

"How did we not hear this?" asked Asher rhetorically, his eyes darting in all directions to ensure the battle was over. He pulled his shirt over his nose and mouth to avoid the smell. "We're not that far from the condo."

"I don't know," Sam replied. He tried to look over the low-rise buildings to catch a glimpse of the tower at 455 CPW. "I can guess when it happened, though. A wild shot or stray bullet from the gun battle hit your building."

Almost all the glass in the aluminum-clad windows on the upper floors had been shot out. A parking enforcement cart had been turned over on the steps leading to the entrance. It had been set on fire. Beyond that, Sam and Asher were able to see signs of fire inside the precinct's entryway.

"Asher, do you know whether they have holding cells here?"

"Probably. I think all of them do." He paused and pointed to the west and east side of the building. The precinct was flanked with windowless concrete towers rising slightly above the office in between. "Those look like they'd hold jail cells."

Sam studied the bullet-riddled bodies strewn about the parking lot. "Is there gang activity around here? Look at how these guys are dressed." The dead were dressed in black and gold clothing, most of which had a three-point or five-point crown associated with it.

"Ten years ago, the Upper West Side, where we are now, was the second-safest in the city behind the Upper East Side. That was mostly because the residents welcomed police protection, whereas other neighborhoods joined the anti-cop movement. Over time, though, the gangs have moved in."

"I'll bet they were here to bust their pals out of the holding cells," said Sam.

Asher nodded and was about to add a thought when Lauren hollered for them from the next intersection.

"Guys! Can we keep moving?"

Crap, thought Asher. Now was not the time for sightseeing. As the sun rose in the sky, more people were exiting their homes. Some were curious about the shoot-out at the 24th Precinct, while others searched for answers as to when it would all end.

He and Sam walked briskly to catch up, and they began moving toward the Lincoln Tunnel again along Amsterdam Avenue. The one-way street was littered with stalled cars. The ground-floor retail spaces had all been looted except those with steel grates or iron gates to protect them. Residents of the upper floors of the older residential units had opened their windows to allow in some air despite its smokiness.

Off in the distance, through the haze, the fifty-five-floor skyscraper at 200 Amsterdam tried to touch the sky. Asher pointed toward it.

"That's where we're headed first," he said.

"What's there?" asked Lauren.

Asher gathered his thoughts and proposed his idea. "There's a company called Cooper Classic Cars here in the city. Their first location was in Greenwich Village, selling mainly foreign sports cars and other small exotics. They provide movie and TV production companies with vehicles when the script calls for it. Once, we got a film car from them to use in a scene featuring Tom and a love interest. During a break-in shooting, a gaffer and his best boy were moving a lighting rig and lost control of it. It fell on top of the car and crushed the convertible top."

"The best boy must not have been the best," quipped Sam.

Asher laughed. "Yeah, sorry. That's production lingo for the guys in charge of lighting and electrical matters. Anyway, Cooper Classics expanded recently to Amsterdam Avenue with a larger facility. In this location, they sell classic muscle cars and trucks."

"You plan on doing some shopping?" asked Lauren, unsure of why Asher was bringing this up.

He sighed before responding, "If any of us object, then we won't do what I propose. Here's what I know about the car dealerships in the city. The FDNY was able to get a resolution passed that required local dealerships near residential buildings to keep a minimum of two gallons of fuel in the tanks of their inventory. Also, they had to eliminate all stored gasoline whether in drums or portable cans. Plus, the keys had to be accessible behind a glass panel. You know, a break-in-case-of-emergency type of deal. That way, in the event of a fire, the vehicles could be moved so they wouldn't provide the blaze any kind of accelerant or explosive potential to put the firefighters at risk."

"Pretty smart," said Sam.

"I think I sense what you're thinking," said Lauren. "I mean, are you okay with stealing a car?"

"I am," replied Asher matter-of-factly. "I can't think of anything else except our survival. If stealing any form of transportation gets us closer to Sam and Cat's farm, then I will do it without hesitation. However, I want us all to agree."

Both Lauren and Asher turned to Sam, who stared at a beer delivery truck featuring Blue Moon beer. All of its side doors had been pried open and the beer inside stolen. The thieves had been so sloppy in their haste they'd dropped more than a dozen cases of the bottled beer on the asphalt, where it soaked into the pores. The irony of this happening across the street from a Catholic Church was not lost on him.

"I say we go for it. They have insurance, right?" Sam's irreverent joke brought a chuckle from everyone as they continued forward, relieved that the first two miles of their journey had not resulted in any confrontations with others.

They still had one hundred forty-eight to go.

CHAPTER FIFTY-FOUR

Sunday
New Jersey

John and Matthew chatted for the first forty-five minutes of their drive to New York. To be sure, the one-hundred-fifty-mile drive into the city would've gone much faster, even in the '56 GMC pickup, had they taken the interstate. John remained concerned about the perils driving on the heavily traveled highways would bring. His dad would think the same way.

He'd been pleased with Matthew's attitude as they got started. He was genuinely interested in learning about how to use the handguns he'd been provided. John would quiz him about what to do under certain scenarios, and Matthew was remarkably accurate in his assessment of how to deal with threats. He practiced dry firing them as well as the loading of the revolvers under timed pressure.

After a while, his son drifted off to sleep, and John allowed him to rest. He reflected on his wife's loving eyes as they'd said their long goodbyes, unable to let go of one another despite the importance of the journey. Her eyes had plead with him to bring her baby girl home. The tears had flowed down Emma's cheeks out of concern for Cat and the thought of losing John and Matthew in the process.

Leaving in the early morning hours had proven to be the right decision thus far. By the time they merged onto U.S. Route 6, they'd not encountered another human being. John reflected on the things his dad had taught him indirectly over the years.

During their trips around Eastern Pennsylvania and Upstate New York, he'd point out landmarks of interest. Route 6, for example, was once the longest highway in America, stretching from Long Beach, California, to the easternmost part of Massachusetts. It was a beautiful drive through Eastern Pennsylvania during the day, one that he and his father had taken many times when John was a boy.

When he and Emma had outlined the safest, most direct route to Times Square, he'd pointed out the last part of the route would be along the Lincoln Highway at the Lincoln Tunnel, which travels under the Hudson River and empties out at Times Square, where their hotel was located.

The Lincoln Highway, like Route 6, had a storied history in America. It was the first transcontinental road for automobiles, dating back to 1913. Across America, travelers were treated to the *Roadside Giants* on the Lincoln Highway. These oversized tributes to Americana included an oversized quarter weighing nearly a ton as well as a twenty-five-foot-tall replica of a 1940s Bennett Gas Pump.

His dad's favorite was the Haines Shoe House near York, Pennsylvania. The replica of a shoe had been built by a shoe salesman as a form of advertisement along the Lincoln Highway. It was once featured on a season of the reality series *The Amazing Race*.

The Cubbison family was always nostalgic. Not only had they made a name for themselves after a century or more of feeding Eastern Pennsylvanians, but they grew up with a love of history and a curiosity of the origins of ordinary highways traversing the countryside.

Once John passed into New Jersey, he began to notice people walking west along the roadside. He woke Matthew to help him keep an eye out for Cat and Sam.

Each time they approached a group of people, they'd slow to see if their family members were among them. At first, John would keep driving. Then, as daylight came, he had Matthew roll down the window so they could ask for information.

One group, a family of six, ambled along the middle of the road. They hadn't expected to see an operating vehicle, so at first contact, they had that deer-in-the-headlights look. John slowed until they moved out of the way to his left.

"Are you guys from New York City?" he asked politely.

The father, heavyset and in his late thirties, replied. His chest was heaving from exhaustion. "Paramus. That's Jersey."

"Is the power out in the city?"

"Duh," replied the oldest child.

Her father shot the child a scornful look. He turned to John. "Can you give us a ride? We're just going to Stroudsburg to her family's house."

John started rolling forward because the man had moved closer to the driver's door. "No, sorry. We don't have enough gas for side trips."

John hastily drove away, leaving the family on the side of the road staring in his direction. He'd loaded three five-gallon cans of gasoline plus the bicycles, which filled the bed of the pickup. Besides, there was no way he was going to pick up hitchhikers travelling in either direction.

As the day grew brighter and they came closer to the bedroom communities stretching near Interstate 80, the number of people fleeing the populated areas of New Jersey and New York grew. John tried several more times to ask questions, and he wasn't able to learn anything useful.

After the last attempt, he promised Matthew he wouldn't do it again. They were about twenty-five miles from the Lincoln Tunnel when he slowed to speak to another group.

"Can you tell me about the city?" asked John, slowing to a crawl. "How is it up there?"

Without warning, one of the refugees pulled a gun from behind his back. John saw him reach awkwardly for the pistol. It got caught in his waistband momentarily, which was all John needed. He didn't hesitate as he pressed the gas pedal to the floorboard.

"Don't fail me," he begged Old Jimmy as the truck lurched forward and began to speed away. Fortunately, the man didn't fire at them although it provided a lesson learned. It was time to switch transportation. He began looking for places to hide their truck where it wouldn't be noticed by the many people traveling on foot.

He followed the route marked on the atlas to the Great Piece Meadows Preserve, a seven-thousand-acre park made up mostly of a freshw ater swamp. All John needed was a dirt road leading into the preserve where he and Matthew could bury the truck in branches and other broad-leafed foliage.

It took them an hour to drive around the preserve to find a suitable place. In the center of the preserve, just past a gun club, was a landscape supply store. The owners apparently resided nearby, as they had a long winding driveway that led into the freshwater swamp. John drove into the preserve as far as he could until he found a four-wheeler trail into the woods. It was the best they could do under the circumstances.

They worked together to top off the gas tanks before removing their mountain bikes from the truck bed. Their camouflage job wasn't perfect, but it was enough, he hoped, to avoid casual scrutiny.

"Here we go, son," said John, who had a little difficulty with his balance as he mounted the bike. He hadn't ridden one in decades.

"Good luck, Dad," said Matthew, laughing at his father's struggles. "Would you rather walk?"

"I'll get the hang of it. It's because we're on this dirt road."

"Yeah, okay. I'll ride behind you in case I need to scoop up any body parts when you wreck."

John laughed heartily. He needed the relief from the tense situation they'd just left behind. He wondered what might have happened had the man started shooting.

He had no idea how bad it could get.

CHAPTER FIFTY-FIVE

Sunday
Upper West Side
New York

"Is this the same Broadway by our hotel?" asked Cat innocently as the most famous street in New York crossed Amsterdam Avenue, creating a similar intersection as Times Square.

"It is," replied Lauren. "It cuts past Central Park and Columbus Square where we walked home the other night."

"Should we get our things?" she asked.

Sam stared down Broadway, looking past the dozens of disabled taxis and people milling about. He hoisted the canvas tote bag a little higher on his shoulder. It was full of food and supplies for the long walk home.

"Cat, unless there's something you just have to get, we shouldn't take the time," he replied. "Besides, we don't have room to carry it in our bags."

Cat thought for a moment and subconsciously tugged at the

straps of the backpack she'd been given. It, too, was heavy with food and clothing from her new friend.

"Nah. There's nothing, really."

After the brief pause, Asher pointed down the street, urging them to continue. The number of people out and about began to concern him.

"Where is it, Ash?" asked Lauren.

"Do you remember Flywheel, the place you took spin classes years ago?"

Lauren was embarrassed. "Yeah, you bought me a membership, and I think I went three times in a year. I was hoping you forgot about that."

"I did. Well, until I saw the dealership had taken the entire ground floor of the building after that fancy kindergarten and preschool closed."

"Now they sell used cars in the space?" asked Lauren.

"Babe, they're more than used cars. They are classics. Vintage collectibles. You'll see, 'cause there it is."

Asher pointed toward the building that contained retail space on the ground floor and a parking garage on the upper levels. The twelve-foot-tall plate-glass windows that once contained the lettering and logo of the classic car dealership had been broken out. Roll-up steel doors were still in place, protecting the vintage vehicles from theft or vandalism.

"Follow me," he instructed. He led them to the street corner and waved for them to follow him down West Sixty-Sixth Street. "We filmed a scene under this tree canopy once."

"How are we supposed to get inside?" asked Lauren.

"We aren't," replied Asher. "Sam and I will. We need you guys to stay visible on the street corner. Try not to make eye contact with anyone or strike up any conversations. If we can't do this quickly, then we'll skip it. Okay?"

Lauren agreed. Asher and Sam handed over their bags. She led Cat to a group of several taxi cabs that seemed to have rolled together when the solar flare hit. By maneuvering around the open doors, they were able to position themselves in the middle of the cabs and hidden from casual passersby.

"Come on, Sam. We're gonna have to jump down about ten feet off a wall. Are you okay with that?"

"Swell," Sam replied hesitantly.

Asher led him up the ramp to the parking garage, and then they moved onto a grassy area in the midst of tall oak trees. To their right was a small homeless encampment, which had been abandoned. The homeless, Asher surmised, probably took up residency in the high-rise apartments adjacent to the car dealership.

"We used to sit on this ledge in between shots to avoid the heat. It was a small crew for a brief, afternoon shot, so we didn't set up the tents and cooling fans like normal. While we waited for the director to fire up production again, I watched the dealership move cars in and out into this utility yard. I forgot about this dumpster being here."

"Do you wanna jump into the dumpster?" asked Sam, looking over the ledge.

"It looks like a soft landing, doesn't it?"

"Yeah, actually, it does. A stinky soft landing." Sam had gotten a whiff of the decaying garbage.

"I'll go first to make sure there aren't any car parts that might surprise us."

"Wait," Sam urged Asher to think it through. "What if we can't get inside? How are we gonna get out?"

Asher pointed to a steel fire ladder that led to the first floor of the parking garage. "We'll climb up there and then jump out through the openings at the front of the building. We'll use the car dealership's awning to break our fall."

"You've thought this through, haven't you?" asked Sam.

"Yeah, sort of," he replied as he eased off the retaining wall and dropped the eight feet into the dumpster. He maintained his balance for a moment before falling on his backside. Asher quickly scrambled upright and provided Sam a thumbs-up.

Sam smiled and joined the escapade. "You only live once," he muttered as he dropped downward. Asher was there to help Sam keep his balance on the bags of trash. The two men climbed out of the dumpster and brushed off the debris and stench.

Sam walked behind Asher as they headed to the rear utility doors. There was a corrugated steel rollup large enough for the cars to be moved in and out as well as a double door for employees to use. It had a simple door handle with no bolt lock.

"Let's find something to pry the door open," suggested Asher. Piles of odds and ends related to the maintenance of the dealer's inventory was stacked on short plastic shelving throughout the utility yard. After some searching, Sam found a four-way tire iron.

"What if we beat the door handle until it breaks?" asked Asher when Sam showed him the tool.

"Well, between removing the doorknob and this, we can pop it open," replied Sam, who produced a grease-covered screwdriver from his back pocket.

The guys went to work, taking turns bashing the lever-style door handle until it surrendered. Then Sam manipulated the locking mechanism with the flathead screwdriver until the door popped open. Seconds later, they were inside a garage full of auto parts and supplies, which led to the showroom.

It was time to go shopping.

CHAPTER FIFTY-SIX

Sunday
Upper West Side
New York

Like kids in a candy store. Whether it was a drunk who broke into a liquor store or a cyberthief having his way with somebody's bank account, a certain euphoria overcame the criminal once they were able to get their hands on the goods. Asher and Sam were no different.

From the apple red '39 Chevy hot rod to the baby blue '66 Mustang convertible, nearly two dozen gorgeous vintage vehicles were neatly arranged throughout the showroom facing Amsterdam Avenue. At first, the men lost sight of their goals, which was to find a vehicle perfectly suited for the hundred-and-fifty-mile trip to Cubbison's Farm.

Sam took more than one occasion to stop and reminisce about a particular vehicle, recalling his glory years as a youth. For Asher, he marveled at the muscle cars and imagined aloud how fast they might go.

However, when several pedestrians on the sidewalk stopped to peer through the steel grates at the vehicles, nearly discovering the two rookie burglars, the men got down to business.

First, they discussed what made the most sense. They debated gas mileage, which was a crucial element because fuel would be very difficult to procure along the way. Sam suggested a diesel truck because they stored hundreds of gallons on the farm, and he knew how to make it from corn, as well.

The diesel criteria limited their options until they came upon an '85 American General Humvee. The olive drab truck with a matching soft top appeared to be straight off the battlefield where it had hauled troops.

The military surplus vehicle was in incredible condition, having been restored to its original appearance. The dealership had enhanced it with the addition of interior upgrades from the consumer model—the Hummer H1.

"It's a beast," said Asher as he strolled around the truck. "Look, it's got tow hooks front and rear."

"Plus a winch," added Sam. "I think these bumpers and the grille guard will help us push other cars out of the way."

"It's a diesel," muttered Asher as he looked inside the spacious interior. "I think this is the one."

Sam readily agreed, and the men moved through the dark offices in search of keys. It was a 1985 model, not quite as old as Sam thought might be necessary to avoid the effects of the solar flare. The keyed ignition with an aftermarket alarm connected to it might be a problem. They'd know in a moment.

Asher slid into the driver's seat with key in hand. Sam made his way to the front of the showroom to give Asher the all clear once any pedestrians had cleared the area. A minute later, Asher was ready.

"Here goes!" he said loudly.

He turned the key, and the powerful six-point-two-liter diesel roared to life. The loud rumble of the Humvee was deafening inside the showroom, even with the windows broken. Sam ran toward him, waving his arms, indicating Asher should turn it off. The motor ticked for a minute as it cooled down from the brief time it was running.

"Did you notice the fuel level?" asked Sam.

"Half full. They don't have a lot of diesel vehicles, so I guess they kept a little more in this one."

Sam stood by the door of the truck and looked around. They'd need to maneuver a couple of cars to the side to make room for the beast of a Humvee to exit.

"The roll-up doors open with a keyed lock together with a chain and pulley system. Let's find the keys to this old Trans Am and the Continental. We can back them up just enough for the Humvee to fit through that opening." He pointed toward a roll-up door directly in front of the truck.

"I'll look in the same place we found these keys," said Asher. "Sam, rummage through the offices and look for anything useful. There's a huge storage area in the back of this beast."

Sam hurriedly walked away. He spoke loudly. "There's a VW Camper van down here. I'll start with its bedding."

They methodically stripped the dealership of anything that might make their trip to the farm easier, or that might be of particular value once they arrived there. They called out to one another as they did so, being mindful of the time that Lauren and Cat had been alone.

Confident that they'd accomplished their purpose, Sam took over the driving duties while Asher moved the cars blocking his path. After a check of the sidewalk, they felt comfortable driving the truck out of the showroom.

Asher nervously fumbled with the lock until it opened. The door rose slightly on its own from the tension created by the chain and pulley system. Then he reached up and grabbed the chain. Asher furiously pulled the chain down to raise the heavy door, which curled up within a metal housing. When it was almost fully opened, Sam fired the diesel motor, and Asher scrambled to the passenger side to join him.

"Hell yeah!" he shouted, slapping the restored dashboard multiple times. Sam put the automatic transmission into drive and forced down the gas pedal. The truck spun the tires on the polished floor until he let off the gas. Despite his inclination to flee to avoid being caught, he realized there wasn't anyone to stop him. So he eased through the opening, careful not to damage the protruding soft top as he drove over a six-inch concrete curb.

Within seconds of Sam wheeling the behemoth onto Amsterdam, heading the wrong way on a once-busy one-way street, people were running toward the dealership to make an acquisition of their own.

Lauren emerged from the protection of the taxi cabs with Cat in tow. "Are you kidding me? A giant Hummer?"

"Nice, right?" replied Asher as he jumped out of the truck to load their bags into the back storage compartment.

"You two are such boys," she responded as they tossed the last of the bags on top of everything else Sam had found inside the dealership.

"It's perfect," Asher said with a smile. He nodded to Sam. "We're ready. Go down about five blocks and turn right. That'll take us directly to the river. Twelfth Avenue is a wide road with turn lanes. We should be able to get around any stalled cars easily."

"If not, we'll just push 'em out of the way."

"Absolutely!" Asher laughed as the guys exchanged high fives.

In the backseat, Lauren whispered to Cat, "Look at these two. You give a boy a new toy and he's happy. Right?"

Cat looked around the interior and peered over the backseat at their gear. She shrugged and looked out the window at the entrances to the apartment buildings that had been broken open. In fact, Cat noticed, every glass window along the sidewalk had been smashed. When she saw a dead body, she quickly turned her head in an attempt to avoid reality.

She just wanted this adventure to be over.

CHAPTER FIFTY-SEVEN

Sunday
Hell's Kitchen
New York

For many years, the neighborhood known as Hell's Kitchen in the west side of Manhattan was a misnomer. When it was first inhabited by Irish immigrants in the early 1800s, it was a notorious slum known for poverty, corruption, and debauchery. Tennessean Davy Crockett once said he'd rather risk himself fighting Indians than venture among the creatures who lived there, who were too mean to swab hell's kitchen.

The name stuck until, over time, the neighborhood was revitalized as young urban professionals, yuppies, as they were once called, looked for inexpensive housing near Midtown Manhattan. Eventually, the negative connotation associated with Hell's Kitchen disappeared.

After the collapse of the power grid, the community reverted back to its roots.

Sam slowly navigated through the streets until he was able to turn onto Twelfth Avenue, the westernmost street on Manhattan and best known for its access to the ship terminals. Eight lanes wide with multiple turn lanes, there was more than enough room for him to maneuver his way through the broken-down vehicles.

Everyone was in high spirits as Asher gave the Pennsylvanians the nickel tour. He told them about the history of Hell's Kitchen and how immigrants played an important role in its development. He talked about the numerous piers that jutted out into the Hudson River to accommodate shipping and cruise traffic.

There was a cross-section of humanity walking slowly toward the Lincoln Tunnel. Some pulled luggage on rollers while others commandeered abandoned shopping carts from a local grocery store.

As they approached Pier 88, the overhead parking for the cruise passengers ended, allowing them a view of the river. All their heads turned toward the west to view the water and the state of New Jersey on the other side.

Sam had to maneuver into the northbound lane to avoid several dozen cars that had stalled at the upcoming traffic signal. He slowly took the truck over the median between two trees until it lumbered to the other side. He started to make a wide turn when suddenly, two men hiding near a graffiti-covered car detail center rushed in front of the truck.

Sam tried to inch forward, but they didn't budge. He and Asher both cranked down their windows and began yelling at the men to move out of the way. He started to put the Humvee in reverse when one of the men grabbed the grille guard and hoisted himself on the hood.

"Get off the truck!" shouted Sam. "I will run over you!"

Asher was furious. He flung the passenger door open and lowered himself out of the truck. He started toward the men with his fists balled up.

"Get off our damn truck!"

"Or what, amigo?"

The voice came from behind Asher, causing him to be momentarily confused. Before he could fully turn around, a fist came at his face as fast as lightning. It caught him on the cheekbone, tearing open the skin and cracking his nose. Blood flew across the front of the truck as Asher spun around to the ground.

Another man caught Sam off guard. He jerked open the driver's door and pulled him onto the pavement. Another joined him, and they mercilessly kicked Sam as he rolled around on the pavement, trying to protect his face from the brutal beating.

Lauren tried to lock the doors to the truck. She grabbed Cat by the arm and whispered loudly, "Hide in the back."

As Cat crawled over the seat back and rolled into the rear compartment, Lauren tried to crawl through the bucket seats across the console to gain control of the truck. She thought if she could back up, their attackers would give chase, providing enough of a distraction to allow Asher and Sam a chance to get away.

Lauren scrambled forward, trying to pull her legs through to get behind the steering wheel. She wasn't fast enough.

A man reached in through the rear doors and grabbed her by the ankle. He pulled her backwards. Lauren screamed and held onto the console and the driver's seat. She kicked furiously at her attacker in an attempt to free herself. He lost his grip; however, Lauren never had a chance. A man stepped onto the side of the truck and hit her hard on the temple with a massive blow from his fist.

Stunned, she let go of the console, which allowed the other men to drag her out of the Humvee. He angrily pulled her legs first, cursing her as her head hit the steel edge of the door frame, and then her entire body crashed the final two feet against the pavement. Her attacker then wickedly laughed as he walked on top of her body to get into the back of the truck, where he was joined by his friends.

Bloodied, but conscious, Lauren heard the men laughing uproariously as they sped away. She raised her head long enough to see Cat's horrified face emerge from the rear compartment to look through the plastic window.

Asher rose to his knees just as Lauren shouted to him, "Cat! They have her!"

Sam was writhing in pain, rolling around on the road with his arms wrapped around his ribs.

Lauren was frightened and incredulous. More than a dozen people had watched the attack, and nobody lifted a finger to help. Even with the truck and Cat gone, no one tried to see if there was anything they could do.

Sam began coughing. Bloody sputum flew out of his mouth and nose. The violent coughing forced Lauren to will her body to forget her own pain to help him. Asher, whose nose was bleeding profusely, crawled across the pavement to help. Sam stopped coughing and seemed to become more coherent.

The three of them helped one another to their feet. That was when Sam began to comprehend what Lauren had said.

"Cat?" he asked, blood dripping out of his mouth.

"She was in the back," said Lauren, who was now crying. The salty tears dripped across the open wounds on her face to sting her slightly. "I thought she'd be safe in the back. I couldn't—" She stopped talking as her sobbing took over.

Asher tried to comfort her, but she pushed him away. "We have to go after her. There's no time!"

Without waiting for their agreement, Lauren began running down the street, willing her battered body to give chase. Behind her the heavy feet of the guys gave chase, Asher catching up to her first while Sam straggled behind. He was having difficulty breathing.

Asher stopped and turned to go back while Lauren continued on. Sam stopped to bend over in attempt to catch his breath. He began waving at Asher.

"Go on! Find her."

"But—" started Asher.

Sam was insistent. "No. Please. I'll be okay."

Asher continued to wipe the blood off his face that drained out of his nose. The pain was intense. The thought of Cat being kidnapped by those thugs was worse. He blew the blood out of both nostrils and broke into a sprint to catch his wife. As she raced past the Intrepid Museum, the massive aircraft carrier that had been docked at Pier 86, Asher caught up to her.

Through her labored breathing, she said, "This is my fault."

"No," he argued. "It's mine. I was distracting everybody by sight-seeing. We should've never let our guard down."

"I see them!" shouted Lauren, pointing ahead several blocks. "They just turned onto Fortieth past the parking garage."

"They must be heading toward the tunnel! Come on, Lauren. We can catch them."

Neither Asher nor Lauren was athletic although they were young and healthy. They put their pain out of their minds as they raced after the kidnappers. Minutes later, they were running between a long row of stalled vehicles that had been lined up to enter the Lincoln Tunnel.

They stopped, their chests heaving as they gasped for air. Asher looked all around him as he tried to determine what had happened to the Humvee. He saw a group of people standing up ahead on the street corner, so he broke out into a run toward them.

"Hey! Did you see a big, green Hummer come this way?"

The people all pointed in the same direction—farther down Fortieth Street.

Asher started to run away from Lauren when she shouted after him, "Where are you going?"

"They're gonna try the eastbound lanes of the tunnel!"

"Asher, we're gonna lose Sam!"

"Go back and get him. Find me in the tunnel!"

Lauren stood in place, debating whether to go back for Grandpa Sam or stay by her husband's side to search for the more vulnerable Cat.

"Okay!" she shouted as loud as she could. "No matter what, don't leave that side of the tunnel. I'll find you!"

Asher waved his arm over his head before dashing between cars to hurdle over the concrete barriers. As he descended a concrete hill toward the tunnel's exit, he soon disappeared.

Lauren stood in the middle of Fortieth Street amidst stalled vehicles and refugees fleeing the city through the Lincoln Tunnel. Despite the fact she was surrounded by hundreds if not thousands of people, she'd never felt more alone in her life.

CHAPTER FIFTY-EIGHT

Sunday
Cubbison's Farm
Harford, Pennsylvania

Emma and Luke's day was coming to an end. They both flopped into the Amish-made rocking chairs that lined the covered porch of the market. The building, which resembled a smaller version of a Cracker Barrel restaurant, featured windows that opened on hinges and two barn doors on rails for an entry. On any given day, the eight rockers that lined the wood decking would be occupied by visitors. As the sun began to sink over the horizon, it was Emma and Luke's turn to relax.

Emma delivered her sweat-soaked son a lemonade with a real bonus. Ice cubes.

"Ain't we fancy?" Luke said with a chuckle as he held the glass up high to admire the three cubes of ice.

"I found some ice trays in one of the kitchen cupboards this morning. After wiping them clean, I stuck them in the freezer for a special occasion. I thought we deserved an honest-to-goodness cold drink."

Luke reached across the arm of his rocker to toast with his mother. They both took a sip, allowing the fresh lemonade to linger in their mouths to savor the flavor.

"You know, I'm really surprised at how much we got done today," said Luke.

Emma swallowed hard and nodded in agreement. "At one point, I'd thought I lost a page or two from the to-do list."

"I liked staying busy," said Luke. "It made the time pass. I hate saying this, but I didn't worry much today. Somehow, I think, um, no, I know everything is gonna be all right."

Emma honestly agreed. She didn't expect them to return this soon. Or the next day, for that matter. During one of their middle-of-the-night convos before John left, they'd discussed the possibility of the truck breaking down and the bikes being stolen. John had warned her it might take ten days to two weeks to walk to New York and find their daughter and Sam before walking home.

"They'll be fine. We have to be patient and do our part to hold down the fort until they get back."

Luke pulled out a sheet from a notepad that was filled with moisture due to the humidity. "I knocked the most important things off my list. Tomorrow, I can help you, or I can start my routine. You know, just like always."

"Same here. Other than watching over the gardens, there's nothing to plant or harvest for a while. If the heat continues, the growing season may be extended. I'm gonna think about what I can plant now to harvest before the first frost. Leafy greens come to mind."

"Mom, we still have the materials to build a small greenhouse. Do you wanna do it?"

"I thought about it, but I wanted to wait for your dad and grandpa to help. I want to put it outside the—" Before Emma could finish her statement, Luke jumped out of his rocker and stepped to the edge of the porch. He cupped his eyes, as he was blinded by the setting sun.

Luke's voice was full of excitement. "Mom! I see them. I see them walking down the road toward the driveway!"

Emma didn't have to look at Sam's pocket watch to be skeptical. It was possible, but the turnaround would've been much faster than imagined.

He hopped off the porch and began to walk briskly toward them. Emma reached behind her to retrieve her hunting rifle. She raised it toward the group of four and squinted her eyes to view them through the powerful scope.

"Luke! Get back here! Now!"

Luke was puzzled. He turned toward his mother and back toward the people approaching. His mom shouted again.

"Luke! Get your rifle!"

He turned in a hurry toward the market. His feet slipped slightly on the loose gravel, causing him to stumble. After regaining his balance, he rushed onto the porch and grabbed his rifle, which had been propped next to his mother's. He reached his hand to his waistband to confirm the presence of his pistol.

Like his mom, he used his scope to view the people coming toward them. Three men and a young teenage boy. All were carrying hunting rifles except for one man who had an AR-15. Luke immediately recognized the weapon he'd asked his father to buy for him on multiple occasions. John never did.

Emma slowly moved to her left toward the barn doors that had remained locked with a chain and a heavy-duty padlock. She eased her body behind a log post holding the porch roof up. Luke moved away from his mom and did the same.

"That's close enough!" Luke shouted to the group, who immediately stopped. He and his mom exchanged glances and nodded to one another in support.

"We're lookin' to buy some food!" the oldest man said as he stepped forward.

Slowly, but noticeable to Luke, the other three laid back a few paces and spread out as the man talked. Luke got the sense they'd rehearsed how they'd approach the family's market.

"We can't take credit cards," said Emma in a raised voice.

"We have cash!"

"No cash either," said Luke.

"We're not selling any food out of the market right now."

The intruders stood silently as the sun began to set behind them. "You were a few days ago. Some of us have been in your store. There's plenty to help out a neighbor."

"Or two!" shouted the man wielding the AR-15.

Emma's mind raced. This was the type of confrontation John had warned her about. They were outgunned by men who appeared more experienced with their weapons than she and Luke were.

"Over the next few days, I'll be doin' some canning. Come back on, um, Thursday!"

"Tomorrow, lady!" shouted another man. "We've got babies to feed!"

"Thursday and bring things to trade. Cash or credit doesn't work anymore."

"Like what?"

Emma was too nervous to remember her list of needed supplies. She blurted out the first thing that came to mind.

"Ammo!"

The men burst out laughing.

"Fat chance, lady!" shouted one.

"I've got some ammo for ya!" hollered another as he cackled, clearly pleased with himself.

The leader turned and calmed down his crew before addressing Emma.

"Here's what you're gonna do," he said. "This time tomorrow night, you're gonna load up some boxes or crates with some of those jars from those shelves inside."

"We want a cow, too!" the mouthiest of the group shouted.

Emma didn't know how to respond, so she didn't. She needed to bide her time, hoping that John would return with the rest of her family. Now was not the time to fight.

When they didn't get a response, the four men turned around and began to walk away.

"Tomorrow! Same time!" shouted the leader over his shoulder.

"Yeah, this ain't over, lady!" yelled another.

Neither Emma nor Luke spoke a word for a moment until the men disappeared into the darkness. It was Luke who broke the nervous silence.

"What are we gonna do?" he asked.

"I don't give in to terrorists," said Emma angrily. She gritted her teeth and snarled as she spoke. "Between now and then, we'll keep an eye out. If they return tomorrow evening, we'll have something for 'em."

She lowered her rifle. As her body relaxed, her hands began to tremble. She'd need to find the courage to back up her tough talk.

CHAPTER FIFTY-NINE

Sunday
New Jersey

It was roughly twenty miles from where John ditched the truck to the entrance of the Lincoln Tunnel. Early on, he went through a relearning curve, if you will, on how to ride a bike. He eventually grew in confidence, and the two were able to pick up speed toward the Hudson River. Except, as they grew closer, the number of people wandering the streets of Secaucus grew exponentially. Quite simply, people had nothing better to do than wander around, strike up conversations, and loot.

John had envisioned the collapse of society following a catastrophe of this magnitude. He'd thought it would take days, as people would be stunned by the sudden turn of events. However, as the second full day got under way since the power grid had collapsed on Friday night, Americans were beginning to realize it would take weeks or months to restore.

Most of the people in the streets were trying to avoid the violence and looting. They were desensitized to it following years of crime skyrocketing in America's population centers. John and Matthew slowed down to avoid confrontations.

At one point after they drove underneath Interstate 95, they saw a late-sixties Camaro drive west toward the Meadowlands sports complex. The car was blaring its horn to force people out of its way. It weaved in and out of stalled cars until it reached the bridge over the Hackensack River, where it ran out of roadway.

That proved to be the end of the road for the vehicle and its driver. A mob of people descended upon the Chevy, pounding on the hood and fenders of the pristine classic car. One young male bashed in the driver's side window with a tire iron. Then he bashed the face of the driver.

Like a pack of wild animals, the onlookers dragged the man into the street and rolled him over, searching his pockets for money. Another onlooker jumped behind the wheel and tried to back away, intent on keeping the car for himself. This angered the young man with the tire iron, who began beating the glass out of the car before jamming the chiseled end into the driver's neck.

Like a train wreck that they couldn't look away from, John and Matthew watched the events unfold from afar. They straddled their bikes, glad they hadn't attempted to drive the vintage pickup into the city. They might've suffered a similar fate as this driver.

They decided to turn off the major thoroughfare leading to the Lincoln Tunnel. The small side streets were not shown on the page of the atlas that John had torn out of the book, but he was able to navigate easily. They focused on keeping the freeway leading to the Lincoln Tunnel entrance on their left while traveling through the township of Weehawken.

John was feeling better about their prospects and tried to push the return trip out of his mind. They were drawing the attention of the locals, and a few shouted at them from time to time. They had just pedaled past a parking garage built to accommodate nearby Union City High School. The side street was packed with parked vehicles as well as stalled cars heading westbound on the one-way street.

"Careful, Matthew. It's a tight squeeze, and there's a speed bump up ahead."

"I'll follow you—" began Matthew when he suddenly cut himself off. "Dad! Watch out!"

Without warning, two men ran down the steps of a porch, leapt onto the hood of a Honda, and flung their bodies toward John. Mathew tried to stop, but he was too close. He applied the brakes and lost control as he turned sideways and landed hard on the asphalt at the base of the speed bump.

"Gimme the bike!" one of the attackers yelled.

John was winded, but he'd wrapped his arms through the frame of the mountain bike. He'd locked his arms together by gripping his wrists. He had no intention of giving it up.

Frustrated, the men began to swing wildly, punching John in the back and sides. A third man appeared from the porch. He was older and not as maniacal as the teens. He grabbed Matthew's bike and tried to jerk it away.

"This dude's got a gun!" shouted one of the initial attackers.

What happened next was something Matthew wouldn't be able to explain. Something came over him that was instinctive and born out of the need to survive. Yet it would come naturally to people who'd been trained by the military or law enforcement.

He rolled over the speed bump and rose to one knee. He pulled both of the .44 Magnum revolvers simultaneously. When the first teen grabbed his dad's weapon, Matthew identified his priority target. He aimed and didn't hesitate to squeeze the trigger.

Each Ruger released a round that sounded more like a cannon as the report echoed off the parking structure on one side and the two-story brownstones on the other. The teen who'd tackled his dad and stolen away his pistol never had a chance. The powerful ammunition was merciless as it tore through his chest, leaving gaping holes in front and back.

The other teen's face was left covered in bloody gore, causing him to freeze in shock. He sat on his knees, unable to move or scream, waiting for Matthew to execute him. Matthew angrily scowled at the assailant as he took a step forward toward the young man.

"No, please!" shouted the old man, who dropped Matthew's bicycle and raised his hands. "Please don't kill my son. Just go."

With eyes focused on the two attackers, Matthew moved closer to John. "Dad? Are you all right?"

John was coughing as he tried to recover from the blows to his chest. His hands were bleeding, as were his elbows. He was sure his insides had been rearranged by the bevy of blows from the teens' fists. Nonetheless, he was able to stand and set his bike upright. The front rim was badly bent, rendering it useless. Frustrated, John shoved the bike to the pavement.

"You idiots! You got the kid killed for a broken bicycle! What's wrong with you?" John was incredulous for many reasons. The bike was the least of his concerns. And, in a way, the dead teen was destined to his fate. He was concerned about the effect this would have on Matthew.

As people flooded into the narrow street from all directions, John retrieved his gun and immediately stood by Matthew's side. "We need to go. Leave the bike."

"But won't we—"

John cut him off. "No. Son, we gotta go. Now. Come on."

Matthew flung the bike down onto the pavement and walked backwards as John led him through the gathering crowd. Both had their weapons drawn, pointing them in all directions to warn off anyone who'd try to attack them.

The two of them started walking briskly until the onlookers cleared out of the way. They began to jog. As the skyscrapers of New York came into view, they picked up the pace until both of them were winded.

John noticed one building towering over the others in the distance. He led Matthew across Palisade Avenue and up a handicap ramp leading to the entrance of Reservoir Park, a manmade lake separating them from the entrance to the Lincoln Tunnel. John searched the area for threats and was pleased to see the only people near them were on the walking trail along the perimeter of the reservoir. There were hundreds of people frolicking in the water to find a respite from the heat.

He turned to Matthew, who still was agitated by the encounter. "Son, you had no choice."

Matthew felt for his guns to confirm they were secured in their holsters. "Dad, he grabbed your gun. He could've killed you."

"I know, Matthew. You saved my life. The fact that guy is dead is on him, not you."

Matthew grimaced and nodded. "If I had known what I was doing, I might've just shot him in the leg."

"And if you had missed because you've got a big heart, we might both be dead." John wrapped his arm around his shorter son's shoulder and pointed across the water. He wanted Matthew to focus on the task at hand and not dwell on the shooting. He imagined there would be time to process what had happened later. "Do you see the tall building in the middle with the pointed thing at the top?"

"The one with the spire?" asked Matthew.

John pulled away and studied his son. "That's what you call the pointed thing?"

"Yeah, Dad. It's a spire."

"Did you know that is the Empire State Building?"

Matthew nodded. "I've seen pictures."

John led his son toward the walking path that sat atop the levee creating the reservoir. There were a few people watching the activity in the water, but none of them appeared to be threatening. Just bored.

They walked around to the other side and past a row of brownstones with a view of the Hudson River. John led the way to an embankment leading down to the roads below that stretched along the water's edge like spilled spaghetti. Cars and trucks sat in all directions, dead on arrival.

Matthew pointed to his left. "I see the tunnel entrance. Over there."

Multiple lanes entered and exited the Lincoln Tunnel. Orange cones were lined up to mark the lane boundaries. Like the surrounding roads, vehicles dotted the concrete in various states of unexpected expiration. But that wasn't what struck John as he stared down toward the tunnel entrance.

It was the hundreds if not thousands of people pouring out of New York City. Nobody was heading in the other direction. Only fools, it seemed, would head into the abyss.

THANK YOU FOR READING PERFECT STORM 1!

If you enjoyed this first installment in the Perfect Storm series, I'd be grateful if you'd take a moment to write a short review (just a few words are needed) and post it on Amazon. Amazon uses complicated algorithms to determine what books are recommended to readers. Sales are, of course, a factor, but so are the quantities of reviews my books get. By taking a few seconds to leave a review, you help me out and also help new readers learn about my work.

VISIT my website to subscribe to my email list to learn about upcoming titles, deals, contests, appearances, and more!

Sign up at BobbyAkart.com

PERFECT STORM 2, the next installment in this epic survival thriller series.
Available for preorder on Amazon by clicking here.

OTHER WORKS BY AMAZON CHARTS TOP 25 AUTHOR BOBBY AKART

The Perfect Storm Series

Perfect Storm 1

Perfect Storm 2

Perfect Storm 3

Perfect Storm 4

Perfect Storm 5

Black Gold (a standalone terrorism thriller)

Nuclear Winter

First Strike

Armageddon

Whiteout

Devil Storm

Desolation

New Madrid (a standalone, disaster thriller)

Odessa (a Gunner Fox trilogy)
Odessa Reborn
Odessa Rising
Odessa Strikes

The Virus Hunters
Virus Hunters I
Virus Hunters II
Virus Hunters III

The Geostorm Series
The Shift
The Pulse
The Collapse
The Flood
The Tempest
The Pioneers

The Asteroid Series (A Gunner Fox trilogy)
Discovery
Diversion
Destruction

The Doomsday Series
Apocalypse
Haven
Anarchy
Minutemen
Civil War

The Yellowstone Series
Hellfire
Inferno

Fallout
Survival

The Lone Star Series
Axis of Evil
Beyond Borders
Lines in the Sand
Texas Strong
Fifth Column
Suicide Six

The Pandemic Series
Beginnings
The Innocents
Level 6
Quietus

The Blackout Series
36 Hours
Zero Hour
Turning Point
Shiloh Ranch
Hornet's Nest
Devil's Homecoming

The Boston Brahmin Series
The Loyal Nine
Cyber Attack
Martial Law
False Flag
The Mechanics
Choose Freedom
Patriot's Farewell (standalone novel)

Black Friday (standalone novel)
Seeds of Liberty (Companion Guide)

The Prepping for Tomorrow Series
Cyber Warfare
EMP: Electromagnetic Pulse
Economic Collapse

CPSIA information can be obtained
at www.ICGtesting.com
Printed in the USA
BVHW030920120422
634068BV00012B/382/J